PRAISE FOR *THE 1*
ON *EVERYWHERE STREET*

"A scrumptious time-travel adventure written with elegance and charm."

– Adam Roberts, author of *By Light Alone* and *Jack Glass*

Connie

Keep Reading!

[signature]

THE LITTLE HOUSE ON EVERYWHERE STREET

F.M.A Dixon

Fitzroy Books

Published by Fitzroy Books
An imprint of
Regal House Publishing, LLC
Raleigh, NC 27612
All rights reserved

https://fitzroybooks.com

Printed in the United States of America

ISBN -13 (paperback): 9781646030743
ISBN -13 (epub): 9781646030996
Library of Congress Control Number: 2020951953

All efforts were made to determine the copyright holders and obtain their permissions in any circumstance where copyrighted material was used. The publisher apologizes if any errors were made during this process, or if any omissions occurred. If noted, please contact the publisher and all efforts will be made to incorporate permissions in future editions.

Interior and cover design by Lafayette & Greene
Cover images © by C.B. Royal

 Regal House Publishing, LLC
https://regalhousepublishing.com

The following is a work of fiction created by the author. All names, individuals, characters, places, items, brands, events, etc. were either the product of the author or were used fictitiously. Any name, place, event, person, brand, or item, current or past, is entirely coincidental.

Printed in the United States of America

For Donna, Ellie and Maisie, my fine, fine fellow travellers!

❧ SONNET CLV ❧

Who can'st escape the ~~mortall~~ claimes of Time
And see his debt from Deaths ._____ struck?
Who mighst by wit alone and conceald ~~time~~
Evade his ___and all ill fortun'd lucke?
Alas, none, my friend. Nay, nere the long-liv'd
Phaenix, nor the red-man'd_____.mighst pay
That _____ and yet survive
To breath Gods sweet air for _____ day.
But one way be knowne to cloake thy bright page
From ___long seeing eie: obfuscate all!
Crosse out thy trackes, erase thee from the ___,
Be ye not found when the _____ doth call.
    ___.-Forsake love, and be as one forsook,
Strike out, or ~~else~~ by Times red pen be struck.

WS ~~1603~~

❧

1

One of the many strange things about the little house on Everywhere Street was that it wasn't very little. Not at all. In fact, it was deceptively large. Everyone said so, especially once they had explored the upper floors, of which there appeared to be several too many, for a house that size, that is. From the outside it seemed that there should be only three floors at most. Or four, counting the basement. But visitors frequently ran out of puff on the West Staircase and found themselves wondering exactly how far they had climbed. Mr Redmayne, who occupied the house with his wife and three children, when asked, always remarked that he had not the slightest idea how many floors there were, never having counted them all. And his guests always took him to be joking, as they knew him to be that sort of a man. However, on this matter he was being quite serious. Count the floors? When on Earth would he find time to do that? And why? At this point Mr Redmayne's wife, Gloriana, would usually intervene and request that her husband should desist from his cruel teasing at once and, after quite artfully changing the subject, take the unfortunate guest by the arm and lead them back down the East Staircase, which only confused them all the more.

Why should a house so apparently, well, *thin-seeming*, at least from the outside, have *two* staircases? And how could it accommodate them both within its narrow architecture? Mrs Redmayne, who was very beautiful and European to boot, possibly French or Romanian, depending, would laugh as if their guest had made the cleverest joke she had ever had the good fortune to hear and treat them to several delicious scones from her kitchen, a confection whipped up only that morning by her own fair and highly skilled hand, in accordance with an ancient Cornish recipe. With hot tea. And cream. Mrs Redmayne was very fond of a traditional cream tea and her enthusiasm for this, like all her famous enthusiasms, was highly infectious.

At which point, any lingering confusion over the number of floors or staircases would be quite forgotten. Afterwards, if pressed, everyone would agree, vaguely, that the house was exceptionally roomy, for its size. On the *inside*. Yes. Remarkably so. And that would be that.

But none of this was by any means the strangest thing about the house. Not at all.

The three children, George, Felice, and Emile, loved the house and believed they knew everything about it, all of its secrets, but they were wrong. Their knowledge was limited, for what was thought to be good reason, for their own protection. But lessons must be learned, even hard lessons, by children and over-protective parents alike. And, happily, their errors in this area are the occasion for this tale. All actions have consequences, Mr Redmayne will remark toward its close. Unpicking them can prove very messy, very messy indeed, not to mention downright dangerous. For everyone. But if you must do it, you'll want to do it right. And to do that you must go right back to the beginning, the very beginning, and start over.

And so, that's exactly what we will do…

2

The little house on Everywhere Street had stood in its present location in New York since 1900. *That,* from Mr Redmayne's perspective, was a very complex statement, very complex indeed, far more complex than it might appear at first examination, especially to the lay mind. But no less true for all that. In fact, all things considered, he postulated one evening, quite pleased with himself, it surely satisfied all the necessary conditions for a true statement. Mr Redmayne was a philosopher and spent the most inordinate amount of time looking as though he was doing nothing at all. But really he was thinking very hard.

"If you say so, dear," replied his wife. "Do eat up your spinach, won't you? It will be quite cold before you know it."

Mr Redmayne looked surprised. "Spinach, you say?"

"Yes, dear. On your plate. We're eating dinner, remember? With the children."

The three children giggled and Mr Redmayne's face was once again a picture of surprise.

"Sorry, I was miles away," he said sheepishly. "Spinach. Yes, so I see."

Mrs Redmayne's culinary repertoire included a stunning number of spinach-based dishes, all of which her children—and to some extent her husband, it must be said—thoroughly detested, as one. On this matter, at least, they were united.

Mr Redmayne, with noticeable reluctance, took a first bite. Then, he laid down his fork on his plate while he ate, a habit that his wife found "very American." Usually her tone made it clear that this was not any kind of endorsement of the practice. Indeed, Mrs Redmayne suspected that left to his own devices her husband might all too readily take to beating his knife and fork on the table as if they were drumsticks, much like George

Washington, whose table manners were known to be generally deplorable.

On this occasion, however, she merely looked at her spouse most disapprovingly but said nothing.

Mr Redmayne went on in any case, quite oblivious. "See, the thing is, a fellow I know asked me the question and, well, I wasn't entirely sure how to reply. Not without telling an untruth. A lie. So, I was thinking it over."

He left it there. All four pairs of eyes were fixed upon him, clearly expecting more.

Mr Redmayne took another portion of pistou creamed spinach bake onto his fork.

The four exchanged glances. Mrs Redmayne took charge. "What question, darling? This fellow, what did he ask you? We're all waiting."

"What?" Mr Redmayne looked around at the four expectant faces.

"Yeah, Pops, what was the question? Don't leave us hanging."

This last was from Emile, the youngest and by far the most impetuous of the three.

Mr Redmayne looked at Emile as though he had never seen him before in his life.

Once again, he laid down his fork while he chewed. "Well, he comes up to me, this fellow I know, and he says, as if all very chummily, 'So, Redmayne, how old's this fabulous house of yours, then?' And I say, 'What?' And he says, 'Your house, the one everybody talks about, it's just off the park, there, isn't it?' I say, 'Yes, it is,' not seeing the relevance. 'Well, okay,' he goes on, 'how long's it been there, would you say?' That's all."

"And what *did* you say, dear? In response."

"All that I could say. I told him I'd have to think about it."

The children groaned, as one. "Really?" cried Felice, quite exasperated. "Papa!"

Why her father couldn't learn to tell a simple lie once in a while was a source of constant frustration to her. She managed it all the time without the slightest problem. Surely he could too?

Most indignant, she turned to her mother. "Mais vraiment, Maman, est-ce que ça le tuerait de ne pas dire la vérité, pour une seule fois? Surtout à propos de quelque chose de si important—pour nous tous!"

But Mrs Redmayne merely smiled at her daughter, albeit in a kindly, knowing way.

"Tu connais bien ton père, ma chérie! La vérité est primordiale pour lui. C'est une des choses que j'aime le plus en lui."

Now the two boys groaned, and this time Mr Redmayne elected to intervene.

"English, *English*! Come on, you two. You *know* the rules—and it is the *house's* rule after all. English everywhere, all the time. Otherwise who knows what might happen? Chaos, most like. And, yes, Felice, it *might* kill me to tell a lie, even just one time, you never know. Consequences, all of our actions have consequences, dearheart, no matter how trivial they might seem at the time. Now, this fellow"—Mr Redmayne paused to note that his daughter had reddened and appeared suitably abashed—"he asked me a question and I wanted to answer it as truthfully as I could, as difficult as that is under the circumstances. So, what could I say? That the house has *more* than one location? That wouldn't quite be true, despite appearances. That the house is where it is, always, and the locations find the house? Strictly speaking, that would be the most true of all. But I can't tell him that, obviously. He'd think me quite mad. And so might I, for saying it. No, what I can say—without fear of a lie or contradiction—is that the house could be found in its present location here in New York since 5:27 a.m. on Sunday, 25th March, 1900. *That* is a true statement. Not the whole truth, I admit, but true enough."

"Really, must you be quite so absolutely precise, darling, on the matter of the time? You know, that might only lead to more questions. Possibly the year itself would suffice? Just a suggestion. And who is this darned fellow of yours anyway? Why is he so interested in our lovely house, do you think? You don't imagine that he suspects something, do you? I should hate to have to move again, not with Georgie doing rather so very well just now in school. I'm not sure I could face all the upheaval, you know, coming so soon after the last time."

"No, no, nothing like that, I'm sure. Just some fellow I chat to at the library now and then. Watkins, that's the chap's name. Yes. Works there, I think. Wears a hat." Mr Redmayne risked a glance at his eldest son, George. "No, dear, I'm quite sure. No need to worry. He's only a librarian, after all. What harm could he possibly do? *Fine* us?"

Mr Redmayne laughed out loud. No one else joined in, but he didn't mind that. He always enjoyed his own jokes far more than anyone else did. That was approval enough for him.

George coughed a tense little cough. "Well, Pops, some librarians have been known to take an interest in matters of historical public record. You know, events, maps, dates, and such—all that sort of thing. Your friend at the library could be looking us up right now, trying to pinpoint the house, the street even, on some turn of the century survey thing or other. It's possible."

"That would be daft, wouldn't it? He's not likely to find us on any map, is he?"

"Exactly, Eric, darling," said Mrs Redmayne. "That's quite possibly the problem."

"Oh, I see," said Mr Redmayne, a little abashed himself now. "I *see*. Well, yes, quite."

And there being nothing else to do about it, he tried another forkful of spinach, which, as his wife had so accurately predicted, had now turned rather cold. Indeed. Quite chilled. Very.

3

Chaos. School mornings, in particular, it has to be said, could be nothing short of chaotic in the little house on Everywhere Street, as is commonly the case in what are otherwise the best regulated and most orderly of households. All happy families are alike, Mr Redmayne used frequently to profess, they're all quite chaotic in their own special way. And just as the Redmaynes were undoubtedly a happy family (the usual minor temporary disagreements notwithstanding), equally they were also on occasion truly and quite uniquely chaotic, especially in the mornings.

Of course, it didn't help that the children attended different schools in what were really—in a way that will soon become more clear—very different areas indeed. Nor did it help that these schools no doubt quite rightly insisted that pupils should meet their particular *local* requirements to the letter. That was their prerogative. Mr and Mrs Redmayne respected that. Rules are rules, after all. But it did make things difficult.

As a consequence Mr Redmayne synchronised everybody's morning routine with military precision. Bathroom visits were scheduled according to a strict rota and tightly monitored. Uniforms would always be first laid out and then donned, or not, as required (Felice and Emile, yes; George, not). Breakfasts prepared (Mrs Redmayne), consumed, typically, in double short order (esp. George, Emile); school bags readied (owner, lackadaisically); lunch packs packed (Mr Redmayne, fussily); and appropriate amounts of currency procured and allocated to each child (Mr R., ditto). A tall, rather imposing grandfather clock stood in the hallway, counting out the morning's all too rapid progress in loudly chimed quarter-hour segments, in a real sense driving it all forward and helping things to run, well, like clockwork.

But it didn't take much—the introduction of some unforeseen element, an unexpected caller, misplaced keys, a lost shoe, *anything*—to upset the finely tuned mechanics of the household arrangements and threaten to throw the entire enterprise out of whack.

In short, *chaos*.

On the morning in question, when this story really begins, the very start, everything was proceeding in the regular fashion. In the cosy basement kitchen, the boys had wolfed their breakfasts down quite unceremoniously, almost without a word between respective mouthfuls of their bacon and eggs. Felice much preferred a lighter 'continental' breakfast these days—croissant, espresso—but, even so, proved no more communicative than either of her brothers. Not that Mrs Redmayne minded. Gloriana was not, by nature, what might be regarded as a morning person, an attribute, if indeed this quality might be regarded as such, to which she had grown perversely attached over the years. Washed, dressed, fed, and out. That was the mantra that played over in her mind each morning. Washed, dressed, fed, and out. With a special emphasis on the *out*.

On this particular morning, however, at the point at which we join them, the 'fed' stage was already drawing to a close. Despite this, neither boy was displaying the least urgency in looking to move on to the 'out' portion of the operation. Unlike them, their Europhile sister had managed to leave the table quite successfully several minutes earlier—without either of her brothers noticing her departure in the slightest—but that did not necessarily mean that whatever she might be doing now in her room was dedicated to the purpose of leaving on time. Still, at least Emile had managed partially to leave the table. That is, he had gotten up from his chair with the intent of doing so and had even gone so far as to take a couple of steps away, but at the last second his keen and roving eye had fallen on the funny pages portion of the newspaper, which had been carelessly left lying open, right *there*, and this had suckered him back in. He stood now, a foot or so away from the source of his capture, swaying back and forth while conscientiously scrutinising the detail of every single cell of every panel in turn, and therefore could be observed in the condition of both half-leaving and half-staying at one and the same time—virtually a quantum state.

Or so his elder brother, George, might have thought, if only he were able to look up—even for an instant—from his copy of *Scientific American*. Alas, he could not. For George, the journal held a gravitational attraction akin to the pull of a supermassive black hole, and it is an established fact that boys held in the grip of one of those rarely make it to school on time. Luckily, for George, the only superior explosive force in nature capable of dislodging a boy caught in this terrible predicament was to hand, in the form of his mother, who, with a mighty, loud and, most of all, persuasive clearing of her throat was able to free his attention from whatever he was reading practically at the first attempt.

"Almost done," he remarked, blankly, without looking up.

Mrs Redmayne advanced toward the table, wielding her tea towel on a clean wet plate without mercy. George's eyes—indeed ever so slightly, his entire head—began to run rapidly from side to side, as if he were now reading at a rate too fast for the stationary human brain to process. As she reached the table he threw the magazine down.

"There! Finished," he said, just in time.

He stood up, still without betraying the remotest sense of urgency in moving on out of the kitchen. Clearly, he was thinking, about Important Things, which is something George did quite often.

"You know, Mother, I now believe that time-travel is technically possible, if functionally impossible. The math stands up. You just couldn't do it in the real world, that's all. Pity."

"Yes, that is a pity," she agreed. "Because at this rate it's going to take a time machine to get the pair of you out to school on time. Now, go on, both of you. Out, out, out!"

Emile looked up from the paper, as if surprised to find that anyone, including himself, was still there. George mussed his younger brother's hair in passing.

"Come on, little Integer. You heard the lady. It's not like we've got the whole day to waste here reading comics, is it? That's called 'Sunday'—to *you*, anyway. Integer."

Emile appeared most affronted. "Don't call me that. I don't like it. I don't know what it means. And I don't spend all day reading comics. Not Sundays. Not *any* day. Not *ever*."

"Do."—"Don't."—"Do."—"Don't."—"Do."—"Don't."— "*Do so.*"—"*Don't so!*"

"Well, if you ever read anything other than a damn comic book once in a while you would know what it means. *Integer*."

"I do. I read all sorts of stuff. Unlike you."

"Don't."—"*Do.*"—"Don't."—"*Do.*"

Despite the intensely Socratic nature of the debate Mrs Redmayne seemed extraordinarily keen to bring it to a rapid end. At once.

She fluttered the tea towel in their direction with the most tremendous animation.

"For goodness sakes, go! Now! The pair of you! Really! Up those stairs! Blessed Blue!"

George chuckled, leaving the kitchen with Emile in tow.

"I do so like teasing mother to the point of her breaking the—"

But whatever he said next was lost on the turn of the stairs. And just as well.

Mrs Redmayne was in no mood to hear another word. Not about anything.

And certainly not about teasing her. Not right then. No. Best not. No. Quite the opposite, in fact. Her husband, on the other hand, was generally immune to teasing of all forms, which equally was just as well, as he was teased a lot. Everywhere. All the time. But really it was as if he didn't even hear it. He was, in truth, the most phlegmatic of men, as will be quite clear by the end of this tale. He fussed, yes. He fussed all the time. Mr

Redmayne was fussing at that very moment, as the two boys came ditheringly slowly up from the basement into the hallway. About the weather. That's what he was fussing about right now. About when and where it was going to rain that day and whether topcoats, as he still insisted upon calling them, should be worn. Or not. He fussed but he didn't get upset. It just wasn't in him. Rarely, anyway. Very rarely indeed. Perhaps once in every century. At worst.

"Rain," he announced, as gravely as if he were announcing that the end of Time had been confirmed to take place at some point in the next fifteen minutes. "Yes, I'm afraid so."

Portentously the grandfather clock alongside him picked that moment to chime the quarter hour. 8:45 a.m. Quite loudly. Neither boy paid it the slightest attention.

George went to the door and looked out through the glass. "Really? Not a cloud in the sky out there."

"Not you. *Him.*"

"Ha! You hear that, Integer!"

But before Emile could frame a response, about how he liked the rain, that in point of fact he preferred any rainy day to any dull old dry day and always had, another voice fatally interrupted his chain of thought. Felice, her head appearing over the banister high up over the East Staircase, peering down, wide-eyed.

"What is it?" she called.

"Rain," responded George, altogether far too gleefully. "For the shrimp."

"Really? Marvellous. What about me?"

"Overcast to begin with," said Mr Redmayne, "but clearing up nicely. Should be fine. All day. Beautiful, in fact."

"*Yes!* I do so hate getting that ridiculous blue hat wet. Makes me look like a partially drowned sailor! It's bad enough when it's dry."

"That's the forecast, anyway. You can never tell. Come on, get your topcoat on, Emile. No dawdling. All of us, I mean. High time we were out. Felice!"

By this point Felice was already skipping rapidly down the stairs.

George had donned his backpack. He was good to go. "Later, losers. Math test today, by the way. Sure to ace it. Again!" "You do that. And less of this 'losers' talk, if you will. Very unbecoming. Emile, I want to walk with you, at least part of the way. Wait there, will you, while I grab my umbrella."

Felice, all in bright blue, kissed her rather distracted father on the cheek as she flashed past, altogether something of a blue blur, with just a hint of red in the knitted bobble on the top of her school hat. Her ridiculous school hat. That she secretly loved. *So* French.

"Bye, Papa. I'll say goodbye to Maman on the way out. Till tea."

"Right, yes, tea," said Mr Redmayne, vaguely, as she headed down the staircase to the basement. After that, Felice would exit via the side door just off the foot of the stairs, as he knew she must. It suddenly struck him what she meant.

"Yes, *tea*. Oh, I see. Till then, okay, yes, bye," he called. "Now...we really *have* to go."

George had already opened the front door, and stopped. A man stood there. A caller. In uniform. Complete with cap. With a white peak. Very smart. Worryingly smart, in fact.

Mr Redmayne, for a second or so, was quite thrown. Emile had his topcoat on now and was waiting. They had to leave by the rear exit, the back door, and soon. Immediately. Who was this deuced fellow in his worryingly smart white-peaked cap? And why on Earth was he standing on the front steps of their house at this most inopportune of moments? What could he possibly be thinking? Mr Redmayne was at a loss. He noticed George, with admirable self-possession, slip past the fellow and be instantly off down the front steps with nothing more than a backward wave of his hand. For a moment Mr Redmayne wished he could do exactly the same thing but he knew that would never do. And would be entirely counterproductive in any case. Back door. Now.

And so, instead, he did what any sensible husband would do in these circumstances. He called for his wife. "Gloriana, dear, we have a caller. At the door. *Front* door. Yes, *now*, would you believe? Can you come up? I need to take Emile. Yes, like I say, *now*. How should *I* know who he is? Sometimes I'm sure you think I know everybody. What? Ask him in? Really? Are you sure? Very well." Mr Redmayne looked doubtfully at the uniformed cold caller in the white-peaked cap. "I say, do come in, there's a good fellow. Sorry to keep you. My wife will be right up. She's just seeing my daughter out. Really now you must excuse me, we absolutely have to dash. School, you know. Come on, Emile. No time to lose."

Mrs Redmayne came up the stairs just then as her husband and son were passing, both with their heavy topcoats on and all in a rush. Emile smiled sweetly if fleetingly at his mother as he dashed past, once again in tow. Then she realised that in her distraction she hadn't closed the side door after seeing Felice off to school.

"Oh, wait a minute," she called but it was too late. Mr Redmayne and Emile were out of earshot, and the caller was right there, loitering in the hallway and examining their grandfather clock as if it were quite possibly the most interesting clock in the world, which, all things considered, it very likely was. But, really, she wondered, what on Earth was Eric thinking by inviting the man into the house at all? Sometimes he didn't have the sense God gave a goose—even if he was something of an adorable goose for all that.

So, for the second time that morning Mrs Redmayne was obliged to clear her throat in a most theatrical fashion. It did the trick. At once, the man in the peaked cap turned toward her and she realised, with a sense of relief so sudden and intense that it surprised even herself, that this was not the day when her worst fears—nor even her second worst or third worst fears—would be realised (Mrs Redmayne privately maintained a mental list of all her worst fears, one through eight, all of which involved her family, the house, and the city constabulary in various improbably melodramatic scenarios). But this gentleman was no gendarme. Not at all. No. Rather he was some kind of local official. That was clear. A traffic warden or a meter reader. Something like that. Very likely the latter, now that she thought about it. Yes, almost certainly. That was it. Mrs Redmayne bestowed upon the poor, unsuspecting fellow one of her best, most enthusiastic of smiles, the impact of which throughout the years had charmed all but the very most hard-hearted of bureaucrats the world over from Bangkok to Berlin. This one today didn't stand a chance. None.

"Yes, can I be of help in some way?" she asked, still smiling warmly and approaching closer.

He looked rather uncomfortable, she noticed at once, the poor fellow, very much so. Her first instinct was to put him at ease. Maybe she should offer him a cream tea? That worked with everyone. Just about. Not that mad monk in Russia that time. True. But he was far beyond the help of a good cream tea. This was an altogether much simpler case, she felt sure.

But the poor chap just looked all the more uncomfortable. All the while he clutched a clipboard tightly, and his eyes, at least to begin with, were kept steadfastly averted down toward that. When he did look up finally, his face was quite reddened. "Well, to tell you the truth, ma'am," he began, extremely sheepishly, "I don't rightly know what to say. I really don't. Actually, it's more than a little embarrassing… And I apologise for this, ma'am, truly I do, but mostly likely you're probably going to wind up getting the biggest darn bill ever, I reckon!"

"Goodness gracious, whatever for?"

"Water. Mrs…?"

"Redmayne. But why?"

He made a short curt note on his clipboard. "Well," he said, looking up again, but for a moment still writing, "Mrs Redmayne, see, it's like this—and this part I can't really explain, not properly—well, not at all, in fact, to tell you the truth. But, listen, ma'am, your house, it's like I've never set eyes on it before, somehow. Not once. All these years… One thing's for sure, I reckon no one back at the depot's ever gonna let me forget about this one. Man, nope. And Mr Morrison, he's my supervisor, ma'am, well, sheesh, no—I don't even wanna think about it…"

Through his teeth he let out a long incredulous whistle at the extent of his own incompetence.

"Nope, nope, nope…" he added quietly, more to himself if anything.

"Now, now, really, come on, there," said Mrs Redmayne, watching him shake his head from side to side in what was in truth a rather unbecoming and somewhat pathetic fashion (while at the same time feeling both rather very sorry for the poor fellow and more than a little guilty by this point). "Now, it's a simple enough mistake. Nothing that can't be put right very easily, I'm certain of that. So don't you worry. Not one bit. Perhaps you would like a cream tea? I always find that helps. Practically every time."

He looked at her a bit oddly then, she thought. "A what, ma'am? No, no, honestly, I just need to find your meter. Hey, like I say, I'm real, *real* sorry about this, but if you show me where it's at, ma'am, I'll be right out your hair. So, ma'am, inside or out? The house, that is…"

Now, he stared at her, as if in expectation. Mrs Redmayne considered very carefully what she would say next. "Well, it's definitely not *inside* the house. No. We would know. I'm quite sure of that." Without intending to, she led him a little further down the long hallway and into the house. "Now, let me think."

She stood still for a second, thinking. He waited. They were placed adjacent to the steps down to the basement and she could see the side door standing ajar down there, which was a farther distraction. What could she say? She couldn't very well let him go outside for a look around. That would be the end. For them all.

A voice, her husband's, came to her rescue, at least temporarily.

"Dear!" he called exceptionally loudly from the back of the

house. "Are you there? Forgot my umbrella. It's simply *pouring* down here, I'm sorry to say—and we're already very late. Can you fetch it? Hat stand, dear." His voice tailed off somewhat at this point, but was still just audible. "And do please hurry, darling, poor little Emile's looking something like a half-drowned mouse already, which is never good. Damn this miserable climate."

The sun chose that moment to shine brightly through the glass on the front door. It picked out the intricate pattern on the colourful Persian rug in the hallway most beautifully.

Mrs Redmayne smiled an enigmatic smile at her guest. She couldn't help but notice that the expression on his face betrayed his confusion—and perhaps a little more than that.

She went for the umbrella, a really fine cane crook model from Smith & Sons. Her gift.

"My husband, he's really something of an adorable goose," she said, brandishing the brolly in what she hoped later had been a totally nonthreatening manner, "but I'm afraid he can be very dramatic about the weather. Do please excuse me, won't you? I'll be right back. Two ticks, that's all. Not a single tick longer, I promise."

Without waiting for a reply she dashed down the hallway, past Mr Redmayne's study, the library and the music room (where, in her younger days, she had so loved to sing), her own study, the game room, the dining room, the great dining room, the drawing room, the scullery, the back-scullery, on through into the middle-parlour, the pre-penultimate back-parlour, the penultimate back-parlour, and then finally the back-parlour itself, and then beyond.

Mr Redmayne was waiting at the back door, looking very much like something of a tall drowned rodent himself, if truth be told, and a very impatient one at that.

Mrs Redmayne handed him the umbrella. "I'm really having the devil of a time with this caller, dear. He wants to read the darned water meter, would you believe?"

But her husband just took the brolly from her.

"You'll think of something. Must go."

And off he went, once again with little Emile in tow. But he was right. It truly was pouring down out there. Cats and dogs. Literally. Well, not literally. But it was certainly torrential. Watching them go, she missed them both already. Big rat and little mouse. Which was silly, as her husband would be home again within the hour. Less.

Perhaps she could stall the perishing meter-man until then? Insist upon the cream tea? That would put a different complexion on everything, she was certain. These were her thoughts as she made her way back though the several parlours. But when she reached the hallway again she had something of a shock.

He wasn't there.

The hallway was quite empty. No white-peaked cap. No meter-man. No anyone.

With a rapidly sinking heart she looked down the basement steps. The side door was now wide open. He was gone.

And they, the happy Redmaynes, were undone. But completely.

Chaos.

4

She would have to go after him, the perishing meter-man fellow. There was nothing else for it. Hang the consequences. And the sooner, the better. Mrs Redmayne didn't think she could even wait for her husband to return. She would leave him a note.

Gone after meter-man. Side door. Sorry. That should cover it.

And then, she added, *With apols for the extreme pithiness of this note.*

Then she added, *Your loving wife, Gloriana.*

Then, *XX.* There. Done.

Now she just needed a good place to leave it, somewhere Eric couldn't possibly fail to notice it. But, looking around, she realised at once that such a place didn't exist, that wherever she left a note for Eric, he would surely fail to see it. In fact, most likely he probably wouldn't even notice that she wasn't home. He'd come in and talk aloud to her for the longest time, complaining about the filthy weather and this and that, all on the assumption that she must be around somewhere; most likely he'd imagine her to be in the kitchen whipping up a fresh batch of scones while she enjoyed the not so rare pleasure of listening to him complain. Yes, that's exactly what he would think. Mrs Redmayne deposited the note on the highly varnished walnut table in the hallway and took down her topcoat and scarf from the hat stand. No time to lose. If he found it, he found it. If not, she would deal with the situation as best she could without him. And, yes, let the darned consequences go hang.

The side door to the house was lower than street level and, after a short ascent, the exit opened out onto an undistinguished, bleak, and rather dusty little alleyway. Mrs Redmayne quickly climbed the short flight of steps and unlatched the tall black iron gate, only pausing for a second to peer both ways along the alley. No sign. Maybe she was mistaken? Perhaps he hadn't come this way at all? Then her heart sank to the ground all over again. The clipboard. Darn. Wasn't that it propped up against the wall at the east end of the alleyway? It very much looked like it was. She went closer and picked it up. Oh dear, yes. *New York City Water Board.* And there, she imagined, was what was supposed to be her name written in pencil across the top. *REDMANE?* For the longest moment she had to fight the urge to correct the spelling, or at least cross out the error (alas, for that she would need her red crossing-out pen). Good spelling was always important, that was as true now as ever it was, but Mrs Redmayne had to concede this might not be absolutely her top priority at that particular time. No time to lose, after all.Now, so, then, which way? Which way would *she* go if she were *him?* That was quite impossible to imagine. She knew exactly which way she would go if she were *herself,* which happily she was. Across the street stood that delightful bakery—La Boulangerie de Papa. That's where *she* would go first, naturally, of course, because that's where she always went first. Who wouldn't? The sheer variety of quite wonderful fresh cream-based confections and light puff pastries that they displayed daily in the window of that one little backstreet bakery put all of America to shame. The world, even. Petit Fours, Pâte à choux, Saint Honoré, dipped in hot caramel, Galette des Rois, with that always astonishing almond cream filling—so light and yet *so* delicious. Mrs Redmayne found herself crossing the quiet road toward the charming pale blue awning of the store. Felice loved this little boulangerie almost as much as she did herself. *So French!* Mrs Redmayne could almost hear her daughter saying it.

She peered in the window—and sighed. Even though it was so early in the morning rows upon rows of the most exquisitely enticing French pastries of seemingly every shape and colour already lay there waiting to be purchased, savoured, and devoured. Who ate them all? That was the unanswerable question. Every back and side street in the neighbourhood boasted such a boulangerie as this. This one just happened to be hers. Who on Earth consumed such a vast quantity of fancies and cakes on a daily basis? It seemed inconceivable but someone did it. And yet all the locals seemed so, well, petite. Mrs Redmayne raised her eyes and, catching sight of her tall, slim reflection in the window, stepped back into the narrow road. She sighed.

This sort of conjecture was all well and good but it wasn't helping her mission. Not at all. No. Right. Concentrate. The poor meter-man fellow hadn't shown much interest in her offer of a cream tea. Improbable as it seemed, the enchanting display in the window before her might not hold his attention quite as much as it would hers. If at all. If this was of no interest to you, poor creature that you were, which way would you go? Which way indeed? Which way?

All at once, a car honked, not a nasty, loud American honk, no—far more like a mischievous seal at play, but it sounded out close enough behind Mrs Redmayne to startle her back up onto the pavement with a little hop and a jump. It scudded right then through a little puddle and almost splashed dirty rainwater up onto her shoes. For a second Gloriana stood there watching the car go past, one of those old-fashioned white Citroëns that always looked like it was smiling at something or other, a good joke or a funny story, either that or it was always really, really pleased to see you, even if you were standing stupidly in its way, and she decided there and then to follow in its direction. Who knows? Maybe the very same thing had happened to the meter-man? That was not impossible, if not very likely. But it was all she had.

So, Mrs Redmayne walked on, determined to pursue her elusive quarry. Shortly, at the end of the narrow street she came to the crossroads. Which way now? About half-a-mile north, she realised at once, lay the famous river. *Water.* Yes. He *was* the *water* meter-man, after all. She went north.

❧

Meanwhile, Mr Redmayne had returned home, thoroughly

soaked and in something of a minor blue funk, and, entirely as anticipated by his wife, he trudged forward through the house complaining aloud about the wet weather, how very rotten it was, the traffic, how very, very terrible that was, the brusqueness of some people these days (really, dear, you would not believe!), and, worst of all, to him, the sad truth that Emile, at eleven, was getting far too grown up to be escorted to and from school these days, even a little part of the way, and soon that aspect of all their children's lives would be over forever, too, and there was nothing that he, she, nor anyone else for that matter could do about it. Nothing. That was that. He had reached the entrance hallway, where he walked back and forth while he divested himself of his wet belongings, taking off, shaking out, and hanging up his wet topcoat, and sliding the partially collapsed umbrella into its slot at the foot of the hat-stand.

All in all, he passed by the note that Gloriana had left for him on the walnut table no fewer than seven times, all the while addressing his absent wife as if she were somewhere in earshot, if out of sight, and because he didn't expect to see a note, he didn't see one. At least that was how he rationalised his complete and utter note-blindness much later that evening, when he and Gloriana reflected on things together privately before going to bed, leading her to speculate aloud that, in which case, no doubt if there had been a monkey sitting on top of the hat-stand, he would have quite missed that too. Which, although the point was well made, he hardly thought a fair comparison.

But, for now, with that discussion still several hours ahead, Mr Redmayne trotted to and fro on the intricately patterned Persian hallway rug, divesting, complaining, quite happily (and miserably) oblivious, until, standing at the top of the basement steps, the morning newspaper in hand, he announced that if Gloriana wanted him she would find him in his study. And the fact that his wife made no response, being at that precise moment quite some distance away from the house and therefore altogether entirely out of earshot, struck him as a matter of no concern either, because in truth he neither required nor expected one. Which was another point that they reflected on privately together later that evening, much to his obvious discomfort.

Mr Redmayne's first task each morning, once the children were safely despatched to school, was to situate himself comfortably in the antique leather Parker Knoll chair in his private study and complete the *Times* crossword within the ten-minute maximum period that he considered respectable for the challenge. The chair itself, the classic, wide-winged 'Oberon' model of Parker Knoll, is worthy of mention in its own right, as it was something of a prized family heirloom, originally belonging to Mr Redmayne's father, no less—Rufus Reginald Redmayne— the architect of the house and now sadly deceased for more than some twenty years. Mr Redmayne, with all due filial respect and affection, had situated the chair under the highly impressionistic portrait of the proudly moustached, rather stern-eyed elderly gent himself, who was thus depicted holding an unlit cigarette and looking down on the observer with an almost palpable degree of disdain. To gaze up at that portrait was to feel with an unnerving degree of certainty that the old man had known something very important that you didn't, something very important indeed. Which, in truth, he did. Many, many very important things indeed, in fact. Too many. But we digress. Probably.

To the casual observer the sight of a middle-aged man in his study attacking the *Times* crossword with gusto may strike them as a scene of mere relaxation, but to Mr Redmayne himself it was far more than that. He saw it as a way of limbering up, of sharpening his faculties, of preparing his mind for the heavy lifting ahead, metaphorically speaking, of course. For the record Mr Redmayne will not be observed undertaking any actual heavy lifting, of actual physical objects at any point ahead, not in this tale nor in any other. No. But mentally speaking, intellectually, he moved the entire universe with his mind, frequently. Daily, in fact. Although he would only blush quite endearingly if you pointed this out to him in person. Also he would cough awkwardly and look down at his shoes for several minutes. So, best not.

On this particular morning the *Times* crossword was proving a routine affair, the usual collection of anagrams, hidden words, double meanings, reversals, homophones and subtractions that he usually so enjoyed, but he quite preferred there to be some element of challenge, some expected dimension that sent his grey matter (if not exactly his pulse) racing. This morning's effort was proving a little too mundane. You could become overly familiar with the puzzle setter's way of thinking, so that the clues yielded few surprises. Sometimes he wished he might travel ahead in time and set his present self a crossword puzzle that would totally surprise him. But then he realised that it would need to be his later self that travelled back in time to do that, otherwise he would already know the entire solution to the puzzle and the whole thing would be quite pointless.

A little like how today's puzzle felt. No challenge at all. A full minute to go and only one clue remained to be solved, number thirteen, down:

Evil Matter Once Again Begins at Home (4,6)

Mr Redmayne's idling grey matter raced and while it did so he quite unselfconsciously twiddled the silver signet ring on his little finger back and forth, this way and that. It helped him to concentrate. He was well aware that a word like 'Begins' in a cryptic clue was a signal to focus on the first few words provided. So, well, yes, an anagram, clearly. Two words, four letters and six. *Evil Matter.* Some of the letters in the solution were already in place from the answers to other clues. Rearranging the anagram was a simple task, virtually automatic. Mr Redmayne inked in the final two words almost without thinking:

Time Travel

There, done! He checked his gold pocket watch. Four minutes and thirteen seconds, deliciously close to a new personal best. Only after a moment or two did the import of the final answer strike him, however. *Time Travel.* If his grey matter had been racing a few seconds earlier it positively pulsed and fizzed now. Time Travel! He had been thinking about that very subject only a few minutes ago, hadn't he? And specifically in this context! Coincidence? As a mathematician he knew that the odds against that being the case were significant, if not quite overwhelming. Coincidences did happen. Who set today's puzzle? He glanced at the top of the page. *Oberon.* Great Galileo's Ghost! Too much coincidence to be mere chance.

Mr Redmayne sprang to his feet. Something—other than himself—was afoot! But what? He went over to the chalkboard in the far corner of his study, on the stand adjacent to his desk, the long, curving art-deco desk that also had once been his father's, and pondered the lengthy and complex mathematical equation that covered the board in its entirety. He spun the chalkboard on its axis and examined the equation's continuation on the reverse side. *Had* he? Really? The clues in the crossword puzzle, every one of them, had played out as if particularly suited to his way of thinking. That's why it was so easy. It made sense. Who else knew him better than he knew himself? Had *he* set it, then, at some future point? As a warning? But about what? And why today? He would have to tell Gloriana, even if she did think him a fearful goose. Something was up. He knew it was. And now! They'd best be on their guard. It would be foolish to be otherwise.Mr Redmayne left his study urgently and stepped out into the hallway. He called down the basement steps to his wife. This time when no reply came, his concern was palpable. The silence only fuelled his growing sense that something was deeply awry. Gloriana seldom went out this early in the morning. Normally she liked to get everything sorted out for the day ahead first and then she might relax with a cup of tea. Or a pot. Only after that would she usually busy herself with any plans for an excursion. Mr Redmayne went down the steps, calling out again as he went. No response. Worse, looking around he could see that the kitchen was clearly empty. What had she been doing when he'd last seen her? She'd brought him the umbrella at the back door. She'd said something or other about something. What was that? How he wished he'd paid more attention. Wait a minute. Hadn't there been a caller? Yes. Oh dear. That was it. He'd wanted to read some meter. Damn. Moving quickly now, Mr Redmayne went back up the stairs to the hallway. He looked to the front door. This time his eyes alighted on the note on the polished walnut table the instant that he glanced in that direction. He picked it up. Great Galileo's Ghost! This was serious! At once Mr Redmayne dashed down the hallway toward the library. What on Earth was Gloriana thinking by going after the chap alone like that? He could be anywhere. Literally. Fiddlesticks! Darn! This was no good. This was no good at all!

He entered the library. Contrary to all exterior expectations the Redmayne's library was not set in a rectangular room, but in a perfectly round room, which many considered an unusual arrangement for a private house, and it was not, to any degree, small. No. Quite the opposite. Two levels of bookcases circumnavigated the circular interior, one on top of the other, reaching from the floor all the way up to the high, domed ceiling. A wonderful, natural golden light suffused the entire room, as vast as it was. In fact, the sheer size of the place alone frequently caused guests to gasp on their first entrance, such were its unexpected dimensions and grandeur, and move them to speculate in a confused way as to how it could possibly be so large. But the Redmaynes maintained that their library had to be large as they owned so many books. It really was as simple as that.

Three ornate clocks were mounted all in a line together on the lower bookcase opposite the door, under the carved crest of a phoenix rebirthing in flames—a vivid tableau itself underscored by the letters RRR. An eagle-eyed observer at this point would note that, curiously, the three clocks were all set to exactly the same time, right down to the rotation of the second hands, a synchronicity that possessed a hypnotic effect that was all its own. But Mr Redmayne clearly had no time to dally on such matters just then. A spiral staircase, resembling a strand of DNA cast in polished brass and blackened steel, provided access to the upper level on the west side, and such was his hurry that he took the turning steps two at a time. With equal haste he made his way around the upper platform to the bookcase located above the east door, where he had entered just a few moments earlier.

There, he stopped, knelt down on one knee as if genuflecting, and at once began to scan the second lowest shelf for a particular volume, running his finger along the spines from right to left. When he found what he was looking for, a rare first edition of Newton's *Philosophiae Naturalis Principia Mathematica*, he pulled the volume forward toward him. A sharp click, just one, the sound of a catch being released, came from behind the shelf, and the heavy bookcase before him swung outwards slowly like a thick door on a hinge, which of course was exactly what it was. Beyond the bookcase lay a gloomy, unlit space.

Wasting no time Mr Redmayne stepped forwards into the gloom, which immediately became illuminated and revealed itself to be a small room most notable for several tall levers, all protruding at odd, precise angles from the floor, and a complicated network of interlacing gears, cogs, and dials of various sizes on the wall behind. A low, throbbing noise was audible, like that of a ship's engine room. Mr Redmayne hurriedly crossed the short distance to the far wall. He took down some kind of gadget, a portable device, from what appeared to be a charging station, and he switched it on and off again, as if to test its power. Seemingly satisfied, he left, taking the device with him, and at once retraced his steps back through the house with the same haste as before. He didn't pause until he reached the side door off the basement steps, which he stopped to open, and passed outside.

The day was fine. Clearly it had rained heavily here much earlier in the morning but now the sky was blue and all seemed well, perfect—quite normal, in fact. Except it wasn't. Not at all. Mr Redmayne studied the handheld device. Three blips were visible on a small square screen and, as he proceeded up the exterior steps and into the alleyway, a fourth blip appeared, which represented himself. The screen depicted a street map overlaid with gridlines of longitude and latitude, and each blip appeared to cause these gridlines to curve toward and beneath it, seeming almost to bend the flat screen in on itself. Only one of the blips was moving. That would be his wife. Felice was clearly at her school. The third blip was stationary, in a nearby park. That would be the meter-man. Unless his wife had dashed out here alone just to sit in the local park, which he strongly doubted, fine day and nice park that it was, the situation was surely as he inferred. Mr Redmayne set off to intercept the moving blip, thinking it would be best if he and his wife dealt with the fellow together.

But what would they do with him, exactly? He expected that depended on the extent of the damage, to him, chiefly, the darned meter-man, although there would be other consequences also. Everything had consequences. How many times had he impressed that lesson on the children? And here *he* was now, equally culpable himself! If only he had been better organised this morning he might not have been quite so keen to pass the chap on to Gloriana. He was indeed as much to blame for this unfortunate calamity as anyone. More so, no doubt. Yes. *Yes.*

And so he went on. Reaching the crossroads, Mr Redmayne checked the device again. His wife was heading south down the main boulevard, on the opposite side of the street. Most likely she had crossed the river to begin with and was now on the way back, having given that up as a bad thing. Really if she hadn't found him in the first few minutes there was a rapidly diminishing chance that she would at all. The city was huge, truly the proverbial haystack. Mr Redmayne peered ahead and spotted his wife in the distance, approaching through the crowd along the busy pavement. Even from afar he could tell how worried and anxious she seemed, and his heart went out to her. They would fix this. They *would.* Whatever it took.

As they neared, and Mrs Redmayne caught sight of her

husband's face, her own changed quickly from an initial expression of pure relief to one of self-reproach and pain. He held out his hand to her and she took it. But she was not yet ready to be consoled. She averted her eyes, looking down, and when she raised them again he could see that they were wet. Her eyes were particularly luminous and beautiful when tearful; still, that didn't mean that he could bear to see them in such a state, knowing the cause.

"My dear, don't reproach yourself so," he said. "None of this is your fault."

"But I left him there alone, dearest, with the side door open. I should never have done that. I should have realised that he might just, well, go out like that."

"How could you have known? No, no, it's my fault entirely. If I hadn't distracted you like that. Anyway, we are where we are. We can still fix this, I promise."

"But, Eric, whatever will we do? Will we have to move again? Everyone was so settled. The children. School. Everything."

"Now, now, dear, let's go find the man first and see how he is, shall we? We'll take it from there. Nothing is decided yet, I promise." He showed her the device. Their own two blips had coalesced into one. "He's in the park, see? There. Hasn't moved in the last ten minutes, at least. Probably in shock."

"That poor man. Whatever can he be thinking?"

"Let's go find out, shall we?"

Hand in hand, the pair set off along the wide boulevard. It *was* a pleasant day, despite the immediate crisis. There were always small blessings to be thankful for, whatever the situation, and the Redmaynes usually tried to keep those in mind. Mr Redmayne was grateful for so many wonderful things in his life, his wife, the children, the house, all their special memories together, and he was determined to protect every one of these things as best he could. Why, this park they were going to now. Even that was full of special memories for them as a family. Sundays, it would seem like half the city was there. That rather ridiculous puppet theatre that his wife and children loved so much but where he could make neither head nor tail of whatever was meant to be going on. The horse-carriage rides that Felice in particular was so taken with. That nice American lady had remarked how positively regal their daughter had looked parading back and forth in that fairy-tale carriage under the chestnut trees. And it was true! She had the demeanour of a genuine princess. Obviously. But then, he would think that. No. The idea of moving again was quite out of the question.

"There he is, dear," said Mrs Redmayne, almost as soon as they had passed through the park's tall iron gates. "Over there, on the bench by the boating lake. See?"

Mr Redmayne nodded. Without a further word the pair went over toward him.

"Hello, there!" called Mr Redmayne jovially as they approached. "Just taking five minutes, I see, to watch the sailing boats. Very relaxing, I always find. Never fails to amuse. Almost as good as the real thing."

The meter-man looked up at the Redmaynes as if he didn't recognise them. His blank gaze at once fell back upon the boating lake. Only then did Mr Redmayne notice that no sail boats were out yet on the water. School day. Too early. Darn.

Mr Redmayne tried again. "Redmayne," he offered, by way of self-introduction. "You were just at my house. Came to read the meter. The *water* meter, wasn't it? Look, old chap, you might remember my wife?"

But the man continued to stare out across the water. "What park is this?" he asked.

The Redmaynes looked at each other uncomfortably. Before either one could think of a suitable reply, the man went on: "I mean, I know *all* the parks on my route, in the whole darn city, in fact. Every single one of them. Or I *thought* I did. I don't know this one. Never set eyes on it before. What park is it?"

Mr Redmayne thought hard about his answer. "Which park, is it? Well, let's see, yes, well, it's the park just off our house, of course. Yes, it is. Now, what's it called again, dear, this park? Exactly? Do you recall?"

Mrs Redmayne gave her husband a sharp look, and he at least had the decency to blush visibly in response. Luckily, he thought, with relief, the fellow didn't seem to notice. Instead, the poor meter-man was staring out across the lake again, and began rambling on, as if in a daze:

"Just now I came down some streets I don't know too. Weird, right? Because, yeah, I mean, like, how's that even possible? I know everywhere. I *got* to, see? Like I was born right around the corner, for crying out loud! Yes, sir! Just right back there someplace, on Eighty-Sixth Street!" He nodded, not very confidently, in the direction of the mystery park's tall iron gates. "So, sir, ma'am, tell me, please, how can I get lost? Here, in New York City? *Me*? Little Artie Geffney!" As he said his name he shook his head so very doubtfully that it was almost as if he didn't know who he was anymore, not for certain. "But Mr Redmayne, sir, I *am* lost—like totally and completely lost. In fact, since I left your house I ain't recognised but one single damn thing and that's the absolute truth." He shook his head again. "See, what it was, to start with, sir, ma'am, I spotted this strange-looking car—that was it, yeah, the car. Real old-fashioned number, foreign, too, you know—wide-grille, fins and everything—Italian, maybe, I'm thinking. So, yeah, like, anyway, I goes over and takes a closer look. Kinda real interesting and all, seeing a fancy Italian car like that or whatever in this neighbourhood. And so right then when it first moves off, going real slow to start with, I can't help but follow after it, just a little ways… And that was it. Man! Lost!"

"Ah," said Mrs Redmayne, nodding knowingly.

The meter-man peered up at her, as though waiting to hear more.

But when no more came, he resumed: "So, right there and then I tried to head back over to Fifth, but, like, man… Nope. Not east nor west. Couldn't be done. Not no way, no how. And, believe me, Mr Redmayne, ma'am, I tried just about every which way I could, I reckon. Nothing doing. And, man, listen, some of the strange things I saw along the way, well, I can't explain them, either! No, sir! Not at all. Like, all those weird street signs, for one. What are *they* all about? And all that foreign writing and such? No way that could be right—this is America! I tell you, none of it made the least bit of sense. So, right about then I started to think, like, you know, maybe I was experiencing some kind of weird episode or some such thing, like you see in a show on the TV. You know what I mean? Yeah, everything considered, I reckoned that's what most probably was going down here. So then I came and sat in this park, just for a while—you know, to try to make sense of things maybe. Get my head together."

"Oh, you poor man," said Mrs Redmayne, "I'm so very sorry. Do come with us, won't you? We'll have you back on Fifth Avenue again in no time. Five minutes, at the most. I promise."

"Really?"

"Yes, really," said Mr Redmayne, very positively indeed, "in a jiffy. Less, in fact. That's a personal guarantee. A Redmayne promise. You just got yourself turned around, that's all, old fellow. Could happen to anyone. Now, pop your cap back on, that's it, there's a good chap. Yes, perfect. First class. Now, come with us. We'll show you the way. Come on."

"Maybe you'd like a nice cup of tea?" suggested Mrs Redmayne. "That always, always helps, I find. A nice cream tea. Yes. Never fails."

Back on his feet, cap straightened, the man nodded to her, if still looking a little altogether too blank for her liking, however, and Mrs Redmayne suspected he might well have proved agreeable to any proposal at all put to him at that particular moment.

"You know, I got lost myself once," Mr Redmayne announced, talking purely as a distraction tactic. "As a nipper, in Shanghai, of all places, would you believe? Gave the Mater quite the scare, I don't mind telling you. Not the Pater, though. Not mean old, gruff old Rufus! Heavens no, not *him*, not by any means. *He* thought getting lost was entirely character building, especially for a small child. Very old-fashioned in his views, was the Pater. Not the sort of thing folk much espouse these days, though, is it? Teaching a boy independence by cutting them loose in a strange, foreign city. Hardly. You won't find that in Mr Spock's manual, I bet!"

"*Dr* Spock, dear. *Mr* Spock's an alien on the television. Quite different."

"Really? That is news."

They had exited the park and were making the short journey west back toward the main boulevard. Mr Redmayne was beginning to feel on the whole a little better about things. The situation might not turn out to be as desperate as they had originally feared. If they could get the chap back into the house and out through the front door without further incident, all might yet be well. Keeping him distracted, that was the key.

"And I'm really quite sure the gentleman doesn't want to hear any stories about your childhood, darling. Not at all. No one ever really does, dear. Not really, I'm afraid. That's about the truth of it. No matter how exotic the setting."

Mr Redmayne harrumphed to himself ever so slightly at this but let it go. They had reached the wide main road and were looking for a place to cross. After a second, he realised that their charge was lingering back slightly, and began to fear the worst.

"Come on, now, old fellow. Almost there. Just across this road here, quick turn around the corner, back in through the house and, voilà, Bob's your proverbial uncle. Good old Fifth Ave!"

The man was peering west above the rooftops.

"Just one thing," he said, hesitantly, indeed more than that—a little fearfully. "Help a poor fella in need out, please, I'm begging you, and tell me the truth. I got to—no, I *need to*—know. Mr Redmayne, *there*. Am I going crazy or is that what I think it is? For real? Right there, see? Over the rooftops. Man, is that, well, like, *the Eiffel Tower* I can see?"

Mr Redmayne's heart sank. "What? Where? Oh, there?"

He looked at his wife. She had nothing.

"Well, it certainly looks like it, I have to say. Remarkable, no?"

And he gave the man his best, warmest, most convincing smile, all the time unsure of what exactly he might be trying to convince him about, let alone whether or not it would work.

5

It would seem that there really were some situations that not even a cream tea might resolve, which was a hard lesson for Mrs Redmayne to have to learn this late in her life. Hard but true. Still, in good faith, she had returned to her house with her husband and their unfortunate, somewhat dazed guest, and together they had set about trying to make him feel a little better about things. They had taken him straight down to the breakfast table in their cosy basement kitchen, sat him in front of the giant cast-iron range cooker and pampered him with fresh scones, a sizeable scrape of clotted cream on a Cornishware blue plate, and a steaming hot pot of tea (none other than Darjeeling Paragon, as you might expect under the circumstances).

But, sad to say, after all that had happened that morning, he didn't seem in the right frame of mind to enjoy their famous hospitality. His confusion, it would seem, was simply too great.

It went like this: the poor man believed, contradictorily, either that (i) only a matter of a few minutes earlier he had actually been in Paris, France, which was clearly impossible; or (ii) he only *imagined* that a few minutes earlier he had been in Paris, France, in which case he was clearly, well, *doolally* (a word supplied by Mr Redmayne, with the best intentions, after their guest had himself struggled to find the right phrase, but for which overly generous act his wife later chastised him roundly). Neither scenario was of much comfort to the fellow, it has to be said. And discussing the matter further, despite what was entirely *his* own (selfish?) insistence on doing so, only seemed to increase his agitation. Some people, after all, are simply constitutionally unable to grasp the silver lining in every basket of eggs, a metaphor that Mr Redmayne himself mixed quite spectacularly, once again with the best intentions. And for which he was, once again, suitably chastised later. And no doubt you might think deservedly so.[1]

But there was no fixing the poor meter-man. The best solution that he came up with to rationalize away his odd experience was that the Eiffel Tower he had glimpsed in the distance had most likely been a Macy's Thanksgiving Day parade balloon; and, yes, that made a certain sense the Redmaynes had to agree. Although, given that the parade was still a full half-year away, and that so much else that had seemed strange to him that morning might be best explained by the possibility of him having *actually been in France*, they doubted that this solution would satisfy him for very long. No, no, and no.[2]

And so, in the end Mr Redmayne led the poor chap out through the front door and down the solid stone steps on to the familiar terra firma of the good old USA. New York City. Bright sunshine, a crowded skyline of tall, tall buildings, the constant hum of busy traffic, all in all the meter-man's natural environment.

Mr Redmayne watched him hesitate on the threshold of freedom for a moment, this skittish little fellow, as if checking that everything was as it should be, before zipping off without a backward glance, much as though he were a wild creature that could not quite believe its good luck in being set loose once again.

And then—*pouff*, he was gone!

But, alas, when Mr Redmayne went back inside the house, he and his wife exchanged a look, and they knew something had to be done.

The children came home in the late afternoon, arriving in the usual order, first Emile, followed shortly afterwards by a happy Felice. Emile appeared quite drowned. It had rained heavily all day, but as soon as he removed his sodden coat he was free of that completely, almost as if it hadn't happened. He dashed off

---

[1] Yes.

[2] No.

to his room at once, muttering something about a new install-
ment of an online manga adventure, whatever that might be,
just released today and so required immediate consumption. His
parents knew they would not see him until dinner, and only then
if called on three or, at most, four occasions. Four being the
upper limit of Mrs Redmayne's established tolerance for calling.

George arrived home long after everyone else and in something of a major blue funk; indeed, his was a mood so black
that his father's practiced grumpiness of earlier that day seemed
in comparison like an interlude of light pleasantries and banter.
The Redmaynes' eldest child stormed off to his room without
so much as muttering a word to anyone, slamming the door
behind him by way of emphasis, and that was that.

His sister, on the other hand, was in such high spirits that
she entirely failed to notice not only George's bad humour but
that her parents were also quite distracted and not at all their
usual selves. She twittered on merrily and at length about some
great success at school, some immense piece of good fortune
through which she had secured a lead part in the drama soci-
ety's coming production for that year.

But it didn't occur to her as odd that neither her father
nor her mother asked any questions about whichever part it
was that she had won, or how, or even about the play that had
been chosen for production. Given that, normally, Mr and Mrs
Redmayne fixated on every minute detail of their children's
lives, that *was* strange, if unremarked by all.

And so went dinner that evening, with each of the Redmaynes
distracted by some concern of their own, so that as an occasion
it was quite flat and ordinary. Altogether mundane, in fact, as is
frequently the case for so many families busily negotiating the
everyday demands of their hectic lives, rather than a celebration
of being together, as it so often was normally for the special
family in this tale.

But this would be the last occasion for a long, long time
that any of the Redmaynes took one another for granted, given
everything that happened next.

After dinner, and after the children had cleared up, Mr and Mrs Redmayne retired to the library. They considered the day's events and what they might do. An option existed, but it was not to be undertaken lightly, for it could have serious consequences. On the other hand, it could fix everything, painlessly and at a stroke.

Gloriana was very concerned for the wellbeing of the poor meter-man, because they—as a family—were responsible for the events that had affected him so badly. At the same time she didn't delude herself that she would be acting entirely selflessly. What the fellow knew posed a risk to them all. He could be back, tomorrow, with others, and that would be the end. Best to head that off, for him and for them, if that were possible. And they knew it was.

Mr Redmayne remembered, eventually, the curious matter of the crossword puzzle, and how that one clue in particular this morning had tipped him off that trouble was afoot. *Evil Matter.* He explained what he thought that it had meant, who had put it there, today of all days, and why—as a warning, he postulated, of what was about to happen—and what they should do about it, which was no less than the very radical action they were now contemplating. All of this Mrs Redmayne found persuasive. No coincidence, it couldn't be, no; rather a very intelligent steer about what to do. A clue indeed. And who else could have sent such a clever clue but himself, Mr Redmayne concluded proudly. Who indeed?

So, they were agreed. Everything was decided. They would act. For better or worse.

Should they tell the children? Mr Redmayne, on the whole, thought not. Emile most likely wouldn't even notice. He joked that what they called the prospect of yet another identically rainy day in London was simply *tomorrow.* And then he chuckled for a long moment about what he regarded as the cleverness of his remark, while Mrs Redmayne waited patiently for him to stop. And when finally he did stop she said that she agreed

about not telling the children, because what they were about
to do presented too much temptation for a young person, any
young person, to be able to resist. It was a profoundly powerful
thing, not to be meddled with lightly for fun or adventure. And
young people were constitutionally unable to resist fun and
adventure. And so, the matter was settled. No, they would not
be told.

And that was that.

Midnight would be the best time to carry it out, on that
point they concurred.

It was essential, of course, that they all be inside the house
when it took place, otherwise, well, best not think about that.
To this day they both frequently lamented how poor Charles
Dickens had, with the most unfortunate timing, picked one such
occasion as this to pursue his clandestine nocturnal wanderings
in the dark streets outside and hadn't been seen or heard of
since—and the Good Lord only knew what had become of
him. Charles Dickens was—or had been—the Redmaynes' cat.
The children, to that day, still asked about him from time to
time, or at least Emile did, a question that their parents typically
prevaricated about in response, in a half-hearted mumbley sort
of way.

Still, the idea of any such similar fate befalling one of the
children themselves, was, quite rightly, to Mr and Mrs Redmayne,
unthinkable. Accordingly Mrs Redmayne undertook to check
on the three in their beds shortly before the time, just to make
absolutely sure. And then she would rejoin him here, in the
library, so that they would be together when it happened.

Mr Redmayne nodded, and she left, while he retired to the
secret room, behind the bookcases, to make some necessary
preparations. Everything had to be exactly right. No room for
the slightest miscalculation. None.

And none was made. It was, after all, only a small readjust-
ment. Mr and Mrs Redmayne carried out their plan. As midnight began to chime Mr Redmayne made the final twist to the
great mechanism of cogs and gears and levers, turning a great

brass key counter-clockwise in its equally great brass lock. Mrs Redmayne slipped her cold hand into his, and together they watched as everything in the room switched momentarily into reverse. At that moment any hawk-eyed observer in the library itself would have noticed the hands on the three ornate clocks spinning backward simultaneously, each lapping the hour of twelve not once but twice.

The die, for better or worse, was cast.

And when the great grandfather clock in the hallway struck the final chime of midnight just then, it did so not to call the close of the day it had just measured out, but the close of the day before.

6

When the Redmaynes awoke on the following morning there seemed nothing to mark the new day as in the least auspicious, except for the fact that it was not a new day. To the innocent, unsuspecting eye, however, it started out much like the day before and most probably much like how the day after it would begin also. Washed, dressed, fed, and out. The same routine applied. Only if you happened to know, as Mr and Mrs Redmayne of course knew, that the present morning was indeed the *very same morning* as the one before, did it assume a fraught quality, one in which the potential for mishap and even calamity felt very real—that is, at least as far as Mrs Redmayne was concerned in any case.

What could possibly go wrong? That was the troubling question that had kept poor Gloriana awake for much of the long, long night, especially when the same single word answer came back to her again and again. *Everything.* If only she had felt that her husband was equally affected by what they had done, if he had displayed the remotest sign of anxiety or concern, then she might have felt a little better about it herself. Partners in crime. But, alas, he did not, and so she did not. Mr Redmayne slept, much like he always slept, like an angel, a lord, as carefree as a lark. No tossing and turning for him. Not at all. In the wee, small hours, Gloriana looked over at his contentedly slumbering form and felt both a little envious and more than a little irritated. *Had they done the right thing?* No point asking her husband. His office was closed until morning.

And even then, when morning came, finally, *again*, he appeared quite oblivious, getting dressed and going about his business as if without a thought in his head, to the point where Mrs Redmayne felt sure that he had entirely forgotten what they had done the night before, their changing history together and potentially altering the destinies of millions (no, billions) of people. When she could stand it no longer and challenged him on this, the blank look on his face confirmed her suspicions on the matter. The fact that they had turned back time had slipped his mind as easily as a dentist's appointment.

Despite his many protestations to the contrary, quite how this momentous act could sit so lightly with him was a mystery to her. And when at last he confessed that it may have slipped his mind a little, at first, dear, as he thought it might, but that he had taken the precaution of tying a knot in his handkerchief, as a *memoria technica*, to remind him that they had done something, or other, well, she thought she might throw the contents of her dressing table at him, and at this point he sensibly withdrew. And Mrs Redmayne seethed quietly to herself as she heard her husband going about his usual morning's chores and tasks, first waking up the children and then heading down the stairs to make things ready below.

Just another day. Clearly.

Except—in a very real sense—it wasn't.

৯

Poor George had also slept very badly. He'd been in a foul enough mood when arriving home after school on what—naturally enough to him, waking up right then—had been the previous evening. And in truth his mood hadn't much improved by the time he heard his father's voice calling him to get up that morning—if anything, the opposite was true! He actually felt far worse, more desperately tired now on waking up than he had at any point throughout the long night. How was that possible? In fact, he thought he would probably be feeling far less tired now if he hadn't gone to sleep at all, rather than finally dropping off at some point after 5:30 a.m. But as it was, he just felt exhausted, zombie-like, which did nothing to help his mood at all.

And now, he only had to go and do it all over again, didn't he? *School.* The cruelty of it all. Life, as many a seriously hard-done-by teen will testify, was so unfair. Especially when your math teacher was an idiot, as was George's. Mr Kelvin. Mr Kelvin of the stupid, corny mathematical symbols on his stupid, corny tie. Mr Kelvin of the test questions that were technically unanswerable because they stupidly lacked a key piece of stupid data. Mr Kelvin who had stubbornly (stupidly) refused to admit that he was wrong and had handed him an F on his stupid test yesterday just because George had equally stubbornly (bravely) refused to supply (technically) incorrect answers to the stupid problems that stupid, stupid Mr Kelvin had set the entire stupid class. And now George had an F on his record forever, as though he was one of the stupid mouth-breather sports jocks who always hid at the back of class grinning nonstop like loons about something inane. An F! So *very* unfair! He, who was so far beyond anyone else in the class at math (including Kelvin) that the idea of him failing it was quite ridiculous. It wasn't like they ever did any interesting math. No dynamical systems, no computational theorising. Nothing advanced. Only basic stuff he'd taught himself years ago. Geometry! Trigonometry! Calculus! Math for dolts. Stupid! Just then, hearing his father's voice calling him again, George struggled upright in bed and began fumbling with the switch on his bedside lamp. At once he winced. Light, blinding, pain, tired. Stupid. Everything was stupid. Except him. Usually. Except maybe a little. Sometimes. He got up, stepping gingerly through the debris of discarded computer parts that perpetually littered the floor of his room.

Days like yesterday shouldn't be allowed to happen. That was the lesson George was taking away from this. None of it was his fault. None at all. Why should he pretend any differently? Especially when he was obviously right and everyone else was just as obviously wrong (i.e. Wrong!). He *could* have given some answers, yes, the wrong answers (technically) that Mr Kelvin was clearly expecting the class to give. But to do that, George would have been required to overlook the glaring flaws in all of the questions (glaring to *him*, anyway), and he simply couldn't do it. No, the truth was important. That's what his father had always taught him, after all. Even if old Kelvin hadn't quite appreciated being made to look like a fool in front of the entire class and at once started to shout (like many of George's teachers, Mr Kelvin apparently believed that shouting equated with better teaching[3]). Now, George just had to find the right moment to break the bad news to his parents. An F. For: *Fail*. Darn. His mother, especially, would be disappointed, he knew. Very. Maybe over breakfast? George paused in the doorway before exiting his room. Hmm, maybe not. Later, then? Yes. Tonight would be better. By far. On that thought he went downstairs.

As it was, breakfast passed much like it had yesterday. Everyone was absorbed in their own thing. Felice nibbled at her croissant as daintily as a bird, as usual, except that today she looked especially pleased with herself while she was doing it, which frankly George found more than a little annoying. His brother, the Integer, was lost in some comic book or other, of course, the *Astonishing Adventures of Enrique and the Epic Ninja Space-Time Pirates*, or something like that. And as for George's parents, well, if anything, for some reason they were even more focussed on getting everyone out on time than they were usually. His mother fussed and hurried them along constantly, practically shooing them away from the table and out of the kitchen, long before they were properly finished. And his father! Not only was he waiting for them out in the hallway with their so-called topcoats ready, but he'd taken the extraordinary step of packing their schoolbags too! Everybody had to get out in good time today, he said, looking sheepish for some reason. It was especially important today, he insisted, given… *something or other* (inaudible). Yes, so, no dillydallying. No exceptions. None. Emile was to take himself to school today. Yes. He was quite old enough now. No arguments. And he should take the umbrella too. The big one. The weather was going to be very much like it was yesterday. Everywhere. Exactly the same for all of them, in fact, so dress accordingly and be off.

---

[3] A standard tenet of teacher training. It has to be. What else could explain it? Nothing, that's what.

Now. No time to lose. And with that he was gone himself, out the front door. All of a sudden, just like that. Very strange.

Consequently George couldn't have found a good moment to mention the problem with his stupid math test this morning even if he had actually wanted to do that. Which, of course, he didn't. Mostly. And so he didn't. And about that he felt glad. Mostly. Eighty percent glad. Eighty-five, possibly. That was enough. Probably. Wasn't it? *Was* it, though? He couldn't decide. Move on.

One more rather strange thing caught his eye, however. On his way out George spotted his father talking on the street. This was unusual in itself, a rarity. And not only that but the often slightly eccentric pater seemed to be making a determined effort to turn someone around, away from the house. Not that the house was that easy to spot from the street, unless you knew where to look to begin with, or unless it wanted you to see it. But something in his father's manner seemed a little off. He barely nodded to George as he passed. That was odd in itself. And there was something vaguely familiar about the man he was talking to, as well, some short, bland, chubby official-looking dude in uniform and a white peaked cap. Clutching a clipboard to his chest like it was a shield. Weird, but never mind. George had other concerns to think about, other far more pressing issues to address. Fix, if he could. School, for one. An F in math, his best subject, other than IT, of course. And poor old Kelvin. Very quickly, then, wandering along Fifth Avenue, George was lost in thought about all of that, his own preoccupations, wondering if there might be anything he could possibly do to repair the damage he'd caused yesterday with his stupid Redmayne pride, stubbornness, and downright refusal to be wrong. The truth above all, or some such family nonsense. Damn.

Not that he actually expected there would be. Not really. No. Life wasn't like that, was it? What's done was done. You didn't get a do-over. Except in the comic books. And those he didn't read. Too lame. Totally. Stupid.

❧

Poor Felice was having a very bad day, a very bad day indeed. And it had all started out so perfectly fine too. On the way to school she was still in a very good mood, even though for some reason her parents had harried and bothered her into leaving far earlier than was her usual routine. Old people! There really was no way of explaining their behaviour sometimes. Still, despite that, her day had begun very positively on the whole. She always enjoyed the walk to school. On a day like today, when the air was all fresh and clean after some early rain, it was almost too lovely for words. The little, winding streets, the shops—she *so* loved all the tiny boutiques and tiny knickknack stores that lined both sides of the rue de Trompe L'Oeil—and all of the hustle and bustle of the people that she passed. Felice found it amusing that she would see the same faces every day as she negotiated her route, strangers that she didn't know in the least but who became a fixture in her life just because their morning routines coincided with her own—the always rushing, beehive-haired woman with her angelic-faced daughter; the kindly old Chinese man sweeping the street outside of his patisserie, who smiled at Felice as she went by.

It was like a kind of secret clockwork, everybody moving independently (or *so* they thought) but still in perfect order, and this idea she found interesting, even if she was a little off schedule today herself on account of being out early (against her will). But even this was interesting, too, because everything was now just a little bit different and therefore new things could happen. She looked up and down the narrow French street. All of it, everything the eye could see, was just *so* interesting—all the time! And, of course, beautiful too. That's exactly how she felt. Perfect, yes, all of it. The world was just perfect—and this another perfect moment to cherish and keep always. She wished she could paint it there and then. *Click!*

Instantly she committed the scene to memory, like a photograph. She would paint it later, but exactly as it was.

Sometimes she felt that it was almost as if time had stood still.

Needless to say, much of Felice's good mood stemmed from the fact that she was still basking in her glorious triumph of the previous day, when she had beaten out her arch-nemesis Claudia Bouffant to the part of Agnes in the annual school play.[4] Sweet, innocent Agnes! Felice was born to play her. Yesterday had been a great day, one of her best. She hadn't expected to get the part, not really, but she'd had hope. Claudia was such a super-achiever, great at everything, if a little cold, well, glacial actually, at least toward Felice. And beautiful, to boot, damn her, in a so very French sort of way (which is, of course, the best way) (damn her, again).

But it didn't seem to Felice that Claudia actually enjoyed any of the things that she worked so hard to master—it was like she just wanted to be first, all the time. And she had no doubt been the favourite to get the lead part, for sure. Then Fate had intervened (good old Fate). And Felice had been there to witness it with her own eyes. Sweet!

No, that was mean. Felice checked her watch. She must have been dawdling. Daydreaming (she did so love daydreaming). But not much farther to go. Felice turned the corner onto rue de L'École and began to hurry. It had been just right about here, she remembered. Claudia had come around the corner on the other side of the street. Felice ran through the incident in her mind's eye, seeing it again in perfect detail. Right about there, it happened, in fact. Exactly. That huge muddy puddle there at the side of the road. Claudia hadn't spotted it, and when she was right alongside that mean little white Citroën with the shark-like smile and fins had zoomed by and splashed a virtual kerbside tsunami up onto the street, soaking poor Claudia in the process. Felice had only been able to hold a hand up to her mouth in horror. And then the car had flashed right on past her too, looking for all the world like it was thoroughly pleased with itself. Grinning, even. Felice literally had not been able to believe her eyes. Poor Claudia! She was so soaked through that she'd been forced right then to turn around and go home to

[4] *L'École des femmes*, by Molière. But you knew that.

change! Such bad luck. Felice stopped for a moment, reliving the scene.

And then—what? It was happening again! No! Surely not! But Felice spied Claudia coming around the corner on the other side of the road, just like yesterday. And, also just like yesterday, at the very same time there appeared the little white Citroën, still in the distance, but approaching. Surely Claudia would see it this time? Especially after yesterday. Surely? But, no. She appeared to be oblivious. What was the matter with her? As if transfixed to the spot Felice stood watching the scene unfold before her: Claudia trudging along, unaware, somehow, and the car sneaking up at speed behind her. It was going to happen again! No! Felice broke the spell. Alarmed, she ran across the road, waving her arms and calling out to Claudia like a mad thing.

"Stop! Look out! Claudia! The puddle! Car! Stop!"

And just in time!

Claudia stopped dead, clearly taken aback by the agitated, arm-waving, wailing banshee running toward her at speed. In a heartbeat Claudia's eyes took in the large puddle immediately ahead at the kerbside, and then at once came the car, scudding through from behind her, sending a frightful splash of rainwater arcing high up onto the pavement and crashing down between the two girls with a mighty *whoomph*, soaking the short stretch of sidewalk between them. In an instant, it was over. Claudia looked up at Felice, her face betraying her confusion.

The car was gone, no doubt still grinning, if now perhaps a little ruefully.

"Claudia, I don't believe it. How could you nearly let that happen, especially after—" began Felice, but then she checked herself. Who was she to judge anyone else's total daydreaminess? The same thing could very easily happen to her. Three times probably. No need to make a big fuss. Still, a thank you of some sort might have been nice. No matter. It would be their secret. Never to be mentioned. No.

After a second, Claudia seemed to have recovered her

composure. She came toward Felice (was that a glimmer—the faintest hint—of a smile of gratitude on her face?) (possibly) and they turned to walk into school together. Neither of them said a word for a moment. Awkward still, no doubt about yesterday. Silence.

"So, about Agnes," ventured Felice, tentatively, still secure in her triumph. "No hard feelings?"

But Claudia, arching a single raised eyebrow, only gave her the most enigmatic smile in response. And then she swept off in typically aloof fashion.

A response that Felice could but interpret in only one way—and admire in equal proportion.

So French!

And, for the rest of the day, that was as good as it got for Felice. Because, after that, everything went rapidly downhill and in the strangest possible way, with the undeniable strangeness kicking in almost at once, immediately after registration. Because, in place of the lesson in éducation civique that Felice was expecting to have first thing (along with the rest of her class, or so she assumed), their professeur launched instead into their première langue vivante étrangère, their first foreign language, which happened to be English; and which, as might be anticipated, Felice naturally found immensely boring, given her great advantages in that subject (its dullness as a lesson enlivened from time to time only by some of her classmates' more original linguistic errors, especially any made by Claudia, which Felice particularly treasured on account of their great rarity—and, not to mention, Claudia's obvious and extreme sense of embarrassment).

But, any change at all to the timetable was a shock, and quite unprecedented in her experience—in anyone's experience, in fact. The timetable *never* changed. It was probably illegal. At any moment les gendarmes would likely burst in to the classroom and arrest the professeur, the normally utterly inflexible Madame Méchant, for daring to deviate from the national teaching schedule, as it was a known fact that every French pupil everywhere must take the very same lesson at the same time. Or was it? Might that be only a myth? Felice wasn't sure. But, in any case, to her surprise, no one else in the class seemed to find the change of the least interest or note. Heads were down and eyes were actively being averted from those of Madame M., so that they might not get called on, all in the usual (boring) way. Nothing was different. Not in the least. Felice studied the room. Maybe she had missed an announcement yesterday, or something? Everyone else was just carrying on as normal. Much as Felice might have enjoyed seeing Madame getting carted off kicking and screaming for her many crimes against teaching (not least for all the times she had referred to her pupils as *nuls*, nothing, a regular occurrence), it didn't seem likely. No. Pity.

Just then a titter ran though the room, reaching a sort of polite, murmurous crescendo before being at once suppressed by Madame M.'s stern, laser-eyed gaze. This wasn't that unusual, except for the source—little Lucie Lagneux, who usually had the art of remaining unobtrusive down to a tee. Except, that only yesterday, for the first time ever, Lucie had done the very same thing, in the very same class. Now it looked as though she had made getting caught out by Madame into a habit. Poor Lucie! She did blush so, at the slightest provocation. So red-cheeked! Felice found herself reddening in sympathy. Still, you'd think she would have learned her lesson yesterday. Her temperament wasn't suited to the spotlight. Not at all. Now Madame had her square in her wicked sights once again and nothing could be done about it. Felice's heart went out to the girl. All eyes were on her. It was too painful to watch, just like yesterday...

Little Lucie Lagneux, her pale amber eyes fixed firmly on her desk, visibly squirmed under everyone's attention. "Pardon, madame?" she managed, in a small voice, the English halting, unsure. "I think maybe I am not being understanding of you."

This all seemed terribly familiar. It was almost like history was repeating itself. Or not even almost. It actually was.

Madame glared. "Of course you do not understand. It is because you are nothing. What are you?"

"Nothing, madame."

"That is correct. Yes, you *were* nothing yesterday and you *are* nothing today. I believe you *will still be* nothing tomorrow also, child. Of course, you will. Unless you improve, yes, particularly in your command of the English tenses. Now…"

Oh dear. Was this how it was going to be now, every day? Poor Lucie! Felice looked around at her classmates. None of them appeared to think that Madame picking on Lucie in the exact same fashion day after day was going too far. Using the exact same words too! What sort of message was that to reinforce on a daily basis? To anyone? It was practically bullying. It *was…*

What? Next came sweet Malou Bellerose. Madame crossed the room to stand directly in front of the unsuspecting girl's desk. That was just like yesterday too. Yesterday, Malou had written a note that she's intended to pass across the class to Jeanelle, her meilleure amie, but Madame had intercepted it and forced her to read it aloud to the entire class, just like she always did in such cases, except that yesterday she'd also forced poor Malou to translate it into English as well. Malou's English was abysmal. The pain! It had taken her ages and made no sense. Felice couldn't believe that Malou had let herself get caught in the exact same way so soon! It was actually becoming a little spooky, too, the way it was unfolding, because even *that* was exactly like yesterday. But *exactly…* Madame holding out her hand, Malou reluctantly surrendering the note, Madame glancing at its contents and then passing it back to Malou with the instruction for her to translate it aloud in front of the class. Felice looked around again. Nobody else seemed to have the same sense as she did that what was happening was, she didn't know what, familiar. A repeat.

In truth, Felice was beginning to feel more than a little spooked herself just now. After a second or so Malou had begun her stuttering translation—and it was exactly the same as yesterday, faltering word for faltering word. But no one else seemed to be registering that fact.

Felice didn't know what she expected. Something. Some raised eyebrows, maybe, some acknowledgement of *what, this, again?* But nothing like that was happening. Nothing! Everybody was just, well, going with it, as though it was the first time. While Felice couldn't help but feel a little like she were watching a TV show that she'd seen before but nobody else had. Déjà vu, in extremis.

What, what if she were going mad? That was it. Her strange lifestyle had finally caught up with her. Everything had consequences, that's what Papa had always warned her about, wasn't it? Everything. And so maybe that's what this was, this strange feeling of having seen things before. Consequences.

But then—*phew!*—something happened that broke the spell. Finally.

Claudia intervened. She was sitting in the seat next to Malou and, with an air of the most tremendous impatience with her poor neighbour's stuttering performance, she had snatched the note away and started to translate it herself—aloud, impeccably, and without the slightest hesitation.

It was a silly note, something about doing something or other on Wednesday afternoon, in town. Nothing that couldn't wait.

But Malou seemed grateful to Claudia all the same and even Madame appeared to be satisfied by her star pupil's intervention. Humiliation completed.

And Felice breathed again. That certainly hadn't happened yesterday. She was just being silly. And that was nothing new, Felice being silly. That could happen on *any* day. Any day at all! *Phew!*

But this, sadly, was only a temporary respite. Felice's day didn't turn really, really bad until lunchtime, when everyone, including many of her so-called friends, had conspired to give *her* part in the school play to Claudia.

To Claudia! Her part. Agnes!

Without telling her, for some reason they had restaged the auditions! Secretly! Why would they do that? And when she'd objected, strongly, no one would acknowledge in any way that they'd given *her* the part only yesterday. In fact, they didn't seem to have any idea what she was talking about. They thought she was trying it on in some way. It was almost like yesterday's auditions hadn't even happened.

It was all so strange and crushing and terrible!

But, most of all, it was just *strange*!

7

George, on the other hand, had enjoyed a very good day and consequently he felt very badly about it, very badly indeed. By the time he'd gotten home from school he truly was in quite the state, no other words for it will suffice.[5] His mind was racing, no, much, much more than that, exploding… His day, his very good day, had also been a very strange day, very strange indeed, and there could be only one explanation for it—or, at least, having systematically and logically discounted all other explanations, only one remained that he was prepared to accept.

Somehow, *somehow*, as crazy as it sounded, he had time-travelled—yes, *time-travelled*—back in time one whole day. Twenty-four hours.

That was the only—the one and only—way to account for all the very strange things that had been happening to him all day long—yes, as crazy as that sounded.

And he knew exactly how crazy it sounded!

But, the thing was, he had evidence. Proof! Right there, in his hands. *Actual proof*, yes, that he—George Rufus Reginald Eric Redmayne—was a time-traveller. Yes, a time-traveller! That much was a fact now, as far as he was concerned. F-A-C-T—FACT!

What George didn't know, however, as he sat cross-legged on his bed at home after school, mulling it over deeply, was how, or why. Or indeed if it were only him.

And so he stared hard at the evidence some more—the sweet, incontrovertible proof—still not quite believing his eyes, as if the act of staring would in some way make it give up its secrets. The truth. The real truth. Whatever that was.

---

[5] Well, many others would, actually, but we're going with these. Move on.

In one hand, his left, he held the once crumpled but since roughly straightened out math test that he had brought home from school on what, despite himself, he could only still think of as *yesterday*; and, in his right, he gripped the clean, unrumpled math test paper that he had taken earlier today.

For the hundred-and-twentieth time since arriving home from school George looked from one to the other, and then back again.

And then for the hundred-and-twenty-first.

Indisputably, they were the very same math test paper, identical, with the very same questions and, this was the obvious clincher, bearing the very same date at the top (but with a very different outcome on the second test: *20/20, A*—otherwise, identical, in every way*).

This was proof, actual *proof*, of a sort, at least to him.

He knew very well it wouldn't stand up to scientific scrutiny. It wasn't like he could send them to *Scientific American* or someplace like that as hard evidence of time-travel.

He knew that. They'd think he was an idiot, or a nutcase, or, worse, both.

But from a personal perspective, they were proof enough that he wasn't going mad, that his day had repeated, that he wasn't just imagining it or suffering some kind of mad hallucination, as he'd feared he might be at first.

Now, he was waiting for his sister and brother to come home. If it had happened to him, it might have been the same for them too. And that's what he needed to know.

Because, like any good scientist, he had a theory. And like any good scientist, he needed to test his theory though observation and evidence.

And it was all to do with the house.

Their special house. Maybe it was more special than any of them knew? Or at least more special than he and his brother and sister knew.

As for his parents, well, he felt sure they knew far more than they were letting on. Both of them had been acting really weird

when he'd first come in from school, even by their standards—
acutely interested in his day (and not just Felice's for once),
while trying equally hard to seem not to be.

It was then he knew. *They knew.*

And when he'd said that it hadn't been anything out of the
ordinary, nothing special, really, just fine, they'd both seemed
really relieved—again, while trying very hard not to seem like
they were!

They were so transparent, the pair of them. Terrible actors.

Yes, they knew. He was sure of it. They may even have been
the cause.

The sound of footsteps out on the landing made him sit
up. His father's tread. Mother was far more light-footed.
George reached over and slipped his two math test papers into
the drawer of his bedside table. Then, he lay back and stared
up at the ceiling. Nothing to see here. Move on. Everything's
fine, normal, really. No untoward after-effects of unwitting
time-travel to mention. No. Not at all. None. A very average
day, in fact, all in all. The whole time-travelling thing aside, of
course…

The footsteps came to a halt outside his door. After a
second or so, presumably while his father adjusted his facial
expression to 'natural,' came a quiet knock on the door, which
at once swung open. His father's face appeared in the doorway,
indeed looking so stiffly 'natural' it might very well have been
carved out of wood, or stone. Silence. Awkward. But no one
was admitting to that.

"Hello, son," said Mr Redmayne eventually, in what came
across as a determinedly ordinary tone.

"Hi, Pops," replied George, equally ordinarily.

"What are you doing?"

"Nothing."

"I see." Mr Redmayne glanced around the room as if looking for something he might have mislaid in there earlier, possibly—perhaps among the scattered debris of dismantled computer parts, the ongoing destruction of innocent computers

seemingly forming one of George's pet hobbies. "Well, I just came to see if you wanted anything, that's all. To eat, perhaps, I mean, or drink? Maybe a cream tea?"

"No, thanks, Pops, I'm fine. Really. I'm just a little tired after my, well, you know, *extra*-long day. Or that's how it felt. So, I'm resting."

"I see. Your *day*, hmm, that was fine you said earlier. Wasn't it?"

"Yes, fine. You know, *average*. An average day."

"Average?"

"*Very* average. Nothing exceptional at all. You know, average."

"I see," said Mr Redmayne. "That's good, isn't it?"

"Average," said George. "Neither good nor bad. By definition."

This last remark hung in the air for a moment, unchallenged.

"Average," repeated Mr Redmayne. A lull followed.

Well, excellent, then," he said, after a second or so longer. "I'll leave you to it. Enjoy your rest. We'll call you for dinner. We're all eating together later. No exceptions."

He turned to go.

"Oh, Pops," said George, "one thing…"

Mr Redmayne stopped. "Yes?"

"Yes. What time is dinner? Exactly, do you think?"

"Time? I don't know. The usual, I imagine."

"Okay, thanks. That's fine. It's just I didn't want to, you know, like, start something, and not have enough time to finish. Because then, you know, I'd only have to start it all over again later. I hate that, don't you? Having to start things over, I mean, and then, well, repeat everything. And I do that all the time. You would not believe. Really, some days! It's like I'm doing the exact same thing over and over, time after time. Do you ever have days like that, do you reckon?"

Mr Redmayne eyed his son uneasily. "Sometimes, I suppose, yes, now that you mention it. Although, actually, son, I imagine it might be just the way I happen to be feeling at the time. More all in my head than anything else, I should think. That's the way I tend to see things, anyway. Nothing new under the sun. Not really, no."

"I guess you're right," agreed George, after a long thoughtful moment. "You know, Pops, I'm going to try and see things more your way in future, I think. See things how they really are, if I can. And always tell the truth about it."

This last statement visibly gave Mr Redmayne a moment's pause.

"Well, good, yes," he said, twiddling with the silver signet ring on his little finger, as if he were thinking—and thinking hard. "Quite."

And then, after one last uneasy glance at his son, he finally exited the room, pulling the door shut behind him as he left.

At once, George leapt up from the bed. He ran over and stood with his ear against the door. His father's footsteps were already receding down the east stairway. Immediately George flung open his bedroom door and dashed out onto the empty landing. Then, at a most inadvisable speed, he romped down the west stairway, taking the steps two at a time. George was desperate to intercept Felice as soon as she came in from school, before his parents had the opportunity to do the same. That was essential to his plan.

Because if her day had been anything like his, then it was highly probable that his theory was correct. And if his theory *was* correct, well, in that case it would be best if they could uncover the truth for themselves. That was his thinking. They'd be more free to find out what was really going on. Together. Free from parental influence or misinformation. Parental misdirection.

Parental lies.

Whatever. Besides it might be fun, or at least interesting. And part of him really thought it might be their only chance to find out the truth.

Just then, breathless, anxious not to be discovered, George reached the hallway on the ground floor, only but a few moments ahead of his father, whose heavy tread he could distinguish on the other stairway. He skulked out of sight on the top step of the short staircase that led down to the side door and the basement. He needed Felice to come in *right now*. She was due home any moment. Where was she? George heard his father reach the hallway. Was he coming this way? No. What *was* he doing? He was pottering about. Whistling. *Whistling*. So annoying. And embarrassing. Parents!

George heard the cheerful, chirpy tune grow fainter as his father moved farther off. Then it grew fainter still. His father must have gone into his study, the door of which—as if in confirmation—closed with a quiet click and the whistling dropped out of earshot completely. Relief.

As if right on cue, the side door opened and someone came in. A woman.

Only it wasn't Felice. It was his mother.

8

"George, what on Earth are you doing skulking there?" said his mother, clearly as surprised to see him as he was her. "You look like you're up to no good, whatever it is. Really, you do."

"What? No way. Actually, if you really want to know the truth, Mother," replied George, thinking quickly, "I was down here looking for you. That's all. I think Pops said you had a cream tea for me, possibly. But I couldn't find you. Have you been out somewhere?"

"Yes," said Mrs Redmayne, clearly disinclined to elaborate any further.

"Oh, I see," said George, not at all sure about what he might or might not be seeing. It wasn't like his mother to be evasive about anything with him. This was new territory.

"Were you out looking for Felice by any chance? Is she late?"

"Felice?" Mrs Redmayne's face was a study in blankness. "Felice?"

Oh, come on, Mother, thought George. *You know who Felice is!*

He was about to remind his mother of her daughter's identity when at that moment the girl herself appeared in the doorway. And one look at her distraught face told George everything he wanted to know. Her expression was full of the same anguish and confusion that he had experienced all day long himself. Her day had been just like his. That was the truth of it. His theory was correct!

They had time-travelled! It had to be that!

Now, all he had to do was prevent his sister from blubbering on about it in front of their mother. Not easy at the best of times. Felice was famously forthcoming on all subjects dear to her heart. On all subjects, really. Full stop. And he could see that she was on the point of launching into a typically scalding and no doubt lengthy diatribe—against, most likely, anything and everything—at that very instant.

By luck, their mother was standing between them. Behind her back, George made a face aimed at his sister. He waved his hands silently, if expressively, like an old-fashioned minstrel or a mime. Or, alternatively, for that matter, a lunatic. Such was the extreme oddness of his demeanour that Felice at once closed her mouth, swallowing in mid-formulation whatever rantish thought had been on her mind.

George then held a lone forefinger up to his lips, emphasising that she shouldn't speak.

Felice could only stare at him, looking very cross and very confused in equal measure.

Their mother intervened: "George," she began, sounding quite cross herself, "whatever it is you're doing behind my back, you'd better stop it at once. Or there'll be no cream tea for you. Not tonight. Much as it pains me to say that to my own son."

"That's okay, Mother. I've completely lost my appetite for it now, anyway. You know how that is.[6] And I'm sorry for messing about. I was only trying to attract Felice's attention. See, we did this really, really cool thing at school today, an experiment, kind of, I suppose, and I'm desperate to tell her all about it. That's all it is. And it really can't wait. She'll love it. It involves acting. And, you know, art! And French stuff! She really must come and hear all about it right this instant. *Now!* I insist."

Mrs Redmayne turned and gave her son a long look. "Georgie, are you quite all right? You're babbling like a, well, I don't know what. It's most unlike you, it really is!"

"That's okay," said George. "I'm fine, honestly. I just need Felice to come with me. Like I say, *right now.*"

He reached over and grabbed Felice by the arm. His sister was most taken aback. Her red-bobbled blue beret lay all askew on her head as he pulled her up the short set of steps. Felice just caught the look of astonishment on their mother's face as he dragged her along. They went rapidly down the hallway toward the east staircase.

[6] No, she doesn't. Not at all. No. No.

"George," she protested, all the time trying to wrench her arm free, "George, have you entirely lost your mind? What are you doing? Stop! It's not funny! I've had the most terrible day. I'm really not in the mood for this sort of messing about. Let me go this instant or I will lose my temper with you!"

Wisely, George relaxed his grip and his sister pulled free. He could see that she was both angry and confused. He had to explain himself.

"Listen, I know exactly what sort of day you've had, Sis. I do. Because mine was the same. Believe me, it was. And I think I know *why*."

Her face changed, still very angry-looking but now also at once curious, too, a change that was most immediately obvious in her eyes.

"How?" she began...

George looked around. "Not here," he said. He stood part way up the east stairway, just below the first floor at this point. "Look, come on up to my room. I've got something to show you. Come on. Quick. Before they notice."

He started up the stairs again and, hesitantly, she followed.

"They? George, what on Earth are you talking about? And what do you mean your day was exactly like mine? How can you possibly know what my day was like? I tell you, I had the strangest, rottenest day imaginable. Everything that could go wrong, did! Once or twice I felt like I was losing my mind."

On the first floor landing Felice trailed after her brother into his room and, once inside, George closed the door firmly behind her.

"I know," he said, quietly, and went over to sit on his bed. "I do. I *know*, Sis, because I felt the same way."

"Really?" Felice sat down on the edge of the bed. "Was it terrible, your day too? Really, was it? Because that is exactly what happened with me. Oh, George, everything all day long was just so weird. I mean, *everything*. The way people were behaving, even my friends. So-called friends, anyway. Do you remember me saying last night about getting that part in the play?

Yesterday? No? Really? Well, I did. And today," Felice paused, welling up, "listen to this, George, today, they only went and staged the auditions again! Without telling me. At lunchtime. And they gave my part—my part!—to somebody else! I could not believe it! And when I found out, I went mad, as you might expect. I was so angry. But everyone just thought it was me, for some reason, being weird and unreasonable. Can you imagine that?"

Although he didn't say so, George thought that he could imagine it all too well. Still, he shook his head. His sister took this as her cue to resume her tragic recitation. And while she talked on, he leaned over toward his bedside drawer and took out the two math tests.

For the moment, he didn't show them to her. Not yet. Timing was everything. And he really wanted—needed—her to believe him.

"Well, I raged, I can tell you," Felice ran on, "absolutely raged. At everyone. I said that Agnes was my part, and that only yesterday they had given it to me. And they had no right, no right at all, none, to be so underhanded and give it to someone else, all behind my back too. I said that was mean and sneaky and lacked character. And it was—and it did. Oh, George, how could they do that? And to *me*? How?"

George could see that Felice, her big brown eyes downcast toward the bed, appeared to be on the point of tears. He really didn't want that. Not at all.

He held up the two test papers. "Look, at this," he said. "Felice…"

"What? So? You got another A? Good for you. Well done. Is that it? Is that why you dragged me in here? If it *is*, George—"

"No, idiot. And when would I ever do that? No, look more closely. See, they're identical. Apart from the grade, of course. Look at the date. This, here," he said, holding up the test in his right hand, "is the one I took *yesterday*. And this one, this is the test I took *today*. Do you see? Do you understand? They've got the same date on the top. See?"

Felice took the tests from him and examined them. "So what? It's some kind of mistake. That's all."

"No, it's not. That's where you're wrong. It really isn't. What day is it?"

"Friday, stupid."

"Nah-uh. You might think so, but it's Thursday. Yes, it is. It's Thursday again. These tests are the proof."

Felice was beginning to be interested. "What are you talking about?"

"This is the test I failed yesterday. Miserably too. Stupidly. *Me*, fail a math test? But I did. All my own stupid fault. But today we did it again. No, I did it again. For everyone else it was the first time. And I aced it. Do you see? Today was a do-over, at least for us. No one else."

"What?" Felice was incredulous. "Wait a minute…no, what?"

He could see that, incredible as it sounded, his explanation was perhaps starting to make a little sense of things for her. He went on.

"Unlike yours, see, Sis, my day was perfect. Like, gold. Everything that had been a disaster yesterday turned out perfectly today, because quite early on I realised that something strange was going on, that everything was repeating. As weird and disturbing as that was, it made sense, kind of. My day was perfect because I knew what was coming next. All day long, that's how it was. Didn't you have some weird sense of déjà vu too? Tell me you didn't and I'll shut up."

"Yes, I did," said Felice quietly. "Yes, I did, on many occasions. That's right. But not exactly, no. Something was different." She looked up with a shock. "My God! Claudia! She didn't make it in yesterday. She got splashed by a car on the way to school. But today… Oh, my God! I stopped that from happening. I changed things—and she got the part. My part! George, do you know what this means?"

He nodded cautiously. "I think so."

Felice was beaming. "I wasn't being excluded. They weren't

being mean to me. What a relief! And to think, the things I said to them. Everyone. They must think I'm such a, well, bitch. Oh my God. This is so amazing. We've got to tell Maman and Papa. They'll know what to do. They will. They always do. Maybe we can make it happen again? It has to be the house, right? If we can do that, do it all again, then I can get the part in the play back. It'll be like it never happened. All of it. And this time I won't be saving Claudia, I can tell you. She can drown in that filthy puddle."

George was shaking his head. "Felice, we can't do that. The Mater and the Pater, get this, Sis, they *know*. Both of them. I even think very possibly, somehow, they made it happen. They did. For whatever reason, they did. I'm sure of it. Absolutely. One hundred percent. And you're right, yes, it has to be the house. I mean, we already know that it equalises time, holds everything steady across the time zones—you know, it syn-chronises everything, that's what I mean. That's how we can all go out to school at the same time. That's actually a sort of time-travel when you think about it. When *you* go to school, Felice, in Paris, you're travelling *back* in time, really, and when you come home, you're travelling forwards again. Or maybe it's the other way around, and I'm travelling back and forth? Or both of us are? I don't know. Whatever. Either way, that's really neat when you think about it like that. I just never did before. Funny."

"Okay, right. Great, George. But why can't we tell Papa and Maman? I don't understand."

"Felice, Felice, Sis, listen, they hid this from us. They did. They lied to us. All that talk about the importance of the truth, as well. The truth above all else and all of that? How could they? Look, the house is about more than location. It always has been. It's about *time* too. Don't you get it? This is huge, Felice. Think big. Bigger than just a part in some school play. Any play. If this works how I hope it does, how I think it might, we could do anything, I reckon, yeah? Go anywhere, any time. Think about it. You could be in the original play, Sis, the very first production of…whatever it was, by, you know, whoever. The famous old-time French playwright guy. Think about that. Huh?" George took a moment to let the enormity of this prospect sink in. "No, we've just got to figure out how it works ourselves. Us. Because they won't tell us. They've had their chance. And even if they did, you know, tell us, like now, they'd still control it, I bet. No, if we want to have some fun with this, we've got to figure it out for ourselves. In secret. Just you and me."

Felice looked doubtful but intrigued all the same, George could tell.

Intrigued and tempted, both. But taking a moment to think it through.

"I don't know," she said, shortly, with a sigh. "What about Emile?"

"I know. Why not ask him?" said George. "He's listening at the door."

Felice span round. George was faster. He sprang off the end of the bed and was at the door in a flash—and he flung it open.

Emile was there. Frozen. But only for an instant.

The boy took off, heading at speed down the east stairway.

At once he was gone.

9

"Squirt! No, wait! Stop!" George called after his brother, all the time watching him descend the stairs at an impressive rate. "Wait. Don't, no! Emile."

But it was too late. There would be no catching him and nothing he could do even if he did. George felt as if the whole universe had been almost his, his very own, if only for a minute or two. His to play with! The possibilities! And then it had all been snatched away before he'd had chance to unwrap it even, let alone take it out of the box and have some fun with it. An opportunity cruelly denied. So unfair.

Felice came up behind him and peered down the stairs. "That's torn it, I guess," she said.

"Maybe," said George, starting down the staircase himself. He couldn't give up quite so easily. Not so soon. Not with so much at stake.

Without a word, Felice followed him down.

At the bottom of the stairs they came across Emile standing with their father.

Mr Redmayne peered up at them both expectantly. "Ah, there you both are," he said. "Good. Just in time. Emile was just telling me that you two have been hatching a little plan. And I have to say that I think it's an excellent idea."

"You do? What?" George was confused and tried to catch Emile's eye. But his little brother was having none of it. Emile stared neutrally, quite innocently, ahead. "What's that exactly, then?"

"Oh, come on, George. Really no need to be so coy. I think it's an excellent idea that you—all of you—should be able to have your friends around now and then. Carefully managed, of course, to prevent any geographical confusions, much like your mother and I have people round, you know, from time to time. We should have done it years ago really, if you ask me. Excellent idea. Top marks. Why don't we all talk about it at dinner? Which I believe, unless my faithful nose deceives me, is almost ready." Mr Redmayne sniffed the air at this point, as if by way of dramatic aid. "Yes, I quite think it is. Why don't we go on through and see? Felice…"

"Yes, Papa?"

"How was your day?"

George and Felice had fully descended to the hallway by this point. They exchanged the briefest of glances. Fleeting in the extreme. Infinitesimal, practically. But significant.

"Okay, I suppose, Papa," said Felice. "Very ordinary. Extremely so. Average."

"Hmm," said her father, looking from one to the other, "your brother said something similar, I believe. Still, no matter. Emile, lead the way, there's a good fellow. Onward."

Mr Redmayne turned to head deeper into the house, and Emile grasped the opportunity to race off along the corridor. Behind their father's back George and Felice exchanged another significant look, of greater length this time and accompanied by several silently mouthed and therefore largely unintelligible questions—and, quite possibly, with one or two unspoken accusations thrown in, to boot.

In truth, neither could make much sense of the other. Very little, in fact. More time was needed to confer. In private. Nevertheless, they followed behind dutifully, if argumentatively in a mute sort of way, seeing no other choice.

"Are you really sure dinner will be ready so soon, Pops?" George ventured. "You know, it can't have been fifteen minutes ago that Mother was offering me a cream tea."

"Yes, quite sure. We worked on it together this afternoon. It's something of a surprise and that's why we didn't want to mention it until now. Anyway, I made the rolls, I'll have you know. Me, I did. Delicious, fresh rolls. And, besides, you know your dear mother, Georgie, she'll offer anyone a cream tea at any time. It's her panacea."

"Yes," agreed George glumly. If he never saw another cream tea again it would be too soon—by far. Eons. Still, it didn't seem as if Emile had spilt the beans on their plan, although it was difficult to tell exactly what the treacherous little rat was scheming, if anything. *Kids*.

"No, the thing is," Mr Redmayne resumed, "we thought it would be good if we might have a proper dinner, all together. A chance for us all to talk. Everyone's been so preoccupied lately. You know how it is, the days roll by. Busy-busy, all of us. And it's very easy to lose track of what we're all getting on with at the moment. *Or*, say, if you've any particular problems, or anything, just now…(Mr Redmayne seemed to swallow his words at this point)…Anything at all, (cough) really. You know, anything strange or unusual going on, perhaps? That sort of thing. Well, you could tell us. Tonight, over a lovely family meal. That's what we were thinking. That's all it is."

George looked at his sister again. She shrugged. She had nothing. What was going on was unprecedented. They were deep into uncharted territory once more. No maps existed.

Just then they passed the steps down to the kitchen, and George and Felice paused.

"Papa?" called Felice after her father's retreating figure, clearly puzzled.

Mr Redmayne stopped and looked back at the pair.

"Oh no, dearheart," he said with a sweet, but knowing, smile. "Not downstairs. No, not tonight. We'd rather thought we'd eat in the great dining room, actually. You know, make it into a special occasion. For all of us. Together. Come on. I've already opened up the room. Everything should be ready. Just so. Like Christmas, really!"

George and Felice shared another look, this time more in wonder than anything else. Something was definitely up. Very definitely up. Way, way up. Stratospheric, in fact. Because the great dining room was, as their father had implied, usually opened up only at Christmas, and perhaps very rarely on some other few special occasions over the years, their grandfather's funeral for example, which neither of them could remember, it having occurred before either of them were born.

But such occasions were very rare indeed. To open it up now, on an ordinary school night, well, it had never happened before. It was extraordinary. Quite extraordinary, in fact. Nothing ordinary or even average about it. Not remotely. Not at all.

The pair, now noticeably subdued, perhaps because they were more than a little wonder-struck, followed their father along the corridor, past Mr Redmayne's study, the library and the music room, Mrs Redmayne's study, the game room, the dining room until, finally, they reached the tall, oak-panelled door of the great dining room.

The door was ajar—Mr Redmayne and Emile had already gone inside—and brother and sister exchanged another glance before entering, the meaning of which this time they both understood: *What on Earth was going on?*

Inside, their sense of wonder only increased. The long dining table was set out exactly as it would be at Christmas, adorned with the best white linen tablecloth and the otherwise rarely seen blue serving-china, their mother's favourite.[7]

All in all, the room seemed very festive. All that was missing was the tall spruce tree and its various beautiful decorations (no tinsel, *ever*—Mrs Redmayne abhorred tinsel as an abomination). And the presents, of course. But that would have been going entirely too far.

Taking their places opposite each other at the table, as was traditional, Felice and George exchanged one last long look. Wherever they were now, it certainly wasn't Kansas anymore. That was for sure. And never more so than when their mother appeared a few moments later, bearing a sumptuous feast—on some never-before-seen wheeled trolley type of contraption.

At once, Emile's mouth fell open.

"Do close your mouth, Emile dear," said Mrs Redmayne

---

[7] And often reported by herself as salvaged personally during some Chinese rebellion. Only much later will George realise that this was a clue that he'd missed for most of his young life. Ah well, like they say, *duh.*

matter-of-factly, bringing the trolley-contraption-thing completely into the great dining room. "Redmaynes never gawp. Or gape. You know that. Your grandfather, in particular, thoroughly detested gaping in a youth."

Mr Redmayne leapt up to assist with the serving, a courtesy that allowed his wife to take her seat at one end of the long table. She smiled at each of her two elder children in turn. Rather enigmatically, George thought, or maybe he was just imagining it? In truth, he didn't know anymore.

His father began to lay the dishes out onto the table, one by one.

"Did you remember the rolls, dear?" he asked with only a hint of fuss. "I baked them especially."

"Of course, dear. Lower shelf, see, there, in the greenware bowl? No, the blue and white one. That's it. Wrapped in a muslin cloth. For freshness."

"Ah, yes, I see. You think of everything. Roll, anyone? They come highly recommended, if only by the baker, who I can vouch for personally as a fine fellow. A good chap, or at least he tries to be. Mostly. Means well, always."

With a noticeable—and quite touching to witness—pride Mr Redmayne passed around the rolls. George took one. It certainly felt fresh, a little warm still, even.

A question occurred to him, however, one of many he thought he perhaps should have asked many years ago, but for some reason hadn't. Now he would.

"Mother, if I might ask," began George, breaking open his roll, "but how did you get all of this up the stairs? From the kitchen, I mean? All of this food. You can't have carried it, can you? You know, surely not?"

"Carried it? Heavens, no!" laughed Mrs Redmayne. "The very thought! No, I used the dumbwaiter, of course. Silly."

George was confused. "Wait. The what, now?"

"The dumbwaiter, dear. The monte-plats. No? It comes up from the kitchen into the small dining room. Did you really think I'd been carrying heavy tray-loads of food up from the kitchen all these years? Do start helping yourselves, children. I believe the asparagus to be particularly beautiful tonight. Felice, you'll find the celery rémoulade to be quite très délicieux, I'm sure of it. *Celery*. It even sounds French when you say it, doesn't it?"

Mr Redmayne agreed. "Celery. Yes, it certainly does, dear, now that you mention it, yes, cel-*er*-y. Ha!"

He chuckled to himself while he passed around several more dishes, so many that to George the feast began to appear potentially unending—with a seeming infinite number of dishes. He hadn't yet taken anything, other than his bread roll, which lay open in broken halves on his plate, lingering there like some incomplete thought or yet another unanswered question.

He decided to ask the question.

"This dumbwaiter, really, how come I didn't know it was there? I mean, did you, Felice? No? Not you, either? Well, I've never even seen it, I'm sure, let alone spotted you hauling things in and out of it. Ever, in fact. Why's that? I'm sure I would have noticed."

"Honestly, dear. Of course not. I don't *haul*. I'm your mother. And, well, I don't use it that often, to be absolutely truthful. No, most of the time I use the elevator."

"The *what*!" George was incredulous, half-expecting this to be a joke.

Felice appeared equally at a loss. "Sorry, Maman, what did you say?"

"The elevator." Mrs Redmayne looked across from one nonplussed child to the other. "The *lift*. L'ascenseur. The paternoster? Surely the pair of you aren't going to sit there and tell me that you've *never* used the elevator? At the back, there? No? Well, I can't believe it. I really can't. Whatever do you do with yourselves? You must both walk around with your eyes shut tight."

George stared over at his sister. "Yes, I think we must," he said.

"I've used it," said Emile, much to the astonishment of his

elder brother. "A lot, actually. Some days, you know, I just like to ride up and down in it. You feel like it's going on forever."

"Don't exaggerate, Emile," said Mrs Redmayne. "Not quite forever—although it can give you that impression, I agree, if you let it. And, yes, it *is* very handy for getting up and down, which is quite the point. Have you really never seen it? Really? I find that quite extraordinary, I have to say. It's like you don't know the house at all. Perhaps you can get your more adventurous little brother here to give you the tour later? What do you say, Emile?"

"Sure," said Emile, tucking in to something of an alarmingly full plate, one that featured far too many sausages for his own good, even if they were Herterich's sausages, his favourite. "Love to. Just ask. I'll show you everything."

George scowled at him. Then, he gave it up and began to take some food for his plate.

The table complete at last, Mr Redmayne sat down and joined everybody else.

His family.

"Cel-er-y," he said again, and positively beamed.

"What I want to know," said Emile, chewing hard, "is who is this dumb waiter bloke and why is he such an idiot? Or is it that he just can't talk? In which case I'm sorry for calling him an idiot. No, really. I am. What? You all said he was dumb, not me."

"You're the idiot," said George.

"George, that is no way to speak to your brother. Apologise."

Mr Redmayne looked sternly at his elder son, at least as sternly as he could muster, which, typically, was not very. Not really. No.

By way of apology George offered a sneer at his brother, which was accepted and returned in kind. Courtesy, of a sort, restored.

"No, no, Emile," resumed Mr Redmayne, "a dumbwaiter is actually a type of little elevator, I suppose, when you think about it, and you use it to pull food and plates and dishes, or anything really, up and down between floors. Very common in restaurants, or large, old-fashioned houses like ours. But all that's by the by. What I really wanted to ask you about, actually, was your day and how that was. Anything exciting or unusual happen today? That's what I really want to hear about. Hmm? Anything, you know, *odd* to report?"

Mr Redmayne turned his full attention onto his younger son, as did everyone else, who, while perhaps each hoping that whatever he said next did not betray their clandestine activities, no doubt all had slightly different reasons for hoping so, some less noble than others.

Four pairs of eyes focused exclusively on Emile…

It would be fair to say that the younger Redmayne *fils* was unused to attracting such universal attention. Usually no one seemed too bothered at all about what he had to say, or indeed thought. He looked around the table while he chewed his beloved Herterich's. The collective gaze of his family members might have been a little unnerving if he hadn't been quite so absorbed in that one all-important task. In Emile's world, sausages—especially Herterich's sausages—trumped all. Any other concerns could wait.

"Anything at all," said Mr Redmayne in his most gentle, coaxing voice. "Something out of the ordinary, perhaps, that might have been hard to understand. That sort of thing."

"Yes, anything, dear," added Mrs Redmayne. "You can tell us. That's why we're here."

Emile looked around at everyone and swallowed.

"Nope," he said, and instantly resumed his feast.

All the other Redmaynes around the table seemed to sit back in their seats as one, in relief, possibly; although once again, in truth, perhaps all for slightly different reasons. As for Mr Redmayne, although clearly relieved, his mood appeared tinged with more than a hint of disappointment, or frustration.

Not George, however, who was positively energised. Triumphant. If it hadn't been so entirely out of character with all of the previous actions in his life up until that moment, he might well have been moved to slap his little brother heartily on the back. Well done, shrimp!

As it was, he settled for babbling instead.

"Well, I've really got to say, Mother—*Mom*—and Pops, guys, you know, this is, well, just, well, the most fantastic, I don't know to call it, dinner, I suppose? No, wait, a feast! Isn't it, though? Don't you think? You know, it almost feels like we're celebrating something. Are we? Are we celebrating something? Is that it? Has Christmas come early maybe? Hey, wouldn't that be great if we actually could make Christmas come early? You think? I do. And, you know what else, well, I don't think now that's anywhere near as impossible as I did yesterday. No, I don't. What do you think, Felice?"

Felice shot her brother the most withering, quite instantly sobering, look—a look which, if it could only be bottled, would make her fortune.

It had the desired effect. At once abashed, George shut up immediately and remained quiet for several moments.

Once again, his mother gave him a long look. "Georgie, you're behaving so strangely, I'm beginning to wonder if you might not benefit from something of a tonic. A generous dose of cod liver oil after dinner, perhaps? You always feel much better after that, if I remember rightly."

George blanched. "No, no, really, Mother, no need for that. I'm perfectly fine. Honestly. Just excited, that's all. It's the occasion, I think, eating in here. That must be it. So special, you see. Isn't it? But, well, see, the thing is, remind me, what *is* the occasion? Exactly?"

Mrs Redmayne looked at her husband, who looked at George.

"Well," he began, before changing tack. "Oh, darling, *yes*, I quite forgot to mention, possibly in all the excitement. Yes. The children have come up with the most marvellous idea, all on their own. Together. Emile was telling me about it right before dinner, weren't you, Emile? Isn't that right, everyone?"

None of the children said anything in response and so Mr Redmayne continued.

"Yes, just now it was, in fact, out in the hallway, Emile happened to mention to me in passing that they all thought it would be a jolly good idea if they could have their friends over once in a while. You know, here, to the house. To stay. Of course, it would all need to be very carefully managed. We wouldn't want anyone wandering out into the wrong city, now, would we? That would be quite disastrous. Or perhaps even seeing something they shouldn't out of a window, such as, say, well, hmm, the Eiffel Tower or the Empire State Building..."

"Heavens, no," interjected Mrs Redmayne, whose grave expression suggested she was yet to be in the least persuaded of the marvellousness of the whole idea. "That really wouldn't do at all. Not at all. No. Obviously."

"But it struck me, dear, that it would actually be a very normal thing to do. You see? And that because we're not, on the whole, a very normal family, we should perhaps do one or two more normalish things. Now and then, anyway. For the children, if that's what they would like."

Mrs Redmayne peered doubtfully around the table. "I suppose, if that's what they would like. Normal." She said this last word like it was a condition. "Is that what they would like? Felice, who would you bring home, dear? That girl you're always talking about? Although I wasn't entirely sure you liked her, to be honest. What's her name? Claudia?"

Felice's grimace suggested she would prefer to bring home the bubonic plague.[8]

"Hmm, I see. And you, Georgie? Some Mathlete chum or other, I suppose? One of those?"

George shrugged. He'd sensibly decided to keep his head down and focus on the food from this point forwards.

His mother continued to scrutinise him in particular, however. Closely. "Well, neither of you seem especially keen on the idea, I must say," she concluded. "How very strange..."

---

[8] Maybe one day.

Emile spoke up. "*I* am, though! Really! Yeah, definitely! I'm gonna be bringing home Steven Sparkle. I am. He's my very best friend. From school. And we all agreed it was a good idea, the three of us, didn't we? *Before.* In *your* room. We did, didn't we, George? Felice, didn't we?"

George and Felice exchanged one last conspiratorial glance. Together they nodded their assent. If this was the price of keeping their secret about the do-over day, then so be it.

Mrs Redmayne looked toward her husband at the far end of the table, and smiled. Inscrutably.

"Well, it looks to me like you're as right as ever, dear. I should have known better than to doubt you. That's decided, then. Perhaps we might make the arrangements to coincide with the summer Open House weekend? That's not so very far away, now. *Chéri,* what do you think?"

Mr Redmayne beamed once more, as if the word *celery* might be bouncing around in his head once more in a way that only he could find entertaining. His smile filled the great room.

"I think that sounds like an exceptionally good idea. Everyone happy with that?

Nods, grunts of assent. It was done. Agreed.

And while everyone around the table professed their contentment with the proposal, only one family member actually seemed in the least excited or pleased.

"Yea, Steven Sparkle, here!" exclaimed Emile, with a mouth too full of sausage for any seemly show of enthusiasm. "This house. Wow! He's gonna love it! He really is!"

And so the grand dinner went on, the non-Christmas Christmas feast, long into the evening, in the most special family room in the great mysterious house, where the happy Redmaynes had until now always celebrated only the most important, most very special of occasions together. Until now.

Because on this occasion, other than Emile, no one was really celebrating (and how so very excited the wee young lad had been when toward the end of the evening Mrs Redmayne had unwrapped the Terry's Chocolate Orange—another of Emile's absolute favourite treats). Christmas had indeed come early. For him.

But for the rest, no. Not at all. No.

Unvoiced suspicions and counter-suspicions lurked in the hearts and minds of child and parent alike, and everyone had their own secret agenda.

And in the end, for those secrets, everyone would pay. Without exception. As well as paying for the secrets of another, yet to be discovered.

Toward the close of the evening George asked his father in an innocent enough way if there might be some plans of the house that he could examine, seeing as it turned out he somehow knew so little about it.

And his father had remarked, in a similarly offhand way, that there were certain to be some in the library, somewhere or other, yes, he was quite sure of it, and that he would dig them out for George tomorrow or another day, if reminded. Father and son had nodded each to the other in acknowledgement of this, quite cordially, in fact, but at the same time neither one believed—nor particularly wanted—that anything should come of it.

Indeed, at the end of the feast, as George made his way with his younger brother and sister along the lengthy and, by now, shadowy hallway toward the east stairway, he surreptitiously tugged Felice by the arm when passing the imposing, oak-panelled library door and made her pause outside.

"In there, Sis, see?" he said, in a low whisper. "In there, that's where we'll find the truth."

10

Striking one entire day from the history books might be regarded as unfortunate; striking two involves a special kind of carelessness, one which suggests your focus might have become more than a little self-involved. And so it was for Mr and Mrs Redmayne. Once you start such a thing, where do you draw the line? One thing leads to another, and before you know it, you're striking days from history willy-nilly. The road to hell, as they say, is paved with good intentions. And soon all is lost.

In any case, George's suspicions about his parents' activities would certainly have been redoubled if he had witnessed them exiting the library later that same evening, just as the great grandfather clock in the darkened hallway was chiming out the last hour of the day. In truth, Mr and Mrs Redmayne were behaving in a rather suspect manner, all whispers and softly-softly footsteps as they padded their way fleet-footed along the gloomy corridor toward the west staircase, which led more directly to their room. All in all, they were behaving like burglars in their own home, which is never a good sign, unless it happens to be Christmas. And, unfortunately, despite George's seemingly fervent wishes on the subject at dinner, his parents had not made any arrangements for Christmas to come early that year. Not yet, at least.

The fact is that they had just turned time forward by twenty-four hours; indeed, they had 'reset the clock,' as it were, or at least that was how Mr Redmayne had first explained it. When he went on to explain that, no, that wasn't quite it, they hadn't turned time forward, strictly speaking, no, dear, not at all, but that what they actually had done, technically speaking, was move the house forward through time by twenty-four hours, well, by then his wife had all but stopped listening.

Mrs Redmayne had other things on her mind, did she not? More important things. Far more. George, mostly. She felt certain that her elder son suspected. And she resolved, quietly, to keep an eye on him. But at least 'resetting the clock,' or whatever it was they had done, technically speaking, would restore the pattern of the week, the run of the days, to what the children naturally expected it to be.

Tomorrow morning when Mrs Redmayne woke up it would be Saturday, and having travelled through time twice since Thursday, she suspected she would be glad of the lie-in.

On the face of it, when Mrs Redmayne did wake up, rather late (even when judged against her own very high standards for lateness[9]) on that fine Saturday morning, with the bright, early summer New York sun streaming in like so much gold (yes, gold, she thought, there really was no other word for it) through her bedroom windows, everything appeared to be back to normal.

At least on the surface of things, anyway.

Felice and Emile were both already out, she soon learned from her husband. After some initial uncertainty Felice had very early popped along to the Saturday morning market at La Bastille (goodness only knew what tremendous piece of highly unusual French tat she would come home with this time!); and Emile, well, barely had he muttered something about playing in some unruly Saturday soccer 'match' or other with his new best friend, this Steven Sparkle boy, before he'd dashed out with his cleats slung over his shoulder and a look on his face like he was heading off to the trenches. And maybe, in a way, he was! Those English games can be very rough, can't they? Bit like the Somme with a football. Or so he had heard. Or was that rugger? Quite possibly.

---

[9] That is, if, like some modish people, you regard waking up any time after 12 noon as being 'late', which Mrs Redmayne, as a matter of principle, most certainly did not, and especially not at the weekend. Or holidays. Or Fridays. And so on.

But, yes, anyway, best of all, dear, was George, resumed Mr Redmayne, after a moment's distraction. Yes, George. As a matter of fact, he'd been working very hard in the library since very early indeed, had old George—and on a Saturday! In fact, the most commendably industrious lad had been hard at it since before Mr Redmayne had gotten up himself, which was a first. No one was *ever* up before him. And wasn't that good news?

And on the face of it, it was. Nothing pleased her more than reports of Georgie working hard. He was so very bright, her eldest boy, and could achieve so much if he only put his mind to it. Indeed, there was no limit to what good he might do in the world, how he might change it for the better. Or Felice, to be sure. Or for that matter, perhaps…Emile. Quite possibly. Yes.

But, despite these several good reports, for Mrs Redmayne, still attired in her silk kimono dressing gown and sipping her jet black espresso in the kitchen, *her* kitchen, a certain uneasiness lingered, a feeling of impending doom that she could not easily shake.

And then she thought she was just being silly. Probably. Most likely. A bit of an old goose. Much like her lovely husband. And so she resolved to try to be more sensible from this point forwards, if she at all could. Yes.

Fortunately, over the coming weeks her resolve on this matter was aided by what appeared to be a complete return to normality in the Redmayne household—actually, to something much better than normality, but so pleased was Mrs Redmayne by this development that she neglected to ponder as to why this might be. It was, in truth, the normality she had always wanted and so she welcomed it without question, when keeping an open mind might have served her better.

And so, in Mrs Redmayne's new perfect world, George continued to work incredibly hard on his studies and spent all manner of long, long hours researching in the library. How so very gratifying she found it to see someone make use of that fantastic resource at long last—a rather unique resource in actual fact, containing all manner of rare volumes, many of which were believed lost to antiquity but had been preserved here, largely by Mr Redmayne's father, the collector extraordinaire.

But, regardless of any of that, what made it all the more gratifying to Mrs Redmayne was the fact that George's newfound diligence appeared to be rubbing off on his sister to a really not very inconsiderable extent as well, it had to be said, since Felice had also taken to studying in the family library of late—quite frequently, in fact. And ever more so with each passing week.

All in all, it could reasonably be stated without any fear of contradiction that nothing so warmed the cockles of Mrs Redmayne's proud maternal heart quite as much as popping into the library from time to time with a cream tea or occasionally (i.e. rarely) a hot chocolate for her two scholars, and find the hardworking pair so far lost in their studies that they would look up quite wide-eyed and seem so very entirely startled to see her standing there, bearing her refreshments—an expression of such extreme surprise that by anyone who knew them less it might easily have been mistaken for shock or alarm, so engrossed were the studious pair in whatever it was they happened to be reading. Her two dedicated scholars!

Yes, without a doubt, all of that was going very well indeed and George and Felice were sure to reap the just reward for all of their efforts, a point she seldom neglected to impress upon them both, such were her strong feelings on the matter.

Emile, too, was doing so very well. Never better, in fact. He'd fallen in with a new set of chums from his school and was forever running around and doing something or other with them, as indeed a boy should be at his age. Properly enjoying his newfound freedom in one of the great cities of the world. Mr Redmayne's father, the irascible Rufus, had been right about that much, for all their disagreements. You can't mollycoddle a child. One day they have to find their own way in the world, sometimes literally. Especially if you lived in a house with such special properties as theirs. Yes.

Anything might happen—and you had to be ready.

Mrs Redmayne was always ready. Or so she thought.

So, all in all, everything was going marvellously well. Too good to be true. Even Mr Redmayne seemed to have put behind him at last what they both referred to—privately—as 'the incident.' No lasting consequences seemed to have followed from it. Despite everything, no harm done. Their scheme had been risky but justified by the outcome. They'd taken the chance but pulled it off. Bravo to them. That was how Mr Redmayne frequently spoke of it, so very often in fact that his wife relaxed and began to view it in those terms too.

And, on the face of it, why shouldn't she? They had to get on with things, didn't they? Life was for the living. Mr Redmayne resumed his daily sallies around Central Park, cogitating all the while about difficult things, and Mrs Redmayne's thoughts returned to more mundane matters than time-travel and its consequences, such as organising the summer Open House event, which this year would be of special interest to everybody. Especially Emile.

Now, let's see…yes, hmm, who's left? Well, the Tithemores of Chelsea (naturally), and the Mayfair Wheedles, yes, then, who? Perhaps Eric and Elsie Blanche (the whippet trainers)? (Yes.) And Mr and Mrs Sparkle (mother and father of Stephen, Emile's friend), the Right Reverend Percival Beige-Blythe of Westminster (no, no, he would never do—Eric detested clergy) [red line], Chester Chesterton III (the Right Honourable Member of Parliament for Harrow East) (no, perhaps not) [red line], the Formby-Mastertons (Hat Outfitters, by Royal Appointment) (maybe…), the Jessocks (George and Jessie, of Jessocks' Fine Sausages, Meats & More) (definitely), and perhaps one other, the Whalethorpes of Westmoreland Ave? (Winnie & Walter) (No) (Heavens, no) [red line]. That should be sufficient as it is, I should think. More than sufficient, in fact. Ample. Quite.

Now, then, Paris…Mrs Redmayne raised the tip of her sec-ond-best red crossing-out pen to her lips, while she cogitated long and hard on the list of names before her (frustratingly, the whereabouts of her very best red crossing-out pen[10] remained a mystery—all three members of her family flatly denied taking it, despite her intense and prolonged interrogation of each in turn). Zut. Zut. Zut. Why was Paris always so much harder than London? You should think it would be the other way around.

Perhaps it was precisely because she knew Paris best? Maybe that made her more discriminating? Ah, well. Still, at least she didn't have to worry about New York this year. Eric would take care of that. Eventually, despite his many protestations that it was somehow beyond him...

Every year the Redmaynes staged two Open House weekends, in the summer and winter, to which they invited several members of the local great and the good and treated them liberally to their famous hospitality. In truth, each Open House weekend was actually *three* events, spread out over both days, and were carefully timed so that there was no overlap between the three groups of guests, each representing their own fair city (imagine the scope for confusion should that overlap happen— heavens, no!).

Of course, Mr and Mrs Redmayne were well aware of the potential risks involved in having visitors to the house but they felt it was important to be integrated to some degree in the lives of the cities in which they were established at the time; otherwise, as Gloriana more than once put it, they were nothing more than rootless tourists and may as well be anywhere. (It has to be said that her feelings on this matter were far stronger than her husband's.)

And so to compensate for the obvious risks, the Redmaynes organised and choreographed each Open House weekend as if it were a highly covert but crucial operation in a very dirty but ultimately unwinnable war. Or a wedding. Depending on mood. Either way, they took it very seriously, both of them, but

---

[10] As every teacher worth his or her salt knows, crossing out all and any errors is *most* effective, *most* emphatic, most *final*, when done exclusively in red pen. This, surely, is part of the training. Or if it isn't, it should be. Damn it.

especially Mrs Redmayne, who at least enjoyed it. And for Mr
Redmayne, quite wisely, that was more than enough to make it
all worthwhile.

Mrs Redmayne resumed her list-making for the Parisian
portion of the festivities, her second-best red crossing-out pen
poised... Well, let's see...

...The Bouffants, naturally (parents of Felice's guest), and
Madame Méchant (by all accounts such a special teacher) ("so
French"—isn't that what Felice always says about her?), and
Pierre Pierre, Puppet Master Extraordinaire (how the children
had always so *loved* his marvellous marionette shows in the park,
although Eric always found them utterly incomprehensible)
(of *course* he did, poor lamb), and the quite wonderful Margot
Defage (world famous xylophonist, no less), and Alain Pensée
(celebrated French philosopher and master chef) (you don't get
much *more* French than that, now, do you?), and one more...but
who? Fabien Fabre, the renowned philanthropist and philatelist?
(No) [red line]; perhaps the lovely Leta Lamour? (star of stage
and screen) (no, on second thought, definitely not!) (George
would only behave embarrassingly strangely around her all over
again) [double red line]; Vitas Vieillard, the virtuoso violinist?
Elderly, but vital still in so many ways despite his advancing
years. Yes, Vitas would do nicely, now that she came to think of
it. Needless to say, he'd been in love with her for longer than
she cared to contemplate, since before the war, most likely, she
should think. But, no matter. Fine. Yes, fine. And finished.

With a feeling of satisfaction at a job tremendously well
done, Mrs Redmayne laid down her second-best, red crossing-out pen. *There!*

Now, her thoughts could turn to other pressing matters,
such as the catering arrangements. Truth be told, she enjoyed
this part of it best of all, the deciding what to serve to everyone
(and then making it!).

It struck Mrs Redmayne as curious how culturally specific
the menus had to be. Maybe she should be adventurous and
mix it up a bit this year? Make the French guests eat English

food and vice versa? No, no, no, heavens, no, that would be a double disaster. She chuckled at the prospect.

Or maybe she might serve everyone hot dogs and be done with it? How the New Yorkers would love that (assuming that they actually had any guests from New York!).

Mrs Redmayne looked doubtfully out though the windows at the front of the house. No, she must remain steadfast. Eric knew exactly what he had to do. And it should not be that difficult for a man of his abilities and social standing to draw up a list of guests for an afternoon tea!

No, he was her husband and her confidence in him was not misplaced. She would not worry. Not about this, anyway.

Anyway, she had other things to do and, if she didn't do them, well, they all knew what would happen then. Mrs Redmayne strode purposefully toward the door of her bedroom. Yes, without her taking charge of everything, she knew only too well what would happen.

Nothing. But exactly. *Nuls.*

While any wife's unwavering confidence in the capabilities of her husband is, as a general principle, to be much applauded, especially given the sometimes severe obstacles that many husbands, often on a daily basis, place in the way of any spouse sustaining such a (some might say) rose-tinted view far beyond the honeymoon stage, Mrs Redmayne's faith in her husband may have suffered something of a fatal blow if she had but known that at that moment her favourite red pen was not to be found anywhere within the deep recesses of her bureau, nor was it, for that matter, to be found anywhere in the entire house. Instead, the precious pen could be found concealed within the interior breast pocket of Mr Redmayne's favourite herringbone jacket, with the possession of said 'missing' stationery item being entirely quite, quite forgotten by the borrower, along with the obscure purpose for which he had borrowed it in the first place.

Of course, such highly irregular 'borrowing' of said

stationery item in this offhand way remained contrary to Mrs Redmayne's hard and fast rule that any and all items removed from her desk must be returned at once by the borrower, on pain of severe punishment, a rule regularly impressed upon the other members of her family, who had grown far too used to taking such items without thought of return, as if *borrowing* meant *forever*, and all too often thereafter misplacing them carelessly somewhere about the house, or forgetting exactly what they had done with them. And never, under any circumstances, should any such stationery items be removed from the house itself. Oh dear me, no. No.

The punishment for this latter offence would indeed be severe and was rightly to be feared, so much so that if and when Mr Redmayne did finally discover the red pen on his person, he might be best advised to consider the pros and cons of simply throwing it away.

Alas, such an option was not to be his—as Fate had other plans.

But all of this, was, at this point, by the by, as poor Mr Redmayne had nothing on his mind other than the seemingly impossible task his wife had set him, that of drawing up a list of at least a half-a-dozen people from all of New York City who might be available and willing to attend a tea party at his remarkable house on the afternoon of the twenty-fifth next month.

A half-a-dozen! Who on Earth could be on speaking terms with so many individuals in a city this size? It was impossible! Unimaginable. How his wife managed it year after year he had not the foggiest idea. But manage it she did and now so must he. That much was clear. Infinitely so.

To this end, feeling vastly troubled and weighed down by the tremendous burden of responsibility that he now must shoulder entirely alone, Mr Redmayne had taken himself along to New York Public Library, one of his favourite haunts, along with the Planetarium in Central Park, in order to issue an invitation to the one gentlemen whose name he had on his list, that fellow Watkins, whom Mr Redmayne had spoken with now and then and who had at one time seemed quite interested in the house—and whom, now that Mr Redmayne actually wanted to speak with him, was nowhere to be found.

And so, disconsolate and altogether quite out of sorts, Mr Redmayne had trudged out of the New York Public Library, muttering to himself about how you couldn't depend on anyone these days, hardly, when the one gentlemen whom he had on his list had failed him so grievously and without the slightest warning.

In truth, when he thought about it, it was all a little bit strange. No one else in the Public Library seemed able recall Watkins in the least, let alone have much idea where he might be found. Very odd. And Mr Redmayne had imagined the fellow to be some kind of librarian. How wrong can you be? Very much so, as it turned out. But completely.

Now it hardly mattered that originally Mr Redmayne had planned to cross this mysterious Watkins chap off his list, and would have done already were it not for the fact that (a) he had no one else; and (b) he temporarily lacked a suitable crossing-out pen (until his wife finally found hers, although it was odd and most unlike her to misplace it in the first place). All in all, far too many odd things had been happening lately, and it was high time it stopped.

He came down the library steps, passing between Patience and Fortitude, the two noble-faced, pink marble library lions (and were qualities he felt that he very much needed in his seemingly Herculean task) and came to a halt on Fifth Avenue, looking north, beyond Fortitude, toward his house, if somewhat rather forlornly.

He had left an invitation in an envelope addressed to Mr Watkins at the desk, along with some instructions, should he ever turn up again and should anyone somehow manage to recognise him, both of which events, at the present moment in time, seemed highly unlikely. But what more could he do? Nothing. That's what. Feeling no better, Mr Redmayne crossed the street. New York. He'd always loved New York, no matter what, and, indeed, perhaps best of all the cities where he had lived for any amount of time. London and Paris, of course. Shanghai. Berlin (ah, yes, the doughnuts at the Café Bornträger, just off that nice neighbourhood park). Dublin (ah, Barry's tea in Bewley's). Why, he loved New York even more than that tiny little town on the Cornish coast where he and Gloriana had honeymooned so happily all those years ago. Port Isaac. That was it. Where Gloriana had first developed her passion for a cream tea. He chuckled, and something randomly caught his eye. A display in a bookshop window. New book.

But it was the old black-and-white photograph on the cover—or rather the greatly blown-up version of the cover that was being used as the centrepiece of the advertisement—that had so startled him.

The boy in the photograph, there, at the front, a bystander, staring straight at the camera, he looked exactly like Emile! Exactly. So much so, he could even *be* Emile. It was most unsettling.

Captured on Camera:

Great Moments in New York History

Clearly it was some kind of 'history-lite' coffee table book, no doubt very popular these days. Mr Redmayne stared all the harder at the photograph. The resemblance was uncanny. Even as the boy's father he could easily mistake the lad in the photograph for his son. Funny. Mr Redmayne set off again, only to come to a halt almost immediately. It wasn't possible, was it? Was it? Then, after a moment, he chuckled to himself once again. Of course not. What was he thinking? Ridiculous. Everything must be getting to him. This damn party, be better for everyone when it was over.

And Mr Redmayne set off again for home, chuckling to himself as he went. Wait until he told Gloriana, which of course he would entirely forget to do—an act of forgetfulness that on this occasion perhaps was entirely understandable, given what happened next.

Because, while at that precise moment his wife once again searched fruitlessly for her favourite red crossing-out pen and Mr Redmayne marched obliviously up Fifth Avenue with it long-forgotten in his breast pocket, other agencies had already mobilised against him.

By the time he had rounded the corner at Grand Army Plaza and headed north alongside the park, happy to be heading away from the mob of tourists and horse-pulled carriages that congregated there and wondering if there might be a better collective noun for that unruly combination of people and animals than 'mob,' the die, yet again, had been well and truly cast.

He stopped, deciding whether or not he should take a circuit around the park, as part of the effort to get his creative juices going on that damned list, but he soon realised that wouldn't work at all. Over the tops of the tall buildings crowding the edge of the park, the sky would be very clear and blue—as blue and smooth as sapphire, in fact, without a single cloud in the sky—and almost instantly his mind would be elsewhere, pondering other things.

No, he would go home. At the Sixty-Fifth Street Transverse Mr Redmayne came out from under the leafy trees and crossed the road, turning east. In a moment or two, just a few blocks now, very soon, he would be there. That was always the best feeling of all, to be returning home, no matter where you've been. He kept going, past the tall, grand buildings.

Of course, as the owner Mr Redmayne knew how to look for the house, and strange as it may sound, the house knew how to look for him. You had to be in exactly the right place, turn in just that right way, and there it would be, all of a sudden, and as solid and inevitable-seeming as the Empire State Building (and without the astonishingly long line to get in—altogether far more welcoming). And there it was. Home. Right there. Now.

And then it wasn't. It was as if the entire house had just winked out of existence.

It was gone.

11

And then, equally as suddenly, it was back. Mr Redmayne's heart performed several varieties of calisthenics in his chest, none of which might be regarded as healthy. What had just happened? Without wasting any time he raced up the short flight of steps and pushed open the front door. Breathlessly, Mr Redmayne called out a loud, "Hello, anyone?" but was greeted only by silence.

This wasn't good. Anything could have happened. Anything.

Trying with the greatest difficulty not to panic, he hurried down the long hallway toward the stairs that led to the basement kitchen.

"Gloriana," he called into the void, "Gloriana, are you there? Gloriana."

No response. This might mean nothing, or it could mean one of an infinite number of things, many of them catastrophic. His mind raced through the possibilities. Although the house had appeared to vanish for only a matter of seconds, it could actually have been gone for any length of time. Weeks, months, even years (dear God forbid!). His precious children might now be older than he was himself! Anything was possible in a timeslip, if that was indeed what he had just witnessed. Anything at all! He called out again, ever more anxiously.

"Gloriana, George, Felice, Emile—is anyone home? Anyone?" Once again Mr Redmayne's cries were met only by silence, a silence far more sinister than any he had experienced before.

Anxiously, he approached the grandfather clock in the hallway and took out his pocket watch. He compared the two. At first glance his watch appeared to be broadly synchronous with the clock, at least in terms of hours and minutes, which was a source of instant relief.

But, no, wait, the two second hands! They were out. His watch was slow, by about thirty seconds.

Technically, Mr Redmayne was from thirty seconds in the past, which, while not catastrophic, was certainly very worrying. And very strange. He would need to find out how and why this had happened. No time-slip had occurred in living memory. This was very worrying indeed.

The sound of footsteps on the east staircase caused Mr Redmayne to look up at once. Gloriana—thank goodness!—coming down the stairs with an expression on her face that suggested that she was less than thrilled to have identified him as the source of all the commotion. He didn't care about that, however. He was just glad that she was okay, that he hadn't lost her to some bizarre accident with the house and time.

Unfortunately, Mr Redmayne was so overcome with relief at that moment that all he managed to do was stare at her in a confused way and babble about how very pleased he was that she "didn't look in the least different, that—thank Heavens—she seemed exactly the same," which was such an unexpected sentiment for him to express that it quite provoked Mrs Redmayne to arch her right eyebrow in surprise and speculate aloud whether he might be drunk or suffering some kind of episode. Possibly both.

"Eric, are you quite all right? What on Earth is all this hullaballoo about? Are you drunk? Of course I don't look any different. I don't feel any different. Should I?"

Mr Redmayne gathered himself together. "Forgive me, dearest. Allow me to explain. Just now, I was outside and the house, it—my goodness! Dear, the children, where are they?"

"The children?" Mrs Redmayne began to feel afraid. "They're around. Eric, darling, what is this about? You're starting to make me feel quite anxious."

"Thank goodness, they're here. But are you certain? It's important."

"Well, yes—at least, I think so. George and Felice were in the library, I'm sure; I took them a cream tea not two hours

ago, in fact. And Emile, was, well, somewhere, you know how
he is. Sometimes I feel like I don't see him for days on end, but
he always turns up again, doesn't he? Usually when he's hungry. No, I'm confident no one has left the house. They tell me
when they do. Normally, anyway. Why, dear, what is it? What's
happened?"

Mr Redmayne's wave of anxiety began to subside just a little.

He breathed an audible sigh of relief, peering along the hallway in the direction of the library.

"The library, you say? That's interesting. I wonder if they
noticed anything? But, no, darling, wait, I'm sorry... Listen,
I'm afraid something rather serious has happened. I was just
outside and the house, well, it—"

Mr Redmayne cut himself short. His two elder children had
appeared at the top of the stairs, behind his wife, and they were
peering down at him with excessively bemused and altogether
quite innocent expressions on their faces. Mr Redmayne was
simply filled with relief to see them both again, however, so
much so that he quite failed to notice that they both were somewhat unusually dishevelled in their attire, as if each of them
might literally have been pulled through a hedge backward, and
not that long ago, either. George, especially, looked as though
he could have been sleeping rough for a week, which, to be
fair, was perhaps not that far outside his typical standards of
appearance.

"What is it, Pops?" called George down the stairs. "Do you
know what caused it? The outage?"

"Outage?" Mr Redmayne asked, looking in his confusion
from the children to his wife.

"Yes, dear," replied Mrs Redmayne. "Just now. The power
outage? All the lights flickered and went out. Everything. It was
so unusual. I think we might have an electrical fault. Is that
what you were hullaballooing about? You were making such a
racket."

"I'm sorry, dear. No, I was outside. But I saw it. Has anyone
seen Emile?"

"The squirt?" asked George. "Last we saw him he was in his room. Wasn't he, Felice? Though I'm not sure how long ago that was. What time is it now?"

Mr Redmayne looked first at this watch and then at the grandfather clock alongside him.

"It's ten past," he said after a moment's hesitation.

"Ten past what?" asked George, apparently seriously.

"Twelve, of course," said Mrs Redmayne, and turned around to look at her son. What met her eyes quite took her by surprise. "Goodness, look at the state of you both! What have you been doing? You look like you haven't washed for a week, either one of you. Felice, is that dirt on your face? Actual grime? I can't believe my eyes."

"Well, Maman," began Felice, abashed. But she faltered.

"It's really all my fault, Mother," interjected George. "I had to carry out this experiment for school, for science class, see, and Felice, well, she was helping me. It all went a bit wrong, I'm afraid."

"Experiment? What sort of experiment? Were you testing the attractive properties of the human form for dirt? I don't know. Really, George, I'm beginning to wonder if that school we're sending you to isn't quite everything it's cracked up to be. I do hope there isn't a terrible mess."

"Possibly there is, just a little," said George, sheepishly. "You know science experiments, Mother. One second all fine, the next, *pouf!* Mess everywhere. But, not to worry, I promise we'll clear everything up if there is. Oh, Pops, just a second ago you were concerned about Emile. Do you want us to check on him?"

"Yes, please," Mr Redmayne called up the stairs. "Do that, George. Yes. There's a good fellow. And now, if anybody wants me, I'll be in my study. Darling, could you join me in there in about thirty minutes or so? It's about the Open House. I'm afraid I'm not getting very far with my list. I might need your help."

"Oh yes, about that," said Mrs Redmayne, turning back to

her children, or at least back toward the space where her children had just been standing. Displaying a talent for vanishing that would have impressed many a stage magician George and Felice had instantly escaped, leaving her addressing naught but the empty air.

Her husband, too, seized his chance and went off at once, although he did not go directly to his study. First, he needed to check on things in the library. Something didn't really add up and he need to find out what that might be. It might be nothing, or it might be the end, and, of course, while he hoped it was the former, he had to make certain. Only after that would he bother Gloriana with any of his concerns, as foolish as they might well turn out to be. Or indeed, equally, not.

12

That was amazing!"
Eyes alive with excitement, Felice closed her bedroom door behind her with a slam, far louder than she'd intended. "Just absolutely...amazing! You think we were there? You think we were actually there? This isn't like some, I don't know, collective hallucination, or something? I truly don't know. But it seemed so real. Was it real? Tell me it was real. George, don't just sit there with that unbearably smug look on your face. Say something. Anything. And, by the way, Maman was right. You are filthy. You look like you haven't washed in a week."

"That's rich, Sis. Go look in the mirror. You won't be winning any prizes for style this week, mademoiselle, I can tell you! You look like you haven't washed in a week!"

"Really?" Felice went across to her dresser and peered into the mirror, fascinated. "My God, you're right. My face, it's filthy. How is that possible? We were only there a few hours. Weren't we? George, how long were we gone?"

"I don't know. I don't know if there's a sensible answer to that question, even. How long were we gone for *us*, or for the *house*? Or, more like it, for the people still in the house? I really don't know. We'll have to read up on it. We might have been gone a bit longer than we think we were, possibly, or at least longer than anyone here would think we were. Maybe. I think the house must have some kind of mechanism built-in to ensure the ongoing consistency of time, like, internally, I mean. Or something like that, I think, so that the flow of time stays constant on the inside, no matter what's going on outside. You know, something that would allow for the passage of time on the outside to vary, be variable, I guess? Compared to the passage of time inside, anyway. Wow, the math must be amazing. Really amazing. Wow."

Still peering deep into the mirror, Felice bade him hush with a single sideways swish of her hand. "You want to know what's amazing, Georgie? What's actually amazing? This dirt on my face." She raised a finger to her cheek. "This dirt is over one hundred years old. Think about *that*. Now that's amazing. Seriously. Fascinating. To me, anyway. More than any math. That's just numbers and such, and easy too. This dirt is, like, living history. Well, kind of. ...Oh, you know what I mean."

"I do, Sis. I do. Believe me. Honestly. It's all amazing. Every bit."

Felice turned toward her brother, eyes widening even further. "George, we could go anywhere. Paris in la Belle Époque. Or the Versailles of Louis XIV, the Sun-King! Think about it! My mind is officially blown. I mean, we were right to try London first, so we could get out the back unseen. And it was great meeting that poor little Cockney man and helping him deliver all his filthy coal to everyone. Such funny people. Really. *Mais*, George, *Paris!*"

George nodded. "You know, I think he was maybe most surprised when you said it would be fun. I don't think that word has featured much in his vocabulary until now, if at all. We really may have blown his mind. And, wait, did you spot that other old guy with the outrageous moustache? By the infirmary? He kept staring at us the whole time like we were, I don't know, aliens or something, which probably to him we were a bit. But, Sis, listen, I don't know. Look, I know you're keen, right now, understandably, and excited as hell and all about everything. I am too. I am. But I'm thinking, too, that maybe we should dial it back a little? Maybe? Just for now. A tad? I mean, you know, until we're a bit more sure about what we're doing? Today was great, don't get me wrong. I'm just worried that we don't really understand what we're dealing with. I don't even know if I got the house back to exactly the right time. Even being off by just a tiny amount, that could be dangerous. You saw the Old Man's face just now. Pops, well, he might be on to us, you never know."

"You think?" Felice bit her lip. She came over and sat on the edge of her bed. "I admit, I don't feel good about the deception. Sneaking around like this and hiding things from them. That part of it isn't good, even if they did deceive us first. Do you feel that too?"

"Some, I guess. Today was, you know, incredible. Beyond incredible. But now we know it works, maybe we should cool it for a bit, you know, find out more about it? That's all. I mean, the past's not exactly going anywhere, is it? What's the big rush?"

"I don't know. Maybe you're right. It's just so, well, exciting, that's all. You know? The possibilities are, like, wow. I still can't get over today. We just got home and I want to go back. And then there's everything else, all the other times and places we can go visit. That's, like, off the chart. My mind is racing, I don't mind telling you. Georgie, now we've got the lid off this, I'm not sure we'll be able to put it back on. *Ever.* How Papa and Maman have managed it all these years, I've no idea. Do you? It's like they don't even know about it. But that can't be right, can it?"

George was shaking his head. "No, they know all right. They do. They've *got* to know. No doubt about it. Nothing else makes sense. Why they kept it a secret from us all this time, I can't say. They must realise they can trust us. I'm sixteen, an adult, practically, and you're not too far off that yourself. I don't know, maybe they'd planned to tell us sometime? Maybe. Or maybe not. Who can say? But the fact is, we know now and there's no going back on that. I still think we need to find out more about what we're doing, though. This is big stuff we're messing with. Anything goes wrong and there'll be hell to pay. I mean it."

Felice nodded, albeit reluctantly. "You're right, I suppose. We should find out more, yes. Maybe there are rules about what you can and can't do? Laws? That sort of thing. I don't know. Something. I guess we do have to be careful. We wouldn't want to kill our own grandfather or anything like that. That would be bad."

"Definitely toward the very bad end of the spectrum. For sure. Here, Sis, wait, I got something for you. A souvenir." George reached down into his pocket. After a moment's somewhat overly prolonged searching he produced his mystery gift—a small nugget of dusty black coal, which he held up between his thumb and forefinger, as if it were a rare gem. "Maybe this will keep you going, for a while, anyway? You can keep it on your dresser."

"I will!" Felice took it from him. She cradled it in the palm of her hand. "Always. I mean it. I do. Hold on, I've got something for you too. A special historic souvenir, all of your own—wait for it…" For a second she fumbled around in her little shoulder bag on the bed, then she looked up.

"Ta-da!" she announced, holding out in her hand toward him an empty and rather crumpled-looking, little, brown chocolate candies' bag that had surely once contained M&M's.

George looked blank. "What's that?"

"George! It's what's left of your packet of M&M's, obviously. Idiot! I found it on the seat in the coalman's cart. You'd left it behind. Talk about messing about with history. George, how could you be so careless? That's not like you. It's a good job I spotted it and picked it up. Imagine!"

"Felice, that isn't mine. Seriously. No, listen, it couldn't have been mine because I didn't have any with me. I swear. I don't even particularly like M&M's, do I? Think about it. Have you ever seen me eating them? Ever? And, yes, you're right, I wouldn't be so careless, not with something as important as this. Because, really, it wasn't me."

Felice appeared doubtful, confused. She looked up.

Their eyes met, the same unspoken question forming in their minds.

If not me or you, then who?

George began to speak but stopped, the words formed but not yet out of his mouth. The bedroom door swung open. Dramatically. Emile.

Emile, looking like an angry mouse.

Emile, looking like a mouse angry that his older siblings had taken all the cheese, *his* cheese. A mouse with dramatic tendencies. Which is a lot for a smallish boy to look like, or, for that matter, for a largish mouse.

But he did. Cute but annoyed. And mouse-like.

"What have you two been up to, as if I didn't know. And don't think I don't know, because I do. All your sneaking around, you two. —Hey, what's that you've got there? In your hand? Is it treasure? Let me see. Let me see, Felice, or I'm telling."

"Beat it, shrimp," said George. "This is none of your business. And we haven't been up to anything, if you want to know the truth."

"Then, show me." Emile came properly into the room. "I *want* to see."

Reluctantly Felice unclenched her left hand, revealing the entirely unremarkable small lump of coal. Time-travelling coal. Emile stared at it without comprehension, but only for a moment. Footsteps, on the landing outside. Felice closed her hand at once.

Papa, in the doorway, looking distracted.

"Ah, there you all are," he said. "Good. I do so like to see you all together, getting along. Very nice. And especially this morning, after, well...earlier. Splendid to see, that's all, yes. Anyway, no, what I came by to tell you was that I've looked into that electrical issue, the—ahem—outage, or whatever it was. Yes, that was it. And, well, I must say everything seems fine. In perfect order, in fact. Nothing to worry about, no, not at all, and I daresay there shouldn't be any repeat. So, carry on as normal. That's it. That's all I wanted to come and tell you."

Three pairs of juvenile eyes stared up at Mr Redmayne.

Three impassive faces. No comments appeared to be forthcoming.

No responses of any kind, in fact.

Mr Redmayne inhaled long, waiting, and then after a further second or so—finally—he took the hint and left them to it, whatever it was they all were doing together so nicely.

His children. Together. Everyone getting along nicely. Which is what he liked best. Of everything.

The three younger Redmaynes waited for the sound of his footsteps to recede on the landing. Then, Emile stepped closer to the pair. A quiet mouse. Discreet.

"Tell me everything you know," he said, leaning in purposefully. "Or I tell them everything *I* know. And I *will*, George. You know I will. Both of you do."

And George looked at Felice, and Felice back at George, each at a loss and wondering how something that only fifteen minutes earlier had seemed so fantastic had so quickly become a trap.

But, alas, at times, as all three Redmayne children must shortly discover, such is life.

☙

An hour or so later, in his study, with the morning's almighty scare seemingly behind him (and no harm done), Mr Redmayne gathered his thoughts. The 'timeslip' or whatever it was appeared to be only a momentary glitch. As far as he could tell the mechanism itself was working perfectly, but he resolved to keep a closer eye on its operation in the short to medium term, just to be on the safe side. You couldn't be too careful when you kept all of time bottled up in your private reading room down the hall; by the same token, neither could you worry about it constantly, as you'd soon go doolally, which would be highly counterproductive, to say the least.

Of course, the other possibility was that the time-mechanism had suffered some kind of third party interference, but this was so entirely unlikely that Mr Redmayne didn't give it any serious thought whatsoever. Who even knew about the mechanism and its secret location, let alone how it worked? No, that was all so very improbable as to be out of the question. Case closed.

Needless to say, poor Mr Redmayne may not have been quite so readily dismissive of this latter possibility—nor for that matter of the uncanny resemblance between Emile and the small, skinny, staring figure of a boy in the old photograph in the bookshop window that he had seen earlier—had he but known that at that precise moment his younger son was being instructed in the operation of the time-mechanism by none other than his elder son in the supposedly 'secret' room itself.

But that, indeed, was not to be known. Not yet, at least. Not until much havoc and heartache for all had been wrought—with consequences, disastrous consequences indeed, in fact, for all.

To George's credit he had tried to guard against such consequences, at least as far as Emile was concerned, by not telling him everything, by leaving out certain key details. For example, George didn't tell Emile about the safety-lock, the one lever that held everything in place and prevented the operation, inadvertent or otherwise, of the time shifting apparatus. And this he did for his younger brother's own protection.

And he certainly didn't tell him about the mysterious time-travelling M&M's wrapper, the import of which George and his sister had yet to comprehend for themselves.

Nonetheless, that George was, by withholding key information in this way, acting in a manner consistent with the behaviour of his parents toward them all, and about which he was so very critical, was an irony entirely lost on George's teenage self. Sadly, his failure to be completely forthright, much like that of his parents before him, makes a major contribution to what happens next.

But that part is still to come. At this point in the tale George was by no means certain that his younger brother understood even the little that he did share with him. Of course, Emile was awestruck by the mere existence of the room, this secret room in his own house, where he had lived oblivious of its concealment all of his days to date. That in itself was enough to bowl him over.

Still, George's (partial) account of the mechanics, the numerous levers, the many-sized cogs, the multiplicity of clocks, with the repeated dire instructions not to touch anything, ever, appeared to wash over Emile like a dull lesson in physics, or worse, geography, at school. He said little, but just walked around wide-eyed, staring at everything. It was, all in all, quite a lot to take in.

Emile did ask George one question, as they were leaving the room and closing it up carefully behind them. He wanted to know how come George knew so much about it. How was that? Two months or so ago he hadn't known anything, had he? So how come he knew so much now? And, again, George prevaricated. He said this and that, but was economical with the truth. He didn't tell Emile about the book. The book he had found on a dusty top shelf of the library itself. An old book, written and printed seemingly in 1666. Impossibly so.

Toward a Practical Quantum Mechanics of Spatial and Temporal Displacement
By RRR

He didn't tell Emile, just as he hadn't told Felice, that the book explained everything about the house and how it worked because the author had been the architect and its builder.

Rufus Reginald Redmayne, their grandfather.

He didn't tell them any of that.

And, most importantly of all, he didn't tell them about the heavily creased handwritten note he'd found secreted inside.

Clearly ancient. Signed RRR.

Dated 25th December, 2766.

Addressed to *George*.

13

Emile was, of course, a good boy—at heart, in fact, a very good boy. He didn't mean for anything bad to happen. That wasn't his intention. It wasn't like any of it happened on purpose or anything. Not at all. Mostly it was an accident. A mistake. Something we've all done at one time or another. His mistake happened to be bigger than any other mistake in recorded history. That's all. Or histories, for that matter. Just about. Which is a big burden for any eleven-year-old to have to carry around on his or her young shoulders; although these days he tries, as a rule, not to think about it. Much.

And maybe, actually, none of it was any of his fault, in the end, seeing how things went; or not much, or at least not everything was his fault. It was all just so complicated when you tried to figure it out that in the end you decided it was best not to and just get on with your drawing. What happened, happened. Obviously.

Who could say whose fault it was? In the end?

Maybe it was everybody's fault? Think about that.

Whatever. All of that is still to come.

Crucially, in order to understand why it all happened, we need to realise that, like many eleven-year-olds, Emile didn't much care for it when his older siblings knew important stuff that he didn't, or when they tried to exclude him from things that he thought he had just as much right to be involved with as they did and all just because they thought he was a dumb little kid who didn't know any better and they happened to believe that they were so much more grown-up than he was (and breathe). When they weren't. Again, obviously.

Which is the way Emile saw it.

Plus, well, yes, he may have wanted to show off a bit for his new best friend, Steven Sparkle, who was coming to visit soon, with his parents (unfortunately), during the Open House weekend. And he may have told Steven one or two things about the house that couldn't possibly be true. Except, of course, they were. And Emile may have felt that now he had to prove it, or *some* of it at least. But only he knows that for sure.

In truth, none of that was much on his mind in the weeks leading up to the fateful and indeed calamitous weekend. Life went on around him as normal. His mother fussed busily about this and that, and largely left him to his own devices. A line existed, of course, which Emile knew he should not cross, normally, with regard to revealing any of the secrets about their house.

But he wasn't thinking very much about that, either. What he *was* thinking about, mostly, in no particular order, were the things that Steven and he tended to do when in one another's company, namely: (a) Soccer, which they played a lot of together, at school, mostly (or *football*, as Steven insisted indignantly that Emile should always and without exception refer to it as, on pain of a dead arm, or, for that matter, leg);

(b) Comic books, in particular manga comic books, which they read a *lot* of together (an awful lot of); and

(c) *The Fantastical Adventures of the Amazing Fang Tang Gang*, which was their own comic book adventure story, one that they spent an extraordinary amount of time writing and drawing together and which was based loosely on the trials and tribulations of their everyday lives, except with added monsters—the latter naturally a by-product of their own feverish, eleven-year-old imaginations.

Indeed, so vividly imagined was this fantasy version of reality for both boys that the line between what had actually happened and their cunningly twisted accounts of it began on occasion to blur. At times they were living the fantasy! Neither Emile nor Steven, however, for all of their wild imaginings, had any idea of the truly earth-shaking adventure that lay just ahead, at least for one of them.

If Mrs Redmayne, or indeed Mr Redmayne, had at that time

crossed the threshold into Emile's bedroom (which, as both of them reflected subsequently, they might have at least *tried* to do with a little more regularity, if only they hadn't been so darned selfishly preoccupied), they would have discovered among the clutter (the debris, as Mrs Redmayne saw it), a vast assortment of abandoned sketches and drawings, frequently of the same scene.

For example, you might spy, sketched over and over, Emile (or a figure that you could take to be Emile, if the resemblance were pointed out to you) hiding around a corner from some kind of approaching huge lizard-creature-thing (loosely depicted, in truth, but no less scary for that); or Steven Sparkle, his cartooned, curly red hair projecting outwards like the blinding rays of the sun in full corona, staring down a similar-looking scaly beast and making it cower. Steven, hero!

Alas, neither of Emile's parents did venture into his room, and so they didn't find any of this out, at least not until after the fact. Still, when they finally did get round to it, or rather, when they got round to dispatching George and Felice to do it on their behalf, the search yielded a very useful clue. But, more of that later.

In her defence it should be noted for the official record that Mrs Redmayne was throughout the entirety of this period very busy indeed with organising everything for the coming big Open House weekend thing and Emile knew, as did everybody else (because she told them, regularly), that she wasn't just doing all of this for herself. No, the Open House was for everyone.

This was, after all, she insisted, quite rightly, a Redmayne event—a family activity, not a solo Mrs Redmayne event—and the sooner they each recognised that simple fact, every single one of them, and chipped in to help her, the better.

In consequence, all of the other Redmaynes wisely kept well out of her way and let her get on with it, even if everything she said was perfectly true.

In the end, it worked best that way, they knew.

So, as a result Emile might catch a glimpse of his mother

approaching down the long hallway or emerging from one of the many, many rooms, somewhat distracted, perhaps crossing items off a list as she went (Mrs Redmayne lovingly compiled all manner of lists and equally lovingly crossed all manner of items off them as she went—a true joy even when one only had one's second-best red crossing-out pen to do it with), and Emile would, quite sensibly under the circumstances, duck the other way, characteristically mouse-like, unseen.

Or, Mrs Redmayne might be in her kitchen, literally up to her eyes in whatever she was doing (sometimes that cake-mix did indeed get everywhere), and Emile might wander in, a little peckish, wondering if there mightn't be a tasty morsel of something or other to be had that he might sneak away with, to tide him over, and he would see his mother, right there, larger than life in a Mrs Redmayne sort of way, but somehow she wouldn't see him. Not at all. In those moments Emile might be standing only a few steps in front of her but no indication would follow that she had registered his presence. He could take whatever he wanted and make off with it entirely unobserved—and frequently did.

Indeed, it would be true to say that, at times, in that vast house, the boy may as well have been invisible, because it wasn't only his mother who didn't see him. No.

Because, of course, Emile's father could also for days on end be notoriously myopic about anything going on outside the interior of his head—at such times external reality might only now and then intrude upon his thought processes, just a little. And, by golly, wasn't it even worse when the poor man had been assigned a specific (typically, Herculean) task to carry out, as under these circumstances Mr Redmayne tended to focus on the task in hand to the exclusion of all else (because if he didn't, inevitably his mind would wander to the four corners of the universe, each of which he knew tolerably well, at least in theory).

So, for example, when Emile heard his father tuning the piano in the music room, as was Mr Redmayne's job before every Open House (like his father before him, and Felice, he enjoyed perfect pitch), well, on those occasions Emile knew that it would be pointless to intrude on Pops with any special worry or concern. Or indeed anything. And when his father wasn't preoccupied with a specific something or other, to the exclusion of all else, Herculean or otherwise, very often his private number remained, so to speak, unobtainable. The lights were on, yes. But was he home? Often, no. No.

And Felice was rehearsing. She played the piano like a demon (Debussy, of course, Ravel, some Fauré) (so French, all of them!). Every year at the Open House, Emile's sister gave a recital—so, three recitals in total, no less. And this year (whatever had possessed her!) she had surprised herself after all and invited the Bouffants, and so was thoroughly determined not to perform anything less than superlatively before her arch-rival and nemesis, the dreaded Claudia (who had, to Felice's equal surprise, deigned to accept the invitation).

And not to mention Madame, too—Madame Méchant, from school! Whatever, whatever, had possessed Felice to invite *her?* She would never, never know!

Why, it was almost as if she needed to impress the very people who seemed not particularly impressed by her, or even to like her in the least. But that couldn't be, could it? No. Surely not.[11]

And Emile and George were no longer talking, not even to exchange insults. No acknowledgement had passed between the pair at all for several weeks.

In fact, to George it was almost as if his little brother didn't exist, which was ironic indeed, given what happens next.

---

[11] Yes.

14

As the big day approached, the fateful day, Mrs Redmayne was terribly, terribly busy. And preoccupied. Understandably so—because there was so very much still to do. The vol-au-vents, the petit choux, those things didn't make themselves, let alone the salade niçoise, the white bean and tomato gratin, the vanilla soufflé, the gougères au fromage—and this was only the French side of things. The English menu didn't bear thinking about, and not just on account of the work involved (such very strange names—Toad in the Hole, Spotted Dick—exactly what *that* was she didn't like to think!).

And then she had the music to organise, the charades, the card games (Mrs Redmayne was rather partial to a hand of Belote, her husband markedly less so), and oh, all of the activities in general. It was such a headache.

Luckily, even though she was keen to stress to all that this was a family event—for everyone, not only for her own benefit—to her relief the other Redmaynes seemed somehow to have realised that it would be best just to leave her to get on with it, an outcome with which she privately concurred.

And supported. If very quietly.

In the end, it worked best that way, she knew.

Because now, quite free from interruption, she was at liberty to get on with everything and cross off items from her many lists as she went along, one by one, which was in itself delicious (and a possible party game, she wondered? Hmm, probably not). Because, as she saw it, every single crossed off item was not only a step closer to completion, but potentially, to perfection. Because, yes, one year she would throw the perfect party. That was her secret goal.

Perfection.

Unattainable? Yes, very likely so.

But she would try. Why? Because she must. This was what she did and she did it very well. Alas, even near-perfection came very hard and required absolute attention to detail. Hence, her preoccupation. Hence, the fact that she didn't cross paths with her family very much these days.

But they were around. Eric, well, he was wherever he was and doing whatever it was he did there (very important things, nonetheless). George, he could usually be found in the library, studying hard (bless him); Felice, the music room, rehearsing her quite difficult piece for the piano (over and over) (and over) (bless her); and Emile, well, he was somewhere, she was sure. Knocking about boyishly. And—this bit was crucial—not under her feet every single minute, unlike as had typically been the case in previous years. Bless him too. The rascal.

Sometimes, however, just every now and then, Mrs Redmayne had the strangest sense that perhaps she had just missed someone, that while she had been up to her eyes (quite literally at times!) (darn that flour!) in doing this or that in her kitchen (so busy!), one of her children (Felice, possibly? Emile, yes, most likely) had been right there, if only for a moment.

But, by the time she had looked up from her soufflé mix or whatever she was up to her eyes with, the room would be empty again, or at least it suddenly felt very empty, apart from herself, of course, which didn't really count.

Or she might be walking between rooms, assessing their event-preparedness, crossing something critical off one list or another as she went (sometimes Gloriana thought she needed a list of the multiple lists she had going, just to keep track of them all), and she would come to a complete stop, all of a sudden, and look around. Had someone been there? A second ago?

Out of the corner of her eye just now had she just glimpsed, well, someone or other? Possibly? In the hallway? Or there in the shadows on the stairs?

But, whenever she checked, invariably no one was there. She would be quite alone—and a little uneasy, if only for a moment, feeling a strange shivery chill, as if she had missed or forgotten or indeed almost glimpsed something of critical importance, something that really required her full attention.

And then she would pull herself together. The odd feeling would pass and Mrs Redmayne would move on.

She had a party to organise, after all. And it wasn't going to organise itself. Was it?

No. It wasn't.

The French delegation would be the first to arrive, a party of eight. The three events of the Open House weekend were carefully staggered to avoid overlap between the respective sets of guests. Mr Redmayne did something clever with the settings in the secret room behind the library, a minor adjustment to the time mechanism, so that the house no longer was held in strict temporal synchronisation with all three time zones.

Therefore, when it was 1:00 p.m. in Paris it was no longer 1:00 p.m. simultaneously in New York and London, as it was usually for the Redmaynes. Mr Redmayne was most careful to make only the tiniest of adjustments to accommodate this, a very fine calibration of the standard settings. Anything bigger could be catastrophic. It didn't bear thinking about. And so he didn't. Much.

As it was, all three delegations would be arriving at what they believed to be 1:00 p.m. local time, when in fact they would be turning up at four-hour intervals. Paris first, London second and, finally, New York. For the Redmaynes it made for quite the long day, very taxing on both the old nerves and hospitality— and not to mention, very filling gastronomically.

This year poor Mr Redmayne didn't feel entirely confident that he could eat quite so much as he used to do when a younger man (enviously, he hadn't noticed George suffering any difficulties in this area); and doubted that as the long day wore on he might be able to do so with the required gusto, despite how undeniably delicious his wife's cooking always turned out to be. It would look very odd to the third set of guests if he as host were to just pick at his food as though he never cared if he saw another (blasted) vol-au-vent for the rest of his days.

But, then, as things stood, perhaps on this occasion he might not be called upon to consume the usual three feasts in one day, after all...

Along with his waning belief in his appetite, Mr Redmayne was equally doubtful about the possibility of anyone from New York turning up at all. Sad, but true. And yet somehow or other the poor man hadn't quite found the right moment to break the news to his wife that, with all of New York City's eight million or so inhabitants to choose from, he had only managed to invite one guest, and that this lone individual, whom Mr Redmayne didn't know very well anyway, was most unlikely to make an appearance, seeing how he seemed largely non-contactable these days and hadn't confirmed. Still, Mr Redmayne planned to cross that bridge when he absolutely had to and not before—a policy he usually found to be sound and practicable, most of the time (if a little bit cowardly).

And this was definitely one of those times.

The final adjustment Mr Redmayne had needed to make was to allow Emile to pop out early and collect his friend, this Steven Sparkle, in London. They had all agreed that the boy could come over first thing in the morning and keep Emile occupied, with the strict instructions that he be kept well clear of the French contingent. They didn't want another Shanghai incident (his fault entirely, as a nipper himself). The confusion had been enormous at the time. No, no, they certainly didn't want a repeat of *that*. Mr Redmayne chuckled to himself at the thought. Old Rufus had been obliged to go to enormous lengths in order to smooth things over. No, indeed. But the house was certainly large enough for two small boys to knock about in unseen, getting up to boyish minor mischief. Pranks, whatever. That sort of thing.

Additionally, the arrangement would keep Emile out from under Gloriana's feet, which played to the benefit of all. That was very important. Keep the mother happy, keep the boy happy too. Nothing worse than a bored child moping around the place all at a loose end when you've got all manner of things to do and no time to do them in. Very tricky.

But when he thought about it, Mr Redmayne couldn't honestly recall when he had last seen Emile moping anywhere, to be fair, either in the house or otherwise; or even, when he really thought about it, when he had actually last seen the child at all! He was around, somewhere, for sure, unless he was out fetching that Sparkly boy, which, given the time, he probably was. Almost certainly.

And knowing that this was most likely true, now that he'd thought about it properly, Mr Redmayne felt a little better.

And so indeed it was.

In fact, that morning Emile had been up and out of bed at the crack of dawn in no less than three countries, on two continents, which, even for someone with his advantages, was quite an achievement. The prospect of having his very special pal from school in his very special house was so exciting—the first time anything like this had ever happened—that Emile could hardly wait for the morning to arrive. Exciting, yes, that was true. Very. But perhaps a little bit worrying, too, although he was trying not to think about this last part. Emile had told so many seemingly tall tales at school about his fabulous house and its unusual properties that he now felt under pressure to deliver on them, or on some of them at least, or else be labelled as someone living in a world of make-believe, an exaggerator, a no-good liar; and if not by Steven then without a doubt by everyone else at school once they heard about it.

And, of course, he couldn't very well reveal too much about the house without betraying his family. Maybe just reveal a little bit, then?

Maybe he could show Steven just enough to be convincing? Whatever that was. Just enough. That was his thinking. Broadly. But exactly how much that needed to be, well, he had no idea. Not at all. None.

Not that any of this had really been quite so clearly articulated in his mind by the point that Emile was first up and out that morning and already on the way to collect his friend. Yes, he felt excited, he knew that much—and he felt a bit worried, all at the same time. But that was about it. *Excited* trumped *worried*, any day of the week, in any case. And so, the rest of it Emile pushed out of his mind whenever it came up. He would cross that bridge if and when he had to cross it and not before, which was something that Emile had heard his father say often enough, so that had to be okay, didn't it? Probably. Whatever. He was out to have some fun and that's what he was going to do. The best fun ever. Fun they'd talk about at school for days, maybe even weeks.

Epic, historic fun. The best. Ever.

That's really all that was on Emile's mind on this most fateful of days as he crossed the Millennium Bridge over the desperately murky Thames toward the south bank, with St Paul's Cathedral behind him and the whopping big Tate Art Gallery dead ahead, the really old power station place with the ridiculously tall chimney pointing skywards like a rude finger. Not that Emile cared much about the architecture. Nope, he was just out for the fun.

And waiting for him at the foot of the bridge, there it was. Fun—in human form. Steven.

Steven the sunny boy, in more ways than one. Always with a bright smile on his round freckly face—and, besides that, he even looked like the sun. A bit. Especially with his curly red hair blowing in all directions at once, as it was this morning. In fact, one windy day out in the schoolyard Mr Tomkins, the science teacher, had once described Steven as looking like a "coronal mass ejection," a remark nobody had understood until he'd explained it later in class. It had meant that Steven looked like the sun, which everybody had known anyway. The sun when it was throwing a party, he'd gone on to say, which again had kind of made sense. The sun when it was ejecting huge amounts of electromagnetic radiation and plasma into space, he'd said next, and everybody lost interest. They all knew Steven looked like the sun. No need to go on about it quite so much and try and make them learn stuff at the same time. And so he stopped, Mr Tomkins, finally. Which the class had appreciated.

But that Steven looked like the sun, there could be no denying. And never more so than on a windy day, like on that fateful, gusty Saturday morning when Emile crossed the Millennium Bridge to meet him and take him home.

Emile's friend saw him coming over the bridge and waved, beaming madly all the time, his thick red hair blowing every which way at once in the strong breeze from the river.

The sun was throwing a party, and so were the Redmaynes.

15

The house was ready. The food was ready. Mrs Redmayne was ready. The weekend of the Open House event was, finally, here. And everything was ready. The last item on the last list had been crossed through. The three ornate gold clocks high on the wall in the library, which normally were synchronised, had now been adjusted each to reflect one of the three different local time zones outside the house: 1:00 p.m., Paris; 9:00 a.m., London; 5:00 a.m., New York. That it was going to be a long day for the Redmaynes was something of an understatement, as there had never been a longer day in the entire history of time. And if you thought about it like that, as Mr Redmayne did that morning, it was enough—rather more than *enough*, actually—to make you feel quite tired before you even began.

And so he tried not to think about it like that and on the whole succeeded. But, as it turned out, the day itself in the end lasted far longer—far, far longer, in fact—than he could possibly have anticipated at the outset. But all that is to come.

The final adjustments to the time mechanism and hence to the three clocks had been made after Emile had returned with his friend. Mr Redmayne had made it his personal responsibility to check that they were safely inside the house before he undertook this task. Adjustments of any sort, no matter how fine the calibration, should never be made while any Redmayne was outside the house. This was a strict rule, laid down in his father's original book, which was around somewhere. The idea that they might, as a family, become in the least desynchronised, was unthinkable—and not to mention downright dangerous. Nothing could be worse. And so he had hunted throughout the house for the pair of young scamps, expecting to find them messing around with the elevator (apparently not many private houses had elevators) (remarkable), or with the dumbwaiter (quite out of bounds today), or at a loose end on one of the upper floors, planning mischief.

Instead, after combing the house and beginning to worry, just a little, he found them in the last place that he'd expected. Emile's room. On the floor, drawing something or other. Quietly. Lots of discarded pages everywhere. The Sparkly boy had looked up at him and smiled when Mr Redmayne had first poked his head around the door. A nice smile. Warm. Astonishingly round head. But at least they were back and he could proceed. Which he did.

Mr Redmayne also made some final adjustments to the translator mechanism. He knew how George liked to test it to destruction on days like today, talking either very literally or utter nonsense (and sometimes both together), just to see how it came out. Most of the time the house coped (old Rufus had been a true genius in so many ways—centuries but indeed centuries ahead of his time), but it irritated his wife when it went wrong, especially when guests were involved. Blessed Blue! Mr Redmayne chuckled at the thought. But, no, it would never do, not today. And so he tinkered with that, too, just to make sure. Blessed Blue! Oh, no, no, no. Dear no. No. A pity, but no. And then, finally, he was ready too. 12:55 p.m., Paris time. Battle stations.

He left the library and proceeded out into the hallway. Everybody but Emile was already there. His wife looked astonishingly beautiful as ever, in a very elegant and not at all old-fashioned gown, blue, like the sky on a cloudless summer's day, and he found himself unaccountably filled with love for her and an overwhelming sense that he wanted the day to go perfectly for her sake, the day that he could not possibly know would end in such bitter and terrible tears for all.

"Mon chéri," she said softly to him. "All is ready?"

"It is," he replied, equally softly, in confirmation, and only just caught sight of George signalling his disgust at the pair to Felice by pretending to make himself gag on the index finger

and forefinger of his left hand. Youth! It was true what they say
about it being wasted on the young.

At that moment the great grandfather clock in the hallway
loudly, portentously, struck the hour for 1:00 p.m., and it was
time.

Mr Redmayne went down the short flight of steps to the
side door, opened it and stepped outside. Mrs Redmayne followed him, close behind. It was another glorious day, very fine.
The pair looked along the little alleyway. No one was there. Mrs
Redmayne turned to her husband.

"Maybe they're not coming?" she said, doubtfully.

"Nonsense," replied Mr Redmayne. "Who in all of France
could resist an invitation to one of your splendid dinner parties? No one, dear, that's who. Precisely no one."

And Mrs Redmayne smiled at his confidence. Nonetheless,
she felt a little flutter of anxiety in her heart all the same. Maybe
the name Redmayne no longer carried the cachet it once did
dans le tout-Paris? That was possible, if unlikely. No, she must
remain confident also. If Eric could do it, then so could she.
After all, she was a Redmayne. And Redmaynes should never
succumb to self-doubt. No. Especially not when considering
all of their tremendous advantages. If nothing else, they owed
the world the benefit of their unique perspective on life and
how to live it. They led by example. She would be patient. And
composed. Yes. That was how she would be. And so she was.

Happily, it didn't take long for Gloriana's patience to be rewarded. All at once, they appeared, at the end of the alleyway,
all together, a small crowd, proceeding uncertainly.

"See, there," said one of them, a woman's voice. "I told you
it was down this ridiculous alleyway. Every time, it is the hardest
place to find, and then, suddenly, *there*, you are here. No?"

"What street is this, even, anyway?" said another, a gentleman this time—a genuinely puzzled-sounding gentleman, at
that. "Rue de Partout? Allée du Phénix? Which is it? Both? *Psaw!*
Never heard of either one. And I know all the little streets. Or
at least I thought I did."

"But that's Paris," said yet another. "Surely, it is inexhaustible, is it not? One cannot know it all. Impossible!"

Mr Redmayne stepped forward, his arms spread wide in welcome. "Friends, dear friends, I'm so glad that you could make it—and even more that you could find us! Forgive us for bringing you in this way. We're having some work done on the front of the house, I'm afraid. Essential works. Tremendous nuisance. But quite safe. And, yes, we're perfectly fine going in this way, I can assure you. Please do come along. Yes. This way. Watch the step. That's right. Gloriana will take you in. Margot, Vitas, how very good to see you both! Delighted!"

"Ah, Eric, the pleasure is all mine, truly," said Margot, a tall, lithe lady with the longest face. "But entirely."

Cheeks were kissed on both sides. "Ah, you flatter me, Margot, but I thank you for it. And Vitas, my good friend. Maybe you would honour us all later? I'm sure I could find the Stradivarius, somewhere, if you were so minded, possibly? It would be a rare treat for all of us. And not least for the Stradivarius!"

The elderly gentleman gripped Mr Redmayne by the hand, a firm grip nonetheless. "Ah, Eric. Will I play? For you, maybe. For Gloriana, certainly. Now where is she? My old eyes require sight of her great beauty at once—it has been far too long, I must say. But you look tolerably well yourself, for your age. Ah, there she is. Going in with the others. Let's go in too. I'm sure you do not appreciate your immense good fortune, old friend, seeing her every day, but for the rest of us it is like, I know not what, a glimpse of the divine on Earth. You know? So, shall we?"

"Certainly, Vitas. And I assure you I am in absolutely no doubt of my astonishing good luck. I'm most unworthy, I know. But every day I count my blessings, I do really. Now, let's go in. Yet again Gloriana has prepared the most sumptuous feast. One that only a guest as discriminating as yourself could truly appreciate, I'm sure. Now, if you would, lead the way, sir. I'll follow."

Gently Mr Redmayne ushered his elderly guest down the steps and toward the house. A slight sadness filled his heart as he could not help but notice how far more frail his very elderly friend had become since he had last seen him. But his grip was still firm, there was that. Some life in the grand old dog yet. For sure.

Gloriana had already escorted several of the guests through into the hallway, where George and Felice were waiting. George couldn't help but be a little amused by how nervous Felice appeared, a twist that he hoped might prove reasonably diverting throughout the long afternoon ahead. Was the teacher the cause, this Madame Méchant? Crazy to invite her (the very thought of inviting old Kelvin!). It couldn't be the parents. Madame Bouffant's hair was as humorously gravity-defying as her name had suggested it would be (maybe she held the trademark, he couldn't help but wonder). The father, a nonentity (obviously realised he could never compete with that hair). Perhaps the daughter? Perhaps the daughter?

George's over-critical eyes came to rest on Claudia…and a very strange thing happened.

Everything began to run slowly, as if time itself had slowed down. No, that wasn't it. More like George had suddenly been submerged under water and every movement had become an enormous effort and, yes, slow, very slow, to complete.

And not to mention cumbersome—in the extreme.

Or it was more than that, even: more like as if an explosion had gone off nearby and he'd been rendered temporarily deaf, stunned, confused. In shock.

It was love at first sight.

At least for George. When introduced, Claudia looked at him for no longer than the nanosecond that was required for her to register his (clearly very) plain features and with no more interest than she might show in a choice of clean towel in a guest room. She glanced, yes—a flicker of her deep brown eyes in his direction (one lone eyebrow arched); then, her interest moved on. Instantly.

George's feelings were only intensified by this supreme show of Gallic indifference, however. If possible, he loved her all the more for it.

Somehow he had to get her attention.

"Claudia, have you seen the," he began, then as she turned her beautiful, if quite impassive, face back toward him he realised he didn't know what the object of his sentence was going be, possibly, and he hesitated. "The, the, the house? That's it, the house. I mean, how could you? You only just arrived, didn't you? Like, *duh*. But, see, what I mean is, I think, I could show it to you…I could. Because I know it really well, the house, seeing as how I, you know, live in it. Regularly, in fact. Actually, sorry, no, every day, of course. I mean. I live here. In the house. Every day. With Felice. My sister. Her. I'm George, by the way. Hi. That's all, yeah. Hi."

Felice shot him a look. What was he doing? Was George purposefully trying to sabotage her afternoon before it had even begun? Claudia, perhaps aware of her impact on her great rival's rewardingly awkward brother, eyed him with marginally less disdain than she had a moment earlier, which George interpreted as a positive sign.

Alas, Margot Defage, the internationally celebrated xylophonist and long-time family friend, chose that moment to appear on the scene.

"But, no, this cannot be *George*?" she cried in mock-astonishment. "Little Georgie? No, I won't believe it. I cannot! I refuse! He's grown so tall. And handsome, yes, like his father? Yes? Georgie, last time I saw you, you were only so high, I think, and talking about nothing but mathematics and your computers. Ah, but I see you have other interests now…no?"

Margot's eyes ran coyly from George to Claudia and then back again.

George's mortification was complete.

Mr Redmayne came forward busily just then, ushering them all on.

"Come on, Margot, Vitas, follow everyone else. There you

go, yes. That's right. Everyone, we're decamping to the drawing room for some light refreshments. Just to start things off.
Follow Gloriana. Excellent, good, yes. George, what's the matter with you? You look like you might be unwell. Not feeling
queasy, I hope? I'm counting on you to eat for us both, my boy,
I don't mind saying. Right, well, don't just stand there. Come
along and join the party."

And George, seeing the lovely Claudia—clearly by far the
most lovely girl in all the world—disappear ahead with Felice
without so much as a backward glance in his direction, dragged
his now quite leaden deep-sea-diver's-like feet step by heavy
step toward what he was sure was going to prove the longest
and most miserable afternoon of his short, loveless life to date.

On that point, he was quite right, although not for any reason that he could possibly have anticipated. Sadly not. No. Not
at all.

Safely ensconced in the great drawing room, which had been set
out especially for the occasion, the seven visiting guests and the
four Redmaynes present (Emile remained elsewhere with his
young British chum, the rascals, as instructed) mingled with all
the initial awkwardness that such disparate groups tend to pos-
sess. The elder Bouffants and Madame Méchant formed a little
group of three, clearly overawed by the unexpected splendour
of their surroundings and were trying hard to hide it behind an
air of extreme indifference and a certain, calculated sangfroid.

But the hint of panic in their eyes could not be concealed.

Luckily, Mrs Redmayne had not only spotted this but had
anticipated and planned for it—it wasn't that unusual for
first-time guests to feel intimidated by the house, the sudden
expansiveness of it all, the sheer number of rooms, the, well,
the *fabulous Redmayneness* of everything. It could be a bit much,
she knew.

Hence, the first drink served was a blend of calming cham-
omile, honey, and vanilla tea, her personal recipe. It never failed
to soothe. Armed with that and, for want of a better expression,

the Redmayne personal touch, Gloriana felt more than capable of putting anybody at their ease. After all, she had been doing this for so very long. And she enjoyed it.

"So, dear Madame Méchant, my daughter tells me you are a teacher such as no other in the entire civilised world, without parallel, one who commands the complete and instant respect of her every pupil. And I'm certain your Claudia says the same, surely that must be so, Madame Bouffant? Yes? Ah, I thought as much. Tell us, do, Madame Méchant, if you will. What is your secret?"

Madame Méchant demurred, a little flushed in the cheek.

"No secret, madame. I am sure I am no better nor no worse than any other," she said, full of false modesty and glancing all the while over at her two pupils, who were being heartily amused by Pierre Pierre, the puppet master extraordinaire. Under his expert prompting, light flurries of laughter were rapidly developing into full-blown gales.

"Come, come, you are altogether too modest, madame," continued Mrs Redmayne. "Isn't that so, Monsieur Bouffant? See, madame, we are agreed. You are guilty as charged. There. Accept praise where it is merited, along with our gratitude as parents. Educating children is so very difficult. So much can go wrong—in the wrong hands."

Madame blushed once more. It was a novel experience for her to be praised so, if unexpectedly pleasant. Once again, her pupils' peels of amused delight filled the room. All in all, she somehow felt quite buoyed by the scene...

Maybe, she wondered to herself, looking on, just maybe, she might try to be a little more like him in future, this raffishly bearded master of the puppets, and less prone to treating her pupils without exception like unwilling dogs?

Hmmm, perhaps. She would see. No promises. The training went deep.

All the same, she smiled to herself at the thought. The girls were laughing so. Another way? Possibly. Possibly...

George, on the other hand, was not enjoying the famous

Pierre Pierre's impromptu performance at all. Not in the least. No.

He was being entirely overshadowed and it was excruciating. Every turn ramped up the girls' hilarity, frustrating him all the more. Claudia would never notice him at this rate.

Here *he* was, a potential Master of the Universe, with all of Time and quite possibly Space at his command, just about, as good as, almost, and he was being pitifully outshone by the stupidly goateed old man who ran the puppet show in the park. La Théâtre Des Marionnettes—Hah!

What was he, Pierre, anyway? Thirty? Forty?

Unable to control himself George allowed a sneer to escape in the direction of the great puppeteer, who arched a lone eyebrow in silent acknowledgement.

George wondered how anyone could find the wretched man amusing, let alone his new one-true-love. What did that say about her? And yet, her face, Claudia's, looking at it, the fine colouring, the clear complexion, the high cheekbones, the hazel eyes, she was so very beautiful, so very...*French*...

Still, he had to do something—and now. But what? What? What did Claudia want? George had no idea. He was miserable. Thoroughly miserable.

Felice, on the other other hand, she was enjoying herself beyond her every expectation. Never had she imagined that her great nemesis and arch-rival would deign to treat her with anything other than her standard haughty Gallic contempt, even in her own home.

And yet here they were, sharing a joke, having a good time— together. What did it mean? Were they friends now?

And was it all only because Claudia was impressed by the grand house, the fancy company? Was it? Felice would have brought her home years ago if she'd known. School would have been so much easier to get through. All this time.

Felice looked over at her parents. They were so elegant, both of them. Maman had that doddery ancient violinist clinging to her now but she was clearly handling him with such charm.

And Papa, he was in his element, holding court. The Bouffants looked so *ordinary* in comparison. Felice was lucky, she realised now, so very lucky. Her family was special. It wasn't just the *house*. *They* were special.

The only fly in the ointment was George. Why did he have to be staring at poor Claudia like that? Felice frowned.

It was just exactly how he'd been with that French TV actress, years ago, following her around like an orphaned puppy. At least then it had a certain charm because he was so young. Now it was just embarrassing. Creepy. He was going to ruin everything. They would have to ditch him. First chance. For certain. No hesitation.

Happily for Felice, and much less happily for George, the opportunity she sought presented itself almost at once.

The great Pierre Pierre, the acknowledged master of the puppet, far from content with merely monopolising the attention of the two young ladies, began to humiliate poor George by proposing that the lad might benefit from joining him in his act—he had a vacancy for a new lead puppet, he said, with a laughing, raffish twinkle in his eye, and George would be perfect, didn't the girls agree? Surely they must? Yes?

"Look, see," he went on, smiling wickedly all the while, "he is so wooden, a natural, I think. Phenomenal. I think he would make first a great Pinocchio, and then maybe, one day, if all goes well, a real boy? Yes? Come, George, rehearse with me now. Together we could be very fine. We could be the toast of all Paris! And after—all France! What do you say?"

George, indignant in the extreme, looked in mortification from the face of his newfound beloved to that of his sister— and saw that they were frozen in the attempt to hold back their amusement, but that probably neither of them would be able to hold it in for very much longer.

Time to go.

"Not likely," he said, with as much dignity as he could muster, before moving off. "I think you'll all find I have far more important things to do with my life than entertain the under-fives on their birthdays and at Christmas. Thank you."

Pierre Pierre feigned as if in receipt of a mortal blow and bowed extravagantly.

George heard the two girls explode with laughter behind him.

That man must be the devil himself, he thought angrily. He already has the stupid pointy beard. One day he might wake up and find that his famous puppet theatre in the park had never existed. That could happen. Yes, it could.

"Ah, George," said Mr Redmayne warmly as his son approached and he placed a paternal arm around the boy's slumping shoulders. "Ready to lead off on the first course, lad, the hors d'oeuvre and what have you? Get everyone started, yes? That's a good chap."

George looked at his father as if he had no idea what he was talking about. "I'm sorry, I couldn't eat a thing. Not at a time like this."

"A time like what?" relied Mr Redmayne, genuinely perplexed.

George shrugged, despondently. Before his father could enquire further, Alain Pensée had quite garnered Mr Redmayne's attention with a rather tricky question that required a rather delicate answer; delicate, that is, if an outright untruth were to be avoided in the response.

It was a query about the origins of the elaborate stained and painted glass window that overlooked the entire great drawing room, a scene depicting a medieval king and queen consulting an elaborate set of architect's plans spread out on the ground in front of them. Alain suggested that if he didn't know any better (and few people did know any better, he hastened to add), it rather looked like an original Morris, Marshall, Faulkner & Co window, although he realised that was highly unlikely given that (a) it was located in a private residence, here, in France, and (b) the fact that they stopped trading in 1871.

Also, there was the striking resemblance in the features of the two figures depicted with those of Eric and Gloriana, so it was clearly a knock-off, if a most excellently executed knock-off. But by *who*, that was the question?

Who in the modern-day art world possibly had the skill, indeed the craft, to pull off such a magnificent copy, so magnificent in fact that it could even have an expert like himself momentarily doubting his own judgement—only momentarily, of course. The circumstantial evidence of its forgery was incontrovertible. Naturally. Obviously. So, who?

Pray tell, dear Mr Redmayne, if the question were not impertinent, who?

He *had* to know. He *must*.

Distracted, Mr Redmayne watched his son shuffle off into a corner by himself, wondering what calamity had so doused his spirits. Unfortunately, Monsieur Pensée's thinly moustachioed face was peering directly into his own, with an expression so sharp that he might very well cut somebody with it, if he wasn't careful. Or was that his intention all along? It was so hard to tell with intellectuals. Very rarely did they mean what they said. You couldn't trust them. Hardly.

Mr Redmayne gathered his thoughts with care.

"Well, that's very hard for me to determine," he began, truthfully enough. "You see, it's probably a lot older than you think. I can see what you mean about the resemblances—yes, quite uncanny. But they're not myself or Gloriana, heavens no. Not at all. That's my father, you see, Rufus Reginald Redmayne, and my mother, Boudicca, would you believe? Yes, I know. What great names. And my father was a very mysterious man, I have to say. Anything was possible with old Rufus. I'm afraid he wasn't much given to explaining himself. I do know that he commissioned the window to celebrate the construction of this very house. The plans in the foreground, there, they're the plans for the building you're standing in right now. It's entirely his own design, you know. He very much saw himself as the king in his own castle. King Rufus. Hence the tableau. I'm only the humble caretaker, as it were, I'm afraid. Le Gaspard de la nuit, if you will."

Monsieur Pensée seemed fascinated and disappointed in equal measure.

"Even so," he said. "Surely…"

"Beyond that I wouldn't care to speculate," replied Mr Redmayne quickly, "should truth be told. Now, Gloriana, Felice, I think it might be time shortly to treat our guests to a little musical interlude. And then we can get this party properly underway. Hors-d'oeuvre, everyone? I'm sure they are quite delicious. My beautiful wife went to a lot of trouble and she's a first class chef, as I'm sure even Monsieur Pensée will agree. Isn't that right, Alain? And he has excellent judgement. Yes, see, Alain agrees. So, everyone please do eat. These things don't eat themselves, after all. That's what I find, anyway. Yes, that's it, *do*. Do."

Thus prompted, the guests—not as one, it has to be said— slowly, gradually, steadily moved themselves toward the long table that formed a centrepiece in the room. On the table were spread all manner of tiny delicacies—shapes and colours and textures of every sort.

Mr Redmayne couldn't help but think that his wife had out-done herself this time, but then he thought that every year. But this year, she really had. Quite. Marrying her really was the best thing he had ever done. No question.

Margot approached him from the rear and with great famil-iarity slid her elegant, slender arm into his. "You Redmaynes, Eric. Really. You do know how to live well, I think. Yes, very well. This is all very beautiful, as always. How do you manage it? What is your secret? Tell me, do. I won't rest until I know."

"I don't know what you mean, Margot. I'm just a humble mathematician. Retired, at that. No more, no less."

"Mathematician, *psaw!* You don't live like a mathematician. You don't dress like a mathematician! I never met a mathema-tician other than yourself who didn't dress like they had fallen from the sky into a rubbish skip full of old tramp's clothes. And yet…*you*. You wear the finest tweed, the most expensive cashmere, the best [sigh] everything."

"All my good fortune lies in inheriting this splendid house. That's all. I can assure you that's so. Look, here comes Gloriana. She'll back me up, I'm sure."

"Yes, I am certain of that. She is in on your little secret, whatever it is. Oh, you are so lucky to have each other. Just perfect together. I envy you both so."

"Envy, Margot, you? Come on. You have your xylophone. No one bangs a tune out on one of those quite like you do. We envy *you* and that's the truth, isn't it, dear? Dear?"

Gloriana and Margot exchanged a look that was quite beyond Mr Redmayne's comprehension. Then, he spotted George moping off by himself, obviously not eating anything, and so he decided to toddle over see what the matter was.

Gloriana watched him go. Margot too.

"Like all men, Eric has his blind spots," said Gloriana, patting Margot sympathetically on the arm. "But we don't love them any less for it."

"No," agreed Margot, wistfully, "we do not."

Felice passed within earshot of the pair, with her rather pretty friend from school. Such an unfortunate hairstyle on the mother, given their surname. No doubt it was very her, in more ways than one. Collecting her thoughts, Mrs Redmayne took the opportunity to remind her daughter that it would soon be time for her recital, in the music room. She might want to pop along there ahead of everyone else and make sure everything was ready. Felice nodded.

"Oh, Felice, you are getting to be more like your mother every time I see you. So grown up, so beautiful." Margot stared at her with suspiciously wet-looking eyes. "Oh, excuse me. Poor Vitas, Gloriana. See? We must go and save him from Alain. His stamina isn't what it used to be, you know? No one his age should be forced to listen to Alain all alone. Not for too long. The consequences could be serious. Fatal, even. No, we must intervene. At once. Come now, I insist, help me. I need you."

Felice regarded the two older ladies as they headed over toward the elderly violinist and his intellectual assailant. Then, she scanned the room some more. Everybody else appeared to be occupied. The coast was clear.

"I think we've actually shaken him off," she said to Claudia, her new best friend. "Goodness, I was beginning to think he would never leave us alone. Quick, let's get out of here while we can."

Claudia lingered. Felice followed her gaze over toward her father and George.

George? What could she possibly be thinking? Surely not? Not a chance. No way. No.

But Claudia was biting her lower lip in a way that might only be described, in a teenage way, as 'thoughtful.'

"Your brother," she began, "the wicked little puppet man, he was very hurtful to him, I think. His pride is injured. Maybe we should speak with him, make it up? That would be the right thing to do."

"What? George?" Felice was incredulous. "You've got to be kidding me. Don't worry. He's got the hide of a rhino. Honestly. Usually, anyway. No, really, he'll keep. Believe me. Let's just go. I think Pierre Pierre might be gearing up for his encore. See, he's looking this way. Come on."

With an obvious reluctance Claudia let herself be dragged from the room. Felice realised that she knew nothing at all about her new best friend.

Who could like George? That would be like liking old snot, or dirt. Or equations. Something largely dry and odious in any case—and entirely one-dimensional, to boot. This was not to be encouraged. Bad all around. Disastrous, even. No, she had to keep them apart, for her own sanity if nothing else. Absolutely. Some worlds should never collide.

Quickly Felice led Claudia away from the great drawing room. In rapid succession they passed the drawing room, the great dining room, the dining room, the game room and Mrs Redmayne's study, until finally they were standing outside the imposing solid oak door of the music room.

Claudia had an air about her of being slightly bewildered.

Everything was just so grand and, well, *fabulous*. And *big*. Seemingly the hallway stretched on forever, in both directions, ahead and behind.

"Your house, it is so imposing—and so *vast*. One would never imagine from the exterior that it would be like this, I don't think, no?"

"Yeah, it's a regular Taj Mahal on the inside. I'll give you the tour later, if you like. Right now I have to get ready to play. It's my standard contribution to the entertainment. Every darn year. My duty."

"Then, let us do that. What are you going to play?"

At that moment several curious things happened, almost all at once. Firstly, the lights flickered, which was unusual in itself and could have a variety of causes in that unusual household, none of which were particularly desirable. Secondly, only a matter of seconds later a podgy red-haired boy whom Felice had never set eyes on before came running along the hallway, barging past the two girls without so much as an upward glance.

And off he went at speed toward the rear of the house. The girls couldn't help but watch him go.

"Who was that?" asked Claudia.

Felice shrugged. "Probably my little brother Emile's friend. Rumour is that he has one."

As if in confirmation Emile himself came running past just then, in dogged but no doubt hopeless pursuit. He, too, passed both girls without paying them the slightest attention. Thirdly, unnoticed by all, the grandfather clock in the hallway struck one. Again.

"Boys, really! What *is* the point? None, if you ask me," said Felice to Claudia. She pushed open the door to the music room. "What were you saying? Oh, yes. *Scarbo*. That's what I'm going to play. Or try to, at least. Scary, I know. So difficult. You know, Ravel, yikes."

"You are far braver than I, to play anything in front of these people. Vitas Vieillard, Margot Defage, I mean, they are musical giants. World famous. I could not do it, I know."

"Actually I was far more worried about you and Madam. Imagine! Claudia?"

Felice turned to see her friend standing still in the doorway, speechless. Dumbstruck. Awestruck.

Understandably, perhaps, in fact, as the music room was unexpectedly large on the inside, round, and full of light and space. In the exact centre stood a full-size concert grand piano, in black, a Sauter. As if this wasn't enough in itself to generate astonishment, numerous other instruments littered the periphery: two oboes, a cello, a double-belled euphonium (Mr Redmayne's own, from his college days), a trio of wall-mounted flugelhorns (all his, also), a flumpet (again, his), a trumpet (his, yes, technically) (but only because he'd inherited it from his father) (who'd been presented it as a gift in 1959 by his one-time musician friend, Miles) (so not really *his*, as such, no); a harpsichord (George), an Irish bouzouki (Mrs Redmayne's, curiously enough), and most incongruously of all, a triple-tenor, steelpan drum set (no one's in particular, although Emile had dropped the bomb on it far more frequently than anyone else, at least recently, anyway).

It *was* all rather impressive, it must be said, especially on a first viewing.

Poor Claudia wandered over to the piano as though in a daze.

She played a soft note. Two. Very soft. Three. Pianissimo. It was astonishingly satisfying to hear. A most excellent instrument. Obviously.

She looked up, her face a picture of blank puzzlement.

"Your family, forgive me for asking, Felice, you must be very wealthy? Yes? All of this, everything, everywhere. I mean, how? How is it this way?"

"My grandfather. He accrued a lot of, I don't know, stuff. Over time, I guess. I never met him." Felice took her position on the piano stool. "He travelled, like, everywhere, you could say, all the time. Picking stuff up here and there. Papa too. We all have, actually. I haven't just grown up in France. No, I've lived in England, London—and in New York, for a long time.

And George still goes to school in New York. He's only home for the weekend."

"For the weekend? What? I do not understand. Really? That makes no sense. And you, how can you have lived in these places, and for a long time, you say? You are *so French.*"

Felice beamed. All at once, a warm feeling flooded her being. Her entire life, throughout its considerable ups and downs, she would always think that this was the single, nicest, *best* thing anyone had ever said to her.

Ever. Without exception. And, in many ways, it was.

The door to the music room opened, letting in first some general hubbub and loud chatter, followed almost immediately by the perpetrators of the racket, the party-goers. Felice opened her sheet music at the right place. *Scarbo.* By Ravel. A difficult piece, one of the most difficult. But she had wanted to impress. And at that moment she felt like she could play anything and play it well. Perfectly.

Felice smiled at Claudia, raising her eyebrows as if to say, *Well, here goes…*

Claudia stepped away from the piano. The music room was filling up, and she spotted George, still looking thoroughly miserable. She went over and stood by him, by the flugelhorns. In passing, she offered him a smile, a shy smile, apologetic, a smile that wanted to undo her part in the wicked nastiness of earlier, a smile that said, *Forgive me, let's start again*, a smile that did all of this and yet lasted in total perhaps under two seconds. If that. But was no less successful for its brevity.

George appeared to brighten at once.

All George saw was the pretty French girl smiling at him. That was enough.

So, there they stood, side by side, ostensibly for the purpose of listening to Felice play the piano, although in truth neither of them was thinking very much about that. Not just then.

Mrs Redmayne called the room to order and the hubbub died away. She smiled. Somewhat proudly, it has to be said. And why not?

"Everyone, distinguished guests," she began, "thank you all so much for coming along today to our humble gathering. We are honoured and grateful."

Mrs Redmayne paused. She looked around the room for her husband, but he was nowhere to be seen, which was unusual for a moment like this.

Maybe he was retrieving the Stradivarius from his study? Still, his absence was a little disconcerting.

"My brave daughter is about to play something for you all, a piece by Ravel, I believe. Brave, firstly because of the difficulty of the piece she has selected and, secondly, to play at all in front of such a celebrated audience. Celebrated musically, I mean. Who could forget Alain's exploits on the triangle at the Christmas party that year? I know we never could—and, as a rule, we never do." General polite laughter. "So, without anything further from me, Felice, please—"

Before she could complete her introduction, unfortunately, Mrs Redmayne's eye was caught by the sight of her husband in the doorway.

His face looked ashen.

"Sorry to interrupt, dear," he said, and all eyes turned toward him. "We have some early, I mean, *late* arrivals."

One by one, a succession of people almost no one present had ever seen before came into the music room, looking ever so slightly lost and confused themselves, it must be said.

It was the London contingent. They were exactly on time.

16

Mr Redmayne hadn't liked the look of those same flickering lights that the two girls had witnessed a few moments earlier. Not one bit. And particularly not when there was company in the house. The last thing they needed was some kind of time-slip. Not now. Not ever. But not *now*, especially. Probably it was nothing. He wouldn't have been quite so worried if he hadn't witnessed the strange flickering disappearance of the house when he had been outside a few weeks earlier. As it was, he had felt duty bound to investigate. To put his mind to rest, if nothing else. And so he had slipped out of the drawing room and started in the direction of the library.

Hardly had he set foot beyond the door, however, before the astonishingly red-haired/round-headed Sparkly boy had come hurtling along the corridor, at full pelt, practically knocking into him. And no sooner had Mr Redmayne dodged one wild running boy (quite artfully, at that, he thought) when along came Emile, similarly jet-heeled. Another quick-footed sidestep. Boys! Well, he had been young himself once. But there was a right time and a place for everything. And this wasn't it. Not today. Not right now. And besides, Emile hadn't given him so much as a backward glance. Not like him. Mr Redmayne had watched his son disappear into the deepest recesses of the house. Or maybe it *was* like him, he had thought, suddenly uncertain.

When all this was over, this darned Open House, he would spend more time with Emile, give him more attention. That was a promise. One he should try his very best to keep.

But, right now, the house required his attention. Sadly. Always the house. Occasionally Mr Redmayne had used to wonder to himself whether it was all worth it, all the fuss and bother that came with the house. But, of course, when he

thought it through, inevitably it was. Worth it. Of course. No
getting around that. He went on along the corridor past the
music room, toward the library.

And then he stopped.

Something was wrong. What was it? He could *feel* it somehow, something not being quite as it should—a most strange
sensation. But what?

The clock, the grandfather clock, that was it—it had just
been chiming out the hour. On some level he was always aware
of that. Time.

But right then, hadn't it stopped too soon?

Had it? Surely, yes? Or was he just imagining it?

Mr Redmayne approached the clock quickly. Oh, no. 1:00
p.m.

But that meant—Great Galileo's Ghost!

At once Mr Redmayne started toward the rear of the house.
Checking on everything in the library would need to wait.
Something must have indeed gone very wrong in there but this
was an emergency.

Most uncharacteristically he dashed past the various
rooms—the music room, the game room, the dining room, the
great dining room, the drawing room, the great drawing room,
the several sculleries and parlours (great, middle, pre-penultimate, etc.), all at full speed. Sometimes having such a very large
house wasn't of the utmost convenience. Not at all.

By the time the poor breathless man had reached the back
door, however, he was astonished to find some people were
already *inside* the house, approaching *him*.

What on Earth! This was extraordinary! Unprecedented!

It took a second for everything to sink in, for the situation
to make itself clear. Then Mr Redmayne gathered his wits together and extended his hand in greeting, initially to the large,
bald gentlemen in the vanguard of the group. He thought he
recognised a certain family resemblance to Emile's young friend
(principally, head shape) (round, very).

"Redmayne, hello," announced Mr Redmayne as casually

as he could manage under the circumstances. "How are you? So pleased you could make it. Yes. You must be little Steven's father, Mr Sparkly? Am I right?"

"Sparkle," corrected the large man at once, in a gruff tone that suggested errors arising in connection with his surname were a frequent irritation.

"Spar-*kel*," came a further correction from behind, from a surprisingly tiny woman in a round, wide-brimmed flowery hat, whom Mr Redmayne correctly presumed to be the man's wife.

"Excellent. *Do* come through. Some of the guests are already here, you'll find. Ah, Eric and Elsie, how nice to see you again. How are the whippets? In fine fettle and famously fleet of foot still, I trust? Yes, good, come on through. And *you*, Major. Very pleased to meet you. Redmayne, that's me. Ah, Mr and Mrs Jessock, how lovely you could make it. I do hope you found us okay. Sometimes it can be tricky. Yes. Nice to see you both too. Right. That's everyone, I should think. Come with me. I'm going to lead you straight to the music room. Yes, I am. Yes, several of our guests arrived a little earlier, from France, actually. They're all just right along here. My daughter's about to play. The piano. Plays beautifully, if I say so myself. We'll join them directly. Yes, that's right. Follow me everyone. This way."

Mr Redmayne wasn't at all sure that he was doing the right thing, but didn't really see that he had any other choice. They would just have to wing it. Gloriana was very good at that sort of thing. Normally. But nothing about the next few hours was going to be in any sense 'normal,' he didn't think. No. Not at all. They'd always been so careful to keep various national contingents apart. Until now. Anything could happen. But they'd cope. With whatever. They *were* Redmaynes, after all.

"Actually, Mr Redmayne, your house was a little tricky to find, if you don't mind me saying," said Mr Sparkle, breathing heavily, regardless of whether Mr Redmayne minded or not. "Yes. In fact, I was just beginning to wonder, you know, if this wasn't some kind of prank. Everywhere Street—it sounds a bit ridiculous. I said that to Stella when we couldn't find it. I said,

Stella, what kind of street name is Everywhere Street, anyway? It sounds a bit ridiculous. I've never heard of the like. I bet it doesn't even exist. It's all some kind of prank, I reckon. And then our Steven came running out, and lucky for us he did. He showed us the way in. And so, well, then, here we are. Just like that. Very nice, too, if you don't mind me saying. Large."

He stressed this last point as though it were a particularly prized virtue.

"Thank you. Yes, the street name is odd. Strictly speaking, the house stands on Phoenix Yard, but for some reason it's become known, quite far and wide, actually, as Everywhere Street, and that's how we tend to refer to it ourselves. Still, no matter. Your son went outside, you say?" enquired Mr Redmayne, after a second. "I do hope he made it back in without any difficulty. The back door can be quite tricky too. Still, I expect Emile's with him. And, indeed, yes, as you say, here we are. So soon. The music room."

Mr Redmayne pushed open the door and entered. Luckily things hadn't yet gotten underway. His wife was still making the introductions. Felice was at the piano, however, and looked ready to play. Mr Redmayne caught Gloriana's eye. He wanted to convey to her that although the situation was serious he had it under control. Probably. "I'm sorry to interrupt, dear, but we have some early, I mean, *late* arrivals."

All eyes in the room had turned toward him—and then toward the newly arriving guests as they filed in, one by one.

For a second, Gloriana's expression betrayed her alarm, but only for a second. A look passed between her and Mr Redmayne, and she understood. Situation serious, but we'll manage. We're Redmaynes. After all.

"Friends," announced Mrs Redmayne, "honoured guests all, today we're pleased to receive parties from both Paris and London—together here for the first time. Now, Felice will play, for everyone, and then there will be refreshments. So, Felice, if you will…"

Felice looked up at her mother a little anxiously, but Gloriana smiled at her, by way of reassurance, as a mother should, and she felt better. Ready. The hubbub in the room died away to silence. Felice took a breath. Unfortunately, at that moment the entire house began to shake. Quite violently.

Cries of alarm filled the room. Mr Redmayne saw his daughter spin round on the piano stool, an expression of genuine fear—and incomprehension—on her young face. Panic everywhere. Guests stumbled. One by one the three wall-mounted flugelhorns fell to the ground. Poor Vitas Vieillard took a similarly dramatic tumble. Mr Redmayne saw Gloriana struggling to the elderly violinist's assistance. Something had to be done. The house was tearing itself apart. He could feel it.

He went out at once into the hallway, intending to reach the library. But one extremely violent jolt tossed him down onto his knees. It was no good. Everything was out of control.

And then it stopped. The shaking ceased. Mr Redmayne could feel the house settling, as if catching up with itself. Was it over? He drew himself upright.

Ahead of him, the front door had swung open. Mr Redmayne did not like what he could see outside.

He stepped forward and stood in the doorway. No tall skyscrapers crowded the horizon, no small buildings either—in fact, no buildings of any kind. No Manhattan. All around, the land was as green and virgin as the day the first settler had set eyes on it.

Great Galileo's Ghost! *When* were they?

He had to act. Now. At once. No time to lose.

Mr Redmayne passed back along the corridor as quickly as he could.

The door to the library was also swinging wide open, which surprised him, despite the intense vibrations. The library had been designed to withstand anything and everything. Inside, however, Mr Redmayne found nothing short of chaos. Books were strewn everywhere, lying in cluttered heaps. Disaster.

He cast his eye first on the three clocks on the opposite wall. They all read very different times of day. Then, he looked up behind him for the door to the secret room—and his heart fell. That, too, was wide open. This wasn't possible.

As quickly as he could, Mr Redmayne trudged through the fallen books littering the floor and then took the blackened spiral steps two at a time. He didn't know what to expect inside the secret room—everything had been in perfect order when he had been in there earlier that morning. Calibrated just so. For things to go so badly wrong it would take nothing short of—

—Tampering!

He didn't want to believe it, but it was true.

Actual manual tampering! The key anchoring lever had been thrown lose, to an angle of approximately ten degrees. That was potentially ruinous.

The three time-zone levers, they were where? My God! They were set in three entirely different eras: backwards—backwards—forwards!

No wonder the house had felt like it was tearing itself apart. Who could possibly have done this? And why? He had no idea.

But for now that was a secondary concern. His top priority was to put everything back to how it should be. The *how* of why this mess had happened he would address later.

First, New York. If any of the guests were to step outside now through the front door, well, it would be most unfortunate, to say the least, both for them and for history.

Carefully, smoothly, Mr Redmayne adjusted the lever, allowing the house time to work, to calibrate its position. He even paused for a moment, so as not to overload anything, given the great distances in time involved.

There. Then, he repeated the exercise for London, showing the same great care and precision.

With each successful reset Mr Redmayne's overwhelming sense of anxiety and tension eased somewhat. It was going to be okay. Broadly speaking.

He was fixing it.

Finally, Paris. That intrigued him. The other two time zones were set hundreds of years in the past, Paris in the distant future, possibly half a millennium into the future. Or more, even. Why?

Mr Redmayne made a quick calculation, based on the current position. Sometime in the mid-to-late twenty-eighth century—why on Earth? Nothing made any sense. It was like the work of a maniac—or a *child*.

The house was lucky to still be standing, going racing through time like that in different directions. It was all very mysterious.

But later, later. Yes. For now, he just had to fix it.

Once the appropriate era had been restored to the Paris time-zone, Mr Redmayne reset the anchor mechanism, placing the long lever at a precise ninety-seven degrees, which would hold everything perfectly.

He lingered for a moment before leaving. There was much to think on.

But right now he had to attend to his guests. That was his priority. He so hoped nobody was injured. That would be un-bearable.

Mr Redmayne closed the door to the secret room firmly behind him. And this time he locked it, pocketing the key.

Back in the music room things seemed to have settled down a little after the terrible shock. Guests were standing together in groups of three or four. Someone had found a chair for Vitas. Gloriana was attending to him. Refreshments were underway. The highly acoustic room was filled with the high-pitched, echoey murmur of chitty-chat, of relief—the relief of survi-vors.

Mr Redmayne signalled with a brief nod to Gloriana that order had been restored outside the music room also. He saw that she understood.

Then, he began to circulate among the guests, checking on them individually.

The general consensus appeared to be that they had suffered an earthquake.

"Who would have thought that possible, here, of all places," said Margot. "I tell you, I believed it was the end."

"I know. I said exactly the same thing to my wife at the time, but exactly," agreed a sombre-faced Mr Sparkle, pausing to take a sip of tea from a delicate china cup that looked far too small for his giant hands. "Didn't I, dear? I said, 'Dear, this is the end.'"

His tiny wife nodded in silent, wide-eyed affirmation.

"Well, no harm done, it would seem," said Mr Redmayne, somewhat prematurely as it turned out. Then, he moved on, surveying the room all the while.

In fact, the only injury of any sort that he could detect was to Pierre, who at that moment was having a sticking plaster applied to the bridge of his nose by Felice and her strikingly pretty young friend.

Mr Redmayne went over to assess the extent of the damage.

"Ah, Eric, my friend, there you are. I am glad you are okay. *Me?* Bah, it is nothing. I was struck by a falling flugelhorn, that is all. Right on my pointy beak. Here. See? The real injury is to my pride, I am ashamed to say. Yes. Your son, he saved me. Other flugelhorns, they were falling also. He intervened. I am in his debt. Death by flugelhorn would have been so, shall we say, embarrassing, yes?"

"Yes, indeed. But he's a good lad, is George," said Mr Redmayne, with more than a hint of pride and, again, alas, perhaps prematurely.

Nodding, he took his leave. He was keen to reach Gloriana. They probably needed to bring the occasion to an end sooner rather than later, before some of the conversations between the two parties took a regrettable turn.

"My dear, I'm afraid the day has been a terrible disaster," he said upon reaching her. "I'm so very sorry, but perhaps under the circumstances we should bring things here to a close. And soon."

His voice and face conveyed the true extent of his concern.

"Was it…anything bad?" she enquired, nervously, with a significant emphasis on the 'bad'.

"Worse," he replied, before adding in a whisper: "Tampering."

Gloriana's face blanched.

"Yes, I'm very much afraid so, dear," said Mr Redmayne. "The evidence is incontrovertible."

"Ah, Eric, there you are," said Vitas, from his chair. "Your wife has restored me to life. She is a true angel."

"I know," agreed Mr Redmayne. "She is always that, old friend, I can assure you. Now, please excuse me one second if you will, there is a pressing matter I must attend to, I'm afraid."

Unfortunately, some of the surrounding conversations had caught his ear.

To his left, Margot had just complimented the Sparkles on their perfect French, especially for 'British people,' a remark that provoked uproarious laughter from Mr Sparkle in particular, as if this were quite entirely the best joke he had ever heard, because—as he loudly declared—he "didn't speak a word of any foreign lingo—never—and was thoroughly proud of it."

Meanwhile, over to Mr Redmayne's right, Alain Pensée and the Mayfair Wheedles were embroiled in an escalating comedy of confusion about the improbability of suffering an actual earthquake in the respective cities of Paris and London, with neither party quite understanding why the other city in question was under discussion.

"Because, today," said Alain, as plainly as he could, as if he were explaining the matter to a child, "we have experienced an earthquake in Paris, no?"

"Good Lord! In Paris too?" exclaimed Major Wheedle. "In which case, the epicentre must have been somewhere in the Channel, surely? You know, what do you call it over there—La Manche?"

Matters were proceeding exactly as Mr Redmayne had feared. He had to act. Again. Now.

At once he took up a position at the piano. Initially he tinkled out a few random notes in a seemingly non-attention-seeking sort of way, but soon progressed to his favourite major chords, complete with several 'look-at-me' jazz style flourishes and embellishments.

Quickly he hit his stride.

And then he sang.

"'I had no luck with love—till I found you.'"

It was the first song that he had sung for Gloriana, all those years ago, when courting her, in Casablanca, and was special to them both for that reason.

Their song. She came over and stood by the piano. The room had fallen otherwise silent. All eyes were on the pair. Gloriana sang the second line.

"'Just like a lonesome dove—till I found you.'"

Her singing voice was as soft and clear as an old church brass bell cutting through the night on a foggy evening. In France. Rural France, at that, with rolling green hills in the misty distance and an apple orchard nearby.

The entire room gathered around to watch their performance.

George and Felice were agog. They exchanged looks of astonishment. In fact, they were so astonished that they quite forgot to be embarrassed. Neither of them had so much as heard their parents singing before, at least certainly not in a public way. Not duetting!

And yet, here they were, harmonising, no less.

"'I was all alone in my grand empty home.'"

The singers' eyes were only for each other as they ran slowly through the number. It was quite the performance, the show stopper it was intended to be. By the time they neared the song's climax, no one in the room had a thought in their head about anything else.

George stole a glance at Claudia—and felt his face flush red when she shyly stole one back.

"'So now—I don't know what I'd do if I lost you.'"

Unfortunately the pair did not manage to complete their song. The door to the music room burst open—most dramatically—and in ran Steven Sparkle.

All eyes swung around toward the new entrant, the breathless boy, who was clearly distressed. He stood there panting.

Seldom had Steven ever looked less like the sun.

Mr and Mrs Redmaynes' eyes met anxiously.

Good Lord, Emile, the two boys, they had been quite forgotten, in everything and what-not. All of that.

Emile, however, did not at once follow Steven into the room.

The boy's parents went across to their son, and stood looking at him awkwardly. And then Steven became aware of the many pairs of eyes in the surprisingly large room that were now focussed exclusively on him. Tears did not seem far away. Not at all.

"The house was shaking," he blurted out. "And I got scared, so I hid. And then I couldn't find anyone."

Mrs Redmayne approached the boy. She had a bad feeling, all of a sudden. All-consuming. A dread. Call it a mother's intuition.

"Steven, where is Emile?" she asked, unsure if she could bear to hear the answer.

"He went outside," said the boy. "See, we were playing a game. It—"

Mr Redmayne came over and interrupted him. He knelt down.

"*When* exactly did he go outside, Steven?" he asked. "Think now. This is very important."

"When the house was shaking," replied the boy. "He went outside when the house was shaking. And now I can't find him anywhere."

17

Recriminations followed. Recriminations followed by self-recriminations, followed by anger, disappointment, tears of bitterness, all of this. And regret.

Enough regret to fill all of time and still have some left over. The happy Redmaynes were no more. This was the life—the lives—that they had made for themselves. No one else was to blame.

And at the bottom of it all was the fact that Emile was gone. Lost in time.

At first, having gotten some of the story out of Steven, Mr and Mrs Redmayne were at a loss to understand how Emile knew about the secret room in the library, let alone about how the two boys had come to suppose how it could be used in a game about 'time-travel.' ("Oh, the very thought, very nasty," Mr Sparkle had remarked, taking his tearful son home.) The Open House party had broken up almost immediately after Steven had burst so dramatically into the music room, with the Redmaynes no longer caring how the respective sets of guests would react later when they came to discover their two cities had somehow remained quite earthquake free—all day long, no less.

But George and Felice soon confessed that they also knew about the room and its special uses, that they had known about it for several months, in fact—and that they had already used it once themselves. To visit London in the 1870s (for a school project) (kind of) (-ish).

And that George had shown how it worked to Emile, to prevent themselves from being discovered. And that was how the boy had come to know about it. But, but, George had maintained, in his defence, such as it was, he hadn't told Emile anything about the safety mechanism, the one lever that locked all the settings in place. Without knowing that, how could Emile have moved the three exits of the house through time? How could he? He couldn't. It didn't make any sense. None of it made any sense, did it? Okay, George admitted, after a pause, it might be a bit his fault, this situation, but not all of it was, he didn't think, no...

Possibly you have not had much cause to notice it thus far in this cautionary tale but Mrs Redmayne possessed something of a wicked temper, one to which her family were generally quite motivated to avoid making the least provocation. But it was always there, largely dormant but lurking under the surface, Vesuvius-like. And when it blew the best advice was to stand well clear.

On this occasion, however, as might be expected, the blast zone was quite extensive.

Deceit, lies (technically the same thing but no one thought this detail was worth pointing out at the time), irresponsibility, stupidity, lack of care about others—in fact, downright cold-heartedness, negligence, stupidity (yes, repetition but, again, no comments thought necessary). But, out of everything, it was the deceit. The months of deceit. That was the most damaging. That was what hurt the most. Her own children. Her *own* children to whom she had given everything...

Everything but the truth, George had said then, after the dust had settled for an instant. Both his mother and father had done nothing but lie to him, to all of them, every day of their lives. They'd kept the truth from them, the truth about the house. They'd lied. They'd changed time, made a day repeat over, yes, they did, without telling them—and that had been a terrible deception. They'd kept it from them. Anything could have happened. And all because they didn't trust them, their own children, with the truth. That's why all of this had happened, if they were so keen to apportion blame. And after all the fuss that Pops made about always telling the truth—the hypocrisy!

Tempers were running high. Often at such times there comes

a point when there is nothing left to say. Everything has been said. And afterward nothing can ever be how it was before. This seemed such a moment.

The Redmaynes looked from one to the other, unable to comprehend how they had come to be in this position. And now it struck them all that this was all there was left.

Mrs Redmayne was the first to storm out of the room, followed shortly after by Felice, in sobs of tears. George lingered a moment or so longer, but his father looked too sad to hear a word more, and so he exited also, leaving Mr Redmayne quite alone in his study.

And none of it changed the fact that Emile was gone.

A heavy gloom filled the study, leaving Mr Redmayne in the shadows, all alone at his desk. Outside, the crowded New York skyline obscured the view from his window. Yes, his little Emile was gone. Everyone was gone. If he chose to do so, he could make that so impressive skyline disappear in an instant also. Such power. It was a curse. The house was a curse. Family was everything and the house had ruined his family. It had ruined everything. He didn't know where they went from here.

This was despair. All the trappings of their great life, they meant little, nothing, in fact, if they were not bent toward that one end, to make his family happy. His father's house, in which there were indeed many mansions, how he wished he could bloody-well give it back to him.

But old Rufus, like everything else, was gone—long, long gone in his case. When he thought about it, it struck Mr Redmayne that almost all the great treasures of the house had belonged to Rufus in the beginning. He had hardly added anything to its vast haul of loot in all these years. Even this fine Art Deco statue of the owl in brass that stood in the centre of his wide-winged desk, staring back at him right that minute with its black, hollow eyes—and of which Mr Redmayne had grown so very fond over the years, his favourite piece, in fact—that too had originally belonged to Rufus. *Minerva.*

The wise old owl. It had no wisdom, really, of course. None. It was empty, hollow. Like himself, then. That's how he felt. Hollowed out. He twiddled with the silver signet ring on his little finger and then examined it in an absent-minded sort of a way. It bore the same tableau as the crest carved into the bookshelves in the library—the phoenix rebirthing in flames, underscored by the initials RRR.

No prizes for guessing to whom that precious trinket had originally belonged, then, he thought to himself, more than a little bitterly.

Maybe they should all just abandon the cursed place and go live somewhere quiet, in the countryside or by the sea? Just them. Leave everything behind? Try life on a farm, perhaps? The simple life. Yes. And why not? Gloriana would be happy on a farm, in France someplace—it would remind her of her life as a girl. If she could ever be happy again, that is. If any of them could. As if any of them could…

Mr Redmayne picked up the volume on his desk-top. *A Christmas Carol*, his father's favourite novel. A handsome first edition, with the title embossed in gold-leaf on the frontispiece. Listlessly he flicked it open, as he had done so many time before. Chapman & Hall. 1843, *A Christmas Carol. In Prose. Being a Ghost Story of Christmas*. And there, of course, was the personal inscription, in a flowing hand:

To RRR,
My Ghost of Christmas Future,
CD
Broadstairs, Kent, 1851

He slammed the book shut and stood up from his desk. Time-travel! They exchanged their lives for shameful trinkets such as this! Once again, he examined the portrait of his father that hung over the fireplace. *France, 1898*. That's how the inscription read. Rufus always did have a special fondness for the French. Of all the nations he'd pillaged relentlessly and without conscience, France had doubtless yielded the most wonderful treasures, which was probably why he had so heartily approved of Gloriana. Why, hadn't this very portrait here originally been hung in some Parisian museum or other? Yes, it had, once, since *borrowed* forever. His father's long, stern face still stared down from it quizzically at his son, the great thick red beard and wild moustache accentuating the staunch sombreness of his expression, so much so that it practically resembled an accusation, or a challenge. *Do something, boy! Anything!* In his left hand, the perpetually unlit cigarette—

—In shock, Mr Redmayne took a step away from the painting. He blinked, once, twice, his heart suddenly racing. Tentatively he retrieved the step away that he'd only just taken. Then, he fizzed. He positively fizzed. A very strange noise to hear from the mouth of a grown man. But not entirely unpleasant, under the circumstances.

The unlit cigarette—it had not only been lit, it had burnt down to the nubbins. Just about. A red glow. Rekindled. Burning bright. Mr Redmayne examined the portrait in detail. It appeared unchanged in every other way. But this meant—

Great Galileo's Ghost!

Mr Redmayne ran from the room.

"Gloriana! Gloriana!" He took the steps on the East Staircase two at a time, and then raced along the landing. "Gloriana! We can find him! We can find him!"

When he reached the closed door to their room he barged inside without the least concern for protocol (no knock). "Gloriana, we can find him!"

His wife turned her head around sharply toward him. She was at her dressing table. Her eyes were little more than dark rings by this point. "But how? He could be anytime. You said yourself it would be next to impossible. One little needle in a million or more potential haystacks. That's what you said. One hour ago, you said it. Less."

"I know, yes. But I was wrong. Anything is possible. We're Redmaynes after all. We're going to need the children's help— they're Redmaynes too. Come on. No time to lose. Especially if we want him home by supper. Come on, dear! Follow me.

I'm going to fetch George and Felice and we'll meet you in my study. Five minutes, no later, okay?"

And with that, he vanished. Mrs Redmayne continued to stare at her empty doorway, not really comprehending what was going on. But, for the first time in several hours she felt a lightness in her heart, a hope. She got up.

Mr Redmayne had assembled George and Felice in his study and the three of them waited for Gloriana to join them, which she did presently. A certain tension remained, of course, given recent revelations and things said, and Mr Redmayne was keen to address this first. Mistakes had been made, he said, by everyone. No one was blameless and no one was solely to blame. Yes, George, Felice, we had kept some things from you, but we believed we were acting in your best interests. The house is very powerful and that power can be intoxicating. Just look at his own father. Completely without restraint, in the end. Mr Redmayne glanced up at the portrait that now stared down at them all. He had a theory about his latest discovery, but he felt it best not to share that just yet. That could wait. It was enough that it had rekindled his fire, reminded him who he was, that together they could achieve anything. Even the seemingly impossible.

But when all was said and done, he went on, they were family. They had a bond that nothing could break—in their case, not even Time. That was the lesson that he was taking away from today. They were Redmaynes. They were Time's Masters, not the other way around. That's what they had to remember, and he'd almost forgotten it himself. Now, listen, he was sure that everyone was sorry for their part in recent events. Truly sorry (sombre nods all around the table). Personally he wished he'd been a better parent and paid more attention to his children, rather than allow himself to be distracted by matters of ultimately no consequence, regardless of how important they may have seemed at the time. Maybe, if he had, then none of this would have happened.

But that all was by-the-by. Now they had to put things right and bring Emile home. He had a plan. And if they all worked together it would succeed. So, were they on board? Everyone? Yes? Good. Excellent.

Felice could take it no more. She stood up and threw herself on her mother with a great cry of "Oh, Maman, I'm so sorry!" Gloriana at once returned her embrace, saying, "I'm sure we all are, dear. Yes, we are." And she extended her hand across the table to George, who took it and held it. Mr Redmayne detected a look of reconciliation pass between the pair—and his son's eye even appeared a little wettish, as was his own. But he felt so much better seeing his family reconciled. Indeed, if he had been a cat of any variety at that moment he would have been quite moved to purr. Aloud. Several times. As it was, he had to settle for the silent inner glow of cat-like contentment. Now, they just had to finish the job—and bring Emile home.

"So, pay attention, everyone," he said, "because this is what we're going to do. First off, I think we can discount Paris, and perhaps to a lesser extent, New York—the Sparkly boy suggested that they were playing their game by the London exit at the time of the incident, and although he did seem a bit confused by the entire experience, that's probably the best place to start. The question is *when*."

Mr Redmayne looked around the table. It felt good—liberating—to be able to discuss these matters openly with his family.

"Now, let me see… When I made it into the library, the settings looked at first as though they'd been adjusted altogether quite randomly: two time zones were heading hundreds of years into the past, the other hundreds of years into the future. That's why the vibrations were so intense—the house was literally tearing itself apart. We were rather fortunate it stabilised at all, if you ask me. A very close call. Our atoms—and those of our guests—could have been smashed across all of time. Think about that for a moment."

Everybody around the table took a second to be suitably

impressed by their recent near-miss with such a doom-laden scenario. Mrs Redmayne arched an eyebrow. Felice, two.

"Was Paris in the time zone heading into the future?" asked George.

"Yes, good lad. Which is another reason why I think we can rule it out from our initial investigations. Felice?"

"Sorry, I was just stuck by the idea of Paris in the future. I mean, well, have you been? What's it like?"

"Very French," said Mr Redmayne. "And still more than a bit snooty. Now, assuming we discount Paris—"

"I'm sorry, Eric, chéri, but I don't understand. Why should any of that make it less likely that poor Emile went to Paris? He could be there right now, far in the future? Couldn't he?"

"Well, yes, he could, that's true…but I think that would make it far harder for us to find him, I'm afraid. We must concentrate our efforts where they're most likely to succeed. And if he's gone into the past he's very likely left a trail we can follow, if need be—I mean, in terms of his impact on things going on around him. Everyday things, or history even. It could be small, subtle things, or big, obvious things. We just have to spot them."

Mrs Redmayne arched her other eyebrow.

"You think my little Emile might have changed history?"

"Almost certainly, dear. Yes, I'm afraid so. And when we do spot them, the aberrations he has introduced, they'll lead us back to him."

Felice thought she understood. "You mean, like, if everyone is now suddenly going around hopping on one leg," she ventured, "and they think it's normal, we could go back to when that first started and maybe find Emile behind it all? Or something like that?"

"In principle, dearheart, broadly speaking, yes," said her father, nodding with a greater conviction than his voice perhaps suggested. "Remember, *all* actions have consequences. Unpicking them can prove very messy, very messy indeed, not to mention downright dangerous. For everyone. But if you must do it, you'll want to do it right. And to do that you must go right back to the beginning, the very beginning, and start over. And so that's what we'll do. Ideally, we want to pick up Emile the moment he first leaves the house, or as close to that as we can get. That way we'll undo everything he does—and he'll still be our Emile, unchanged by any of this."

Mrs Redmayne suddenly looked very worried, and daunted. "Oh, Eric, he's only a small boy, our baby. And he's all alone, wherever he is. *Whenever* he is. He could have lived his whole life like that. Lost, feeling abandoned. Anything could have happened to him. Anything at all. And now, right now, out there, is he even alive? Still? This minute? Chéri, it is too awful to think about." She allowed herself a small sob. Just one. "I am sorry. Forgive me."

Felice reached out and held her mother's hand once again. George too.

"I know, dear. I feel the same way, I absolutely do," said Mr Redmayne, visibly choked for a moment or so before gathering himself together again. "But that's perhaps the wrong way to think about it. For everyone else, yes, indeed, all of that would be very true. Inevitably so. But, for us, no, it isn't. Not at all. You see, for us, nothing is written. Nothing is set in stone. There is no *now* we absolutely must live by. And, if I can be quite blunt about the matter, for us, here, no one is ever gone. That's the lesson I've learnt today, quite forcibly, I must say." He glanced up at the staring-eyed portrait behind them. "Also, you have to remember that although Emile might be quite small, at least when he set off, he's also very resourceful and determined. And clever. And he's a Redmayne. Always remember that. We have resources no one else can even imagine. All of us."

Mrs Redmayne smiled at her husband. All four Redmaynes joined hands around the table.

"We may have caused this mess," said Mr Redmayne, "between us all, our follies. But, by goodness, we're going to fix it!"

"But, Eric, how? What is it exactly that we're going to do?"

"Everyone has their part to play. First of all, I'm off to see an old friend of my father's from long ago. We have to start somewhere, and if anyone can help us in the era where I'm thinking of beginning the search, well, he can, I assure you. You'll see, dear. Don't worry. Everything will soon be back to normal and right as rain. That's a Redmayne promise."

18

Felice and George were assigned the task of going through Emile's room and looking for clues. It would be fair to say that this wasn't quite what they thought they were signing up for when their father recruited them to the team. Firstly, it didn't involve time-travel (which is what they hoped/imagined they were being recruited for). Secondly, they had no idea what a clue might look like ("Well, anything, really," their father had said, offering possibly the least useful advice ever given by one party to another. And when pressed, he added, only marginally more usefully: "Anything at all that might help us spot Emile. That's it, really.") And thirdly, Emile's room was a nightmare—a terrible mess of papers, pencils, felt-tipped pens, drawings, discarded carrier bags, sticky sweet wrappers, and randomly abandoned clothes (including a number of suspect items left here and there on the floor that Felice could only assume were actual worn pieces of boy's underwear) (ugh) (ugh) (and, look, there, too, *ugh*). This was most definitely *not* the great adventure either of them had thought it might be. Not at all.

The pair sat on their brother's bed, a relative oasis of order amid the debris. All in all, a useful vantage point for scanning for clues—without risk of potential contamination. Not that much active scanning appeared to be in progress anymore. Felice sat with her knees drawn up under her chin, making herself as compact as possible. George was quiet. He was staring off into space, a bit despondently, or at least that's how it struck Felice.

"You shouldn't blame yourself," she suggested, in a well-intentioned way.

"Thanks. I wasn't. What for, anyway? Exactly?"

"Emile going missing. It was you who showed him how the house worked, after all—you know, the controls, I mean."

George looked at her sharply. "Yes, to protect our secret. That was why. Don't forget that, Sis. *Our* secret. And I didn't show him everything. Which might have been a mistake, as it turns out. No, anyway, it wasn't that. I was just thinking that I couldn't remember the last time I came in here. Can you?"

"I don't think I've ever been in here before. Is that bad? It feels bad."

George nodded. "It's probably bad. I guess we haven't been the best siblings, not to the squirt, anyway. Everyone just gets wrapped in their own stuff. We all do. And now that he's not here…"

Felice's eyes widened. "George, don't you think we'll get him back?"

"I don't know. I really don't. Unless there's, you know, stuff Dad hasn't told us about, a way of tracking a person through time, or something like that, I think it could be difficult."

George thought for a moment about the piece of information that he hadn't told anyone about, the note he'd found in his grandfather's book. It hadn't seemed relevant at the time, and most likely still wasn't. Probably.

It had been addressed to him, but written as if from the far future and then concealed in a book that was seemingly published in the distant past. None of it made any sense. But it was the contents themselves that were the most puzzling, encouraging *George* to *trust his instincts about whatever he learnt from this book about the house and all its secret uses*—that's what was most confusing. Maybe it had been written for a different George from a different era? But then, why would it begin *George, my dear grandson?* He didn't understand. Perhaps he should say something? Even if it hadn't been addressed to him, he had actually taken encouragement from it, weirdly, about what he was doing—as if it had indeed been meant for him somehow.

But how would anyone know that he would ever find it in that book in the first place? George really didn't understand. He might mention it later, to Pops. He would. Yes. It might be important, even if it wasn't clear to him just now how exactly.

"What *I* don't understand, I think," said Felice, hesitantly, unsure if she was ready to admit to George that she didn't understand something, "is, well, why can't we just switch the clock back a day, you know, to the day before the Open House? Then none of this would happen, would it? And we'd have Emile back. Isn't that what they did before, Maman and Papa? With that meter-man guy, I mean, remember?"

"I've thought about that too," said George. "The difference this time, I reckon, is that Emile wouldn't be in the house when we turned the clock back. He's outside. Last time we were all inside—and so we, us, the you and I having this conversation now, we stay on the same timeline, our timeline. If we turned the clock back now, there'd always be an Emile who was out there, our Emile, on the timeline that we started, but abandoned him on. See? We'd never get our Emile back. Unless he turned up one day under his own steam and then we'd have two. What would we do then? Keep one in reserve, just in case it all happened again?"

Felice shook her head. "It's hard. Very hard."

"I know. I was always a bit obsessed by time-travel, I just didn't know why. Now I know it's because I, we, come from a long line of time-travelling plunderers—which is probably what we are, really, when you think about it. Hey, does this look like a clue to you?"

George held up one of Emile's outlandish drawings, one that looked like a giant lizard with fur. And an extra arm. Felice shook her head.

He dropped that particular picture and picked up another from nearby. "Or this, maybe?"

Felice took the piece of paper from him. She scrutinised it for a time.

"I didn't even know he could draw. And it's not bad. How great a sister am I?"

George shrugged. "Yeah, who knew? But maybe you're right, perhaps we should have paid him more attention? I don't know. Easy to say now, I suppose. Look, I'm not sure this is helping. Why don't we go and do the other thing? That might be more useful than this."

"You think? I hope so. I want to do more, though. I do. And I'd feel better if I could. Wouldn't you?"

"Yup, for sure. But you know Pops. We need to stick to the plan—his plan—and hope he's having better luck than we are. That's all we can do, for now."

"He'd better be. That's what I say." Felice took a last, long look around the cluttered room. "Otherwise I'm not going to care what timelines we mess up to get Emile back—*any* Emile. And that's a Redmayne promise. Honestly, George, I'm not going to care. And neither's Maman. So, brace yourself."

George nodded. "I know. Come on, Sis, we've got four hundred years of world history to check, and it's not going to check itself. And it *might* help, possibly, you never know. And Pops, well, we've just got to believe he knows what he's doing. For all we know, he's done this sort of thing before. If anyone can pull it off, he can."

"I hope so. I do. I really do."

Mr Redmayne most certainly had not done this before, however, not retrieved a missing child—his own child, at that—from the vastness of all recorded time. No one had, as far as he knew. Ever. And when he looked at it like that, it certainly seemed more than a little daunting, to say the least—and so, he tried not to think of it in those terms.

Instead, he forced himself to focus less on the big picture ("bad, very bad") and more instead on the detail ("not great, but better"). And the detail, the position of the levers of the time displacement mechanism when he had entered the secret room behind the library, the testimony (albeit emotional and confused) of the Sparkly boy that afternoon, this all suggested to Mr Redmayne that Emile had exited the house in London in the region of four hundred years or so previously. And visiting London in that era (technically Jacobean rather than Elizabethan, and it irked him that everybody thought of it as the latter) was something that he *had* done before, on several occasions, particularly when he was much younger and in the company of his father. Therefore, it was a good place to start, as good as any and better than most. The best that he could imagine.

Despite his familiarity with the era (or, more truthfully, because of it) Mr Redmayne had given his wife strict instructions to drop him at a specific hour on a specific date, remove the house back to the present and return for him precisely three hours—in both his and her time—later. On the dot. Although the house would deploy its standard defences against being spotted by unwelcome eyes, these were far from infallible, as recent experience had proved.

And while Mr Redmayne was confident its eccentric design (for the period) might be dismissed as yet another wealthy goldsmith's home springing up in Cheapside, it would be as well to avoid any unnecessary attention or interest. Or intrusion. Or home invasion. The consequences were just far too potentially disastrous to think about—and they all had enough to think about as it was.

And so, despite Gloriana's initial misgivings, it was agreed.

He would go. She would collect.

And maybe when she did, he would not be alone. That was their hope. Fervent hope, if perhaps somewhat more fervently so on her side than his—his view being more realistic. It would take more than a minor miracle for them to find Emile at the first attempt.

So, Mr Redmayne departed fortified with a modicum of hope if not expectation, and with the portable device that he had used to track the meter-man in Paris that time, the Quantum Displacement Monitor (QDM). Although, of course, he fully realised he would need to be very discreet in its deployment in that era and that it would only be of any practical utility should Emile actually be present somewhere nearby at that time, the device's range being somewhat limited.

Mr Redmayne also carried with him several likenesses of

Emile, in miniature portrait form, which were in truth photographs that Felice had somehow wondrously doctored on
her newfangled personal computer thingamajig to resemble
watercolours. It really was amazing what they learned at school
these days, even if she had seemed rather blasé about it herself. His plan (albeit now Plan B) was to pass these around via
his supposed 'contact' there, one Henry Humphreus, an old
harbour-master on the Thames and long-time associate of his
father's, a man who knew everyone and everything that passed
back and forth on the river (assuming he could be found—
and, more to the point, be found sober); but more than an
element of private doubt remained in Mr Redmayne's mind
as to whether any of this would be in the least useful, seeing
how the Redmaynes would be quite difficult for anyone of the
period to contact with information subsequently, should they
come to recognise the likeness of the boy in the picture. But
perhaps he might yet think of a way for that to happen and
it had certainly made Felice feel a little better to make them.
Which was important too.

Finally, in addition Mr Redmayne departed carrying various
coins of the time in his pocket (a silver crown, a silver half-
crown, four sixpences, three threepences, two pennies and one
local token halfpenny) (all of which he usually kept in a jar by
his bed), and with a kiss on the cheek from his wife, along with
detailed instructions to be very careful. Gloriana was counting
on him not to get lost, or maimed or killed. Or sick ("Don't
drink the water. Would Emile know *not* to drink the water?")
("Yes. Well, probably. Remember Egypt?")

Or jailed. Definitely *not* jailed. Breaking her husband out of
the Tower, or worse, the dreaded Clink, would be a very messy
exercise (about which he hoped she was joking) (maybe she
was, hard to tell?) (No, she wasn't.) (No.)

And, finally, to bring back Emile.

He said that he would do his very best on all counts. Dear. He
would. Yes. And so, thus fully briefed, Mr Redmayne stepped
out of the back door of his remarkable house, into Phoenix

Yard, London, in the year of 1603, in the reign of King James I. Curiously he stepped out with his eyes tightly shut, as was his old habit on such occasions, because he knew that when he opened them again, there would be this—

—the pure, intoxicating wonder of stepping out into what was, in effect, another world. The sights, the sounds, yes, the smells (as remarkably pungent as they were), it was always nothing short of exhilarating. Having reopened his eyes, Mr Redmayne took a few first tentative steps. It was like waking up and somehow stepping into a dream:

Buy my dish of great eels!
Fresh strawberries!
Three rows a penny pins!

The sights, sounds washed over him. How *alive* it all was! How real!

The crowd thronged. A bright day. Very fine. Not at all chilly. Goldsmith's Row, too, if he wasn't mistaken. To the west stood Cheapside Cross, a fine, tall monument, if a little over-elaborate. Good to see it still standing. Again. Mr Redmayne quite understood why any man, in particular a king (and so given the opportunity), would choose to erect such a memorial to his beloved wife. Though God forbid that he should ever find himself in that same terrible position.

He turned to the east. Old St Paul's Cathedral. Stubbornly spireless. Very different to its successor. More traditional. Gothic in the extreme. And still magnificent. Towering over the crowd, over everything. Mr Redmayne took a few more steps in that direction and sensed the house now disappearing behind him, a development confirmed by a glance back over his shoulder.

He was alone.

Except, of course, he wasn't.

People were quite literally everywhere, or so it seemed, bustling industriously about their business. And such an array of people! Different complexions, different voices, different occupations, it always surprised him to rediscover just how cosmopolitan London was in this era, how truly diverse. And yet here it was. Fascinating. It took his breath away to witness it.

Four for sixpence, mackerel!
Old satin, old Taffety!
Fine writing ink!

This latter cry came from very nearby, from a fellow who passed Mr Redmayne right then with a small wooden barrel slung over one shoulder and a thick bunch of feathered quills gripped firmly in his hand, as if it he were presenting his young lady with something of a rather odd bouquet.

Here, dearheart, take these late-blooming quills. For you. I picked them myself. Mr Redmayne chuckled aloud. Actually, in truth Gloriana *would* quite like them, he was sure. *Oh, yes, and here's a barrel, too, dearest, while I'm at it. Of something or other. Ink, most likely. Enjoy!*

Right then, all at once, a jingle of approaching bells startled him. A carriage!

Barely had Mr Redmayne time to step back out of its way before the horse-drawn carriage's iron-rimmed wheels shot a spray of mud in his direction. The driver turned his head and offered his mud-splashed victim something of a wild, piratical, toothless grin in passing. Quite unapologetic. Rude, even.

Some things actually don't change much, thought Mr Redmayne, whatever the era. Human nature, for one. He stood there for a moment watching the carriage roll on down the thoroughfare, aware that already he was now decidedly muddier than when he'd first arrived. Well, at least now he would smell like everyone else, even if he didn't exactly look like them.

Not that he was overly worried on that score. The many odd styles of dress in view were so various and so strange, even on this one street, that people no doubt would likely take him for just another eccentric foreigner. Which, of course, he was in a way. If now a rather muddy one.

Ripe damsons!
Quick periwinkles!

A church bell clanged nearby. Loud. Two o'clock. He had to

be getting on. This wasn't a tourist trip. Not this time. He was a man on a mission, the most important mission of his life.

Humphreus. Then, Mr Redmayne stopped dead in his muddy tracks.

Great Galileo's Ghost! No! What was he thinking?

Not Humphreus, his father's old friend. No, the *device!* The portable device. The QDM! It would tell him if Emile were here. Now. At once. Plan A.

Shame flushed his face. All this time he had allowed himself to be distracted by everything going on around him (although, in truth, it was a little difficult not to be). Still, his poor, missing son might well have been only a matter of yards away from him, or down the next muddy alleyway or around the next corner—and Mr Redmayne would quite have passed him by. He needed to get out of sight and check the device. Immediately. Now. But where?

Not easy. Buffeted now and then by the passing crowd, Mr Redmayne peered ahead. One or two of the passers-by give him something of an unpleasant stare while he blocked the passageway.

Indeed, one rude, indignant fellow, with bright red, blotchy cheeks, whom to be frank seemed more than a little tipsy, went so far as to blow the foul smoke from his long tobacco pipe straight into Mr Redmayne's eyes—before going off with a smug that-told-you look on his face (followed in quick train by a young lad, no more than Emile's age, also pipe smoking, who paused briefly to offer Mr Redmayne an equally insolent look—and who was succeeded in turn by a far younger boy, perhaps all of five years old, also merrily puffing on a pipe of his own) (who at least didn't give Mr Redmayne so much as a sideways glance). They went off—an odd chain of smokers.

Mr Redmayne looked on. At once, another passer-by bumped into him from behind. This was no good. He must get off the street. At once. An alleyway lay handily a short distance ahead, and he made for that. Dark, narrow-seeming, it might suffice for his purpose, he supposed.

But no sooner had he reached it than Mr Redmayne became aware of some violent scuffling in the mud at the neck of the shadowy alleyway—what on Earth! What?

Swine, no less! Actual loose swine! On the public highway!

Three pigs, in point of fact, none of which might in any sense have been described as 'little' (and hence not of the fairy-tale variety), were snuffling and snorting noisily through the mud. And eating something or other when they found it. Presumably offal.

It was not an edifying sight but at that moment it struck Mr Redmayne as a singularly apt image for the era. He hesitated. Beyond, the alleyway seemed otherwise unoccupied, although as it was very dark, he couldn't be absolutely certain.

What d'ye lack, my masters? What d'ye lack?
Buy any shrimps! Get your shrimps!

Still, he went in, pressing past the three pigs, his new travelling companions. Gingerly. One slow step at a time. The mud—and no doubt, far, far worse—squelched up over his ankles and seeped into his shoes (his finest wingtip brogues!), more so and then more so with each and every step.

The unpleasantness of the sensation was beyond the capacity of mere words to capture it. Needless to say, bad!

And the stench! Good lord! All of his days Mr Redmayne thought that he would never forget the stench, that the foulness of the stench would never leave him. Like putrefying cabbage. Worse. Like the putrefying cabbage of the dead—the cabbage that the dead had left in the pantry and forgotten about before they went off and died in a nasty way. Bad, *very*.

Indeed, in such a confined space it was truly pungent beyond belief, almost beyond his capacity to endure it. For long. He kept going.

Happily his new companions had matters of greater interest to occupy themselves with and paid no attention to the latest addition to their ranks. Although if he should fall Mr Redmayne felt quite certain that he would never rise again, and that under those circumstances he might indeed prefer that outcome.

This wouldn't be one of those stories that a gentleman would care to survive and recount later, not to any audience, no matter how sympathetic (to Margot, perhaps, at an Open House event?) (no) (very much, *no*). The alleyway narrowed ahead. He pressed on, only too pleased to be ignored by his noisy porcine neighbours, but was squelching horribly underfoot with every step.

Time-travel. What a lark! Should all go well today, he resolved to bring George and Felice to this very alleyway and ask them to retrieve something that he'd lost here in the mud and the pigs and the filth and the…whatever. Something other than his dignity, that is.

Mr Redmayne stopped. He'd gone far enough. He took out the portable device, the QDM, and switched it on. An illuminated grid appeared on the small square screen—black gridlines of longitude and latitude—but it presented only one pulsating yellow blip, which caused the gridlines to curve toward and beneath it. This blip was him, here in this stinking alleyway. Nothing more.

Disappointing, but not unexpected.

And then—A blip! A palpable blip!

A second yellow blip had appeared on the screen—all at once, as if out of nowhere.

Emile! It had to be! He was here. The poor lad! Oh, his poor son. This was no place for a boy on his own. He was moving. On foot. Heading south, crossing the river. The bridge…

Mr Redmayne switched off the device. His heart and head raced. Then he set off quickly toward the far end of the alleyway, cutting in the direction, he reckoned, of Eastcheap. A short cut he knew well.

Once there it would only be a brief walk to the bridge. London Bridge. *The* London Bridge. He hadn't crossed that since he was little more than a boy himself, hundreds of years ago. Or was it only forty or so years ago? Thirty?

Or had he in fact crossed it that one time with Gloriana, not long after they were first married? That was the problem with leaping around in time like this. It made it so very hard to keep track.

Either way, he had to hurry. He sped up. Within seconds, he was running. Time—there was never enough. He ran. He ran as quickly as the crowd and the slippery conditions underfoot would allow.

Eastcheap. Yes. Through some kind of market, where the mass of people slowed him back down to a walk. Normally this would be very interesting. Very interesting indeed. But Mr Redmayne's steadfast resolve was—first and foremost—to focus on his mission, to retrieve his missing son. His son who was perhaps less than half-a-mile ahead of him.

His breath returning, he took another alleyway, hoping to hit Bishopsgate Street, which he knew would shortly lead him to the bridge—the so-called "City on the Bridge," no less, and he could quite understand how it had come to be called by that name. A marvel of the age.

But in truth it had been a long time since he had been this way and he had been far younger at the time. When the street suddenly split three ways, with a left, a right, and straight ahead, Mr Redmayne grew uncertain.

He didn't really think that either of those two routes diverging respectively to the left and right could be correct, although it was hard to be sure in the crowd. Which way to go?

In the end he trusted his instinct and went straight on; but the road very soon narrowed even futher and consequently became very dark and yet more crowded, overhung as it was on both sides by low-ceilinged, gable-fronted houses and storefronts. This was impossible.

Mr Redmayne took a deep breath. Such a very busy street. Was he still going the right way? He wanted to consult the portable device. Perhaps Emile had stopped somewhere nearby? He peered through the crowd, seeing nothing. Useless.

He felt hot, rushed, claustrophobic. Everywhere around him was very noisy and echoey now; on all sides pushy hawkers of wares and "entertainments" of every type pressed him for his attention—and therefore his money (one such showman asked Mr Redmayne if he wished to view his two-headed sow, an offer he felt able to decline, more or less politely, having had more than quite enough of pigs for one day).

And so he pressed on, unsure. Maybe he had gone astray? By his calculations he ought to have hit the bridge by now—long ago, in fact. Perhaps back where the road had forked left and right? Had he gone wrong there? Should he turn around? His instinct said no. He needed to check the device.

Ahead, he spotted a gap between establishments, which might provide a moment of privacy. A quick look would be sufficient. Mr Redmayne ducked out of the crowd—

—And all at once the soaring blue sky opened up above him. Shafts of sunlight. Birds. Seagulls. And below. Below, *no*! Surely not…

That wasn't terra firma beneath his feet but the Thames! He was on the bridge already—and must have been for a good ten minutes or so, if not longer! The Thames. Right there. The rushing Thames and—my word!—it *was* rushing. True rapids passed between the narrow bulwarks underneath. White water. Positively foaming.

And the view! Good grief! The view was very distracting, to say the least. Nothing short of breath-taking! Mr Redmayne marvelled at the number of sailing ships at dock along the innumerable wharfs—it was like an infinity of masts all bobbing and rocking, stretching along the shoreline as far as he could see. The same for the number of barges on the water, both large and small, and the rowboats. The *wherries*, yes, that was the word.

And looking down on it all on the north bank, way up there on Ludgate Hill, the highest point of the city, stood old St Paul's. It was something to see. They should all come, together. One day soon. He swallowed. Hard. The device.

Facing out toward the river, reasonably secure in his belief that no one could see what he was doing, Mr Redmayne took out the portable device and switched it on, keeping it close to his chest. Two yellow blips. Neither one was moving. Bankside. Emile was in Bankside.

Mr Redmayne turned to the south. Compared to the opposite bank there wasn't much to see. Some few church steeples, and the famous theatres, of course, they were the few structures that rose above the houses and the taverns, the inns. Not much else. The very worst part of old London. Bear baiting and the like. The stews. The Clink.

But this was where he had to go. Emile was there. And it was no place for a boy. Especially one out of his own time. He should hurry. Ashamed again, quickly he pocketed the device and set off.

Mr Redmayne knew his history. He was aware that Bankside lay outside the city walls, and so lay outside the reach of the City Fathers, and that this fact gave licence to all sorts of things that would have been regarded as both immoral and unlawful if they'd taken place on the other side of the river. Not that this stopped anybody from heading there! Far from it.

The nearby inns were full of thieves, robbers, river pirates, and press gangers. Everybody turned a blind eye to everything, unless you crossed the Bishop of Winchester (in a sense, the local Mafiosi Don), in which case you would end up in the Clink, his private prison. And that was no good place to be. Not at all.

In short, this was not the sort of area, nor the sort of people, that you would pick for your eleven-year-old son's first solo time-travelling adventure. Not at all! Danger was everywhere. Mr Redmayne hurried. He went into what was effectively another tunnel on the bridge, much shorter on this occasion, emerging at last before the Great Stone Gate on the south bank of the river.

This last tall feature he still remembered vividly, mostly on account of the detruncated heads perched on spikes at the top of the tower, which his father had frequently used to encourage him to peruse and even count. Now, however, he was determined not to look, and he hoped Emile hadn't either. Emile! Poor Emile! His son! He was coming.

Mr Redmayne came rapidly down off the bridge, ignoring the very public jakes to his left. Turning right, past the Pepper Stairs, he headed at once toward the Bear Tavern and the Church of St. Mary Overie. The sheer weight of human traffic was far less on this side of the river. He felt more confident of finding a private place to view the portable device, perhaps in the grounds of the church, and he hurried in the direction of its tall spire. Everything seemed oddly familiar, even how surprisingly green it was over here, too—the town almost at once gave way to fields and trees, and some very well-kept orchards by the look of it. Gardens.

Déjà vu. He knew these, he felt sure.

The Great Pike Gardens, that was it. He remembered, yes. It was coming back to him. Several large fishponds were located nearby. For some reason his father had insisted on bringing him here, again and again. And just as well he had, as things turned out, wasn't it? Mr Redmayne gained the grounds of the church, which thankfully were as quiet as he had anticipated. He checked the device.

The other yellow blip hadn't moved, not an inch. Emile was less than two hundred yards away from him. Mr Redmayne took off. He traversed Clink Street as speedily as he could, passing the dark, dreaded prison, and turned first right and then left past Winchester Palace. The river was very close by now. He could see it. Several inns stood ahead on the side of the bank. Was Emile in one of these? If so, it surely could not be of his own volition.

All of the inns had odd signs on their fronts, not wooden hanging signs, as might have been expected; instead these were painted on the front walls, facing the river. Mr Redmayne crossed them off mentally as he passed: the Beares Heade, the Crosse Keyes, the Gunne, the Castell upon the Hope. At this last one he stopped. It stood at the junction of two streets.

Was this it? Surreptitiously, under his jacket, he glanced at the device. No, it was further on – and behind.

He went on. A number of narrow alleyways led off from the

bank side, between the houses and the inns. Based on his calculations, and a strange certainty that he had been here before,
right here, this very spot, Mr Redmayne stopped outside one
such alleyway. Cardinals Hatte Alley.

Dark, narrow, it seemed very familiar. He *had* indeed been
here before, a lifetime ago, as nothing more than a child himself. He was sure of it.

An inn stood at the end. He remembered it now. Yes. Vaguely,
but it was coming back to him. One of those dull places you
get dragged along to as a youngster when you're not particularly
interested or paying attention.

Emile was here? Surely not. That made no sense.

A sudden stark realisation struck Mr Redmayne like a punch
in the face, and he felt, well, right then, he didn't know what he
felt exactly.

Afraid, confused, compelled.

Still, he went on down the alleyway. He couldn't *not* do it.

The Cardinals Hatte. That was it, with the all too gaudily
painted sign of the Cardinal's red cap on the wall outside. He
remembered that. What? How? Wait. It was all coming back to
him. His stomach turned a cartwheel and then completed the
reverse manoeuvre for good measure.

He hesitated, frozen, momentarily unable to go either backward or forward.

Next, when he pushed open the wooden door, it was like
his whole life exploded back into his face. Noise, laughter, mayhem. Something of a mini-riot, if largely self-contained. But
it was a scene he recognised—because he'd seen it all before.
More than once.

And at the bar stood not his son, but his father.

19

With considerable trepidation, Mr Redmayne crossed the gloomy threshold of the inn. His long-lost father. Rufus. Even though the figure had his back to him, Mr Redmayne was certain of his identity. He knew he couldn't be mistaken. The shape of his father's head, the particular shade of red of his hair, the way he was standing, all of these things were so deeply ingrained in Mr Redmayne's psyche that he recognised the man at once.

He would know him anywhere—and he hadn't known him for what felt like a long time, a long, long time. His poor departed father. *Here.*

Mr Redmayne couldn't help himself. He approached the low serving bar and stood next to the unsuspecting man who was his father, who wasn't *yet* his father, by the look of him.

A sideways glance revealed that he was young, perhaps as much as twenty-five years younger than Mr Redmayne was himself. Young Rufus's attention was caught by some high-spirited shenanigans on a nearby table, where a rowdy troupe of men were gambling. Dice. Each throw raised the general din, the shouts, the laughter, to a new level. Unless Mr Redmayne was very much mistaken, what appeared to be a small monkey in a bright red suit (with ruffs) was embroiled in the game somehow, in the action, flitting from player to player, up arms, on shoulders, across the table, back and forth, stealing drinks, coins, anything, much to everyone's loud amusement. Chaos.

His father was smiling. Head averted, yes, but clearly visible still was the familiar, slightly upwards curve of the lip to the left. To the uninitiated observer it might be barely detectable but, after all this time, it was damn good to see. Again. More than any son had a natural right to expect. Far more. Mr Redmayne knew that he shouldn't be here.

Everything that Mr Redmayne believed about the absolute necessity of preserving the timeline, of non-interference, of all actions—no matter how insignificant—having *consequences*, this all told him that he should walk away now. Just turn around and walk away. Before it was too late.

And then it *was* too late.

Mr Redmayne's father turned his head back toward the bar and his manner at once stiffened. Perceptibly. He glanced at the new stranger next to him and then over his shoulder toward the door beyond.

Then, he stood staring straight ahead. He raised his tankard to his lips and took a drink. A sip.

Mr Redmayne searched for something to say—anything—but came up empty. Nothing seemed appropriate. What *do* you say to your long-deceased father as he stands next to you, now far younger than you are yourself, in a disreputable tavern in Jacobean London? No greeting card exists to mark this occasion. You are on your own.

"Pleasant day, sir, no?" was the best that Mr Redmayne could manage, given the difficult circumstances.

His father eyed him cautiously. "Your attire is most unusual, sir. Are you a *traveller*, perchance? Maybe you are a Spaniard? I have heard tell they dress wondrous strange. That must be it."

"A traveller, yes. But not from Spain. No. Indeed, I hail from far closer to home—far, far closer, in fact, than you might expect, my friend."

Mr Redmayne's father eyed him cautiously.

"I see. But heed my words, if you will, and be guided that you would be wise not to mistake anyone in this establishment for your friend, sir, not even the damned monkey. Perhaps especially not the damned monkey. Believe me, he is the worst of them all, by far."

An explosion of wild cries and chatter, more simian than human—a moment of true uproar—seemed to confirm this point.

Both men's heads turned in that direction.

"That, for what it may be worth, is my sincere advice to you," continued Mr Redmayne's father, once the din had sufficiently subsided, "should you choose to frequent dubious establishments such as *this*, and mix with such men as *these*, any one of whom would happily press-gang you for a farthing. That, and seek a new tailor. Your present attire will as likely see you hung from the yard-arm at dawn as press-ganged, as an enemy of the Crown, no less, I fear—or, equally possibly, of me. Spies do not prosper in these dangerous times, not here, nor in any other quarter, as I am sure you well know. Especially spies foolish enough to work alone. And you do appear to be quite alone. So, my friend, beware."

"Sir, my apologies. You mistake my purpose. But entirely. I came looking not for you but for another. And, as for my clothes, I had only a little time to prepare for this trip. Your own outfit is far more…convincing, very much so, I must agree. The ruff becomes you, I should never have guessed. But, as you are not he whom I seek, I will at once take your leave. Be certain, however, that I am pleased indeed to have had this conversation, more pleased than you might appreciate. Truly."

Mr Redmayne made as if to leave, but hesitated. He was taking a last look, making a final commune, with the dear departed. This chance meeting was more than any man had a right to expect. But bringing the encounter to an early conclusion was still difficult for him.

He swallowed, hard, long, feeling the imminent and inevitable, iron bite of Time. Walk away. Now.

At last, he commenced his final farewells. But it was very hard.

"Perhaps we will talk again sometime? Yes, surely so. In fact, I have every confidence that will indeed prove to be the case. So, sir, I say Adieu. Till next we meet. Good day."

Mr Redmayne's father studied him closely, a canny, cold-eyed stare, but these same staring eyes betrayed the depth of his curiosity.

It was as if he didn't know what to make of this odd

performance, this curious interloper before him. All at once his manner changed, the guardedness, the stiffness, fell away.

"Damn it, you're not TDA," he said hoarsely. "Who the hell are you? And how did you find me?"

"Only a traveller, as we said. Much like yourself. Very much so. And I found you quite by accident. Now, sir, I really must be off. My business is elsewhere, and pressing."

Mr Redmayne took a first, tentative step away from the bar.

His father, however, clearly had other ideas. He grabbed his son by the wrist and held up his hand, as if for them both to view. His grip was as firm as ever it was. The bulldog's clenched jaw. The vice.

"That ring you wear, I have one the same. See?"

He held out his own hand, adjacent to Mr Redmayne's. Two silver rings. Two silver phoenixes rebirthing in flames. Identical.

"A crest of my own design," he went on. "Humbly or not, I believed it unique. And, sir, let me tell you, I still do."

He turned his gaze toward his son's face, a searching look. At the same time, he relaxed his grip.

"This makes you…what? My—"

"I must go," said Mr Redmayne. "This is not a conversation any two men should be having. You know that. You do. Truly. The consequences could be calamitous. And not just for both of us right here and now—for others too! Others still to come. If we change anything—anything at all…"

"Fiddlesticks! Consequences be hanged. Answer the question. Here and now. My what? My…son?"

Mr Redmayne nodded, as though reluctantly, inevitably. Eyes lowered.

At that moment another riotous explosion from the table to their rear filled the room with sound—laughter, shouts, cries, chatter. Mayhem.

"My son," said the elder Mr Redmayne as the noise once again subsided. "You know, I think I can see it now, a certain resemblance, yes. You remind me of my father's brother, Raeburn, or perhaps even my father himself, in a poor light at least. Come, this calls for a celebration. To a table. We must sit and talk. It's not every day that your as-yet-unborn son tracks you to a Jacobean hostelry. Melchisedeck, two of your ales!" He turned around toward the bar. "And none of your usual Peacock slops, mind you. This fine nobleman here is my kin, a traveller from a far-off place, who has journeyed long and perilous to make my acquaintance. So, two tankards of the best Merry-Go-Down, man, if you will. Bring them to the snug."

Mr Redmayne's father laid a copper coin down on the counter.

The large, heavily mutton-chopped, bald man behind the bar subjected the pair to a moment's seemingly disapproving scrutiny but soon retired without a word toward a stack of thick, round wooden barrels piled one on top of the other to his rear.

Then, Mr Redmayne's father led away through the dark, small, low-beamed room toward another, at the back of the establishment, seemingly even darker and smaller, in the full expectation that his son would follow. A private place. Clearly. For meetings of all sorts, all purposes.

The obedient son, still, even under these oddest of circumstances, Mr Redmayne obliged, despite the fact that nothing about this encounter struck him as a good idea.

It had already gone too far. Far too far. At the same time he wanted to stay, at least a little while longer. He had the time. Perhaps something over an hour. Emile was not here, in this city in this era, so by lingering in this inn for a time he was hardly impeding his mission.

And, then, also, his father was right. An unusual meeting such as this did not take place every day—in fact, no doubt it would prove unique in all history. No matter what covert encounters this dark little room had witnessed before, murders, trysts, betrayals, it had not witnessed one such as this. Never.

And when it was done, it would be done. Forever. There was that.

So, the unusual pair, father and son, sat together at a table in the gloomy cloistered room, in Southwark, in 1603, a place and time in which neither one of them belonged. Men out of time. The elder being the younger, and vice-versa. With all manner of such awkward contradictions and complications to negotiate before they could talk plainly one to the other.

It took a second, but then the elder (younger) Redmayne began: "Tell me, what do I, *did* I, call you?" he asked.

Mr Redmayne raised an eyebrow in surprise.

"You wish, now, Father, that I should name myself? Whatever I say now will surely influence you when the proper time comes, no? And then, should you be in a contrary mood, I might find myself suddenly with another name, when I happen to be attached to the one I already have, thank you very much. So, no, call me what you will. That will suffice."

"Very well, *Will*," responded the senior Redmayne, "I *will*. And perhaps it would be best if you were not to address me as Father. That word might easily be misunderstood and get us both hung, or worse, if overheard by the wrong person. Here, now, I go by the name of John, John Raven, out of Canterbury. This makes *you* Will of Kent. Of Faversham, to be precise, if pressed by anyone. Understand? Good. Here comes that impossible oaf Melchisedeck with the ales. Say nothing. Even a damned oaf may be dangerous in these dark, unruly times. And I have little wish to visit the Tower today, or the Clink. Not again."

The rather more than generously framed, bald-headed barkeep came up to the table and deposited with a splash two wooden tankards of ale. In the small candlelit room the man now struck Mr Redmayne as positively gargantuan in build. For a moment he lingered by the table, casting sinister, far larger than life shadows on the walls behind and on the rush-covered floor.

"Thank you, Melchisedeck. That is all. Leave us."

With a begrudging grunt, the man departed. It amused Mr Redmayne to witness such a typical display of imperiousness from this very youthful version of his father. So, then, he had always been this way, it would seem. All the same it was a little uncanny to see all the familiar mannerisms on one so, well, ju-venile. But, good, in a way too.

And, as there was nothing else he could do right now toward retrieving Emile, certainly not until the house returned in an hour or so, he thought he may as well imbibe.

He sat back and sipped the ale, which was hoppy. Very. But not bad. The wooden vessel added a certain something too. Splinters, perhaps.

"If you are not prepared to tell me even your name," said the elder Redmayne, "then am I to assume you might be unwilling to reveal when and where I died?"

Mr Redmayne choked on his ale, spluttering.

"I shall take that as a no," said his father. "But I *am* dead. That much is evident from your performance in the other room. You had great difficulty in bidding me farewell. It seemed obvious that you hadn't seen me for some time. What, twenty years?"

Mr Redmayne, aghast, silent, could feel his father scrutinis-ing his face for a clue. A sign. Some indication. He wouldn't tell.

"More? Less? Ten years? Damn it. Very well. If you won't tell me when, at least tell me where. And I won't go there."

"You know very well, *John*, that I can reveal nothing of the sort, nothing that could change your future—*our* future. Not at all. The consequences would affect all of our lives. Perhaps disastrously. My family. Your family. Think about what you are asking."

The elder Redmayne took a sip from the wooden tankard of ale, his eyes maintaining their steady scrutiny of his son's face.

Once again the rowdy boisterousness of the gamblers in the other room exploded into wild shouts and riotous laughter; although, at least now, thankfully, thought Mr Redmayne, smiling wryly to himself, it had grown somewhat muted. Ruffians. Literally. To a man. All of them. Ruffians.

"You smile as though content," said his father, "and yet you would let me die. I see. Was I that delinquent a parent? I can't imagine I am much cut out for the role. Tell me true. No, don't. No matter. Forget it. I don't care. Let's try another tack. What makes you think that this conversation wasn't always meant to happen, that it hasn't already happened, in your timeline? *Our* timeline. Think on that. Son."

If Mr Redmayne was a little taken aback by this idea, which he was, he tried hard not to show it. Too much was at stake to gamble on his father being right. But all the same, the change in the portrait in his study, in his *father's* study, had that come about because of this meeting? Had it? All of it, in fact? Everything? His mind raced with the possibilities. Had he already changed history just by being here? Or was he merely fulfilling his destiny, their destiny? Darn it!

Would he be damned if he did, or damned if he didn't?

Another outbreak of cries and shouts from the other bar—this time heavily punctuated by plainly outraged monkey chatter—interrupted his train of thought.

"Those men," he said in an irritated way, "must they be quite so rowdy? With their damned dice and their insufferable monkey? What are they? Brigands?"

"Them? They're the so-called King's Players. They're of no importance. Ignore them. I do. I make a point of it."

Hardly listening, Mr Redmayne turned his head toward the doorway to the other bar. "You mean…"

"Yes, yes, *yes*… He's why I'm here, in fact. Tell me, do you have a scrap of paper and a pen? You must do."

"What? I'm not sure, at least I don't think so. No. Listen, you don't mean to say, in that next room is?…" Mr Redmayne searched distractedly through each pocket of his jacket in turn. "Really?"

He found an old envelope and without paying attention placed it down on the table. On the back at some point he had made a list of names and then crossed out every one—his list of potential guests for the Open House. That doomed event.

Emile. Poor Emile.

"Yes. Pen?"

"No, I really don't—"

To his surprise, Mr Redmayne's searching hand pressed

against the long, thin shape of a pen lying horizontal in the inside breast pocket of his jacket.

When he reached in and fished it out, his surprise was even greater. A thousand-fold greater. Ten-thousand-fold greater.

"Gloriana's best red crossing-out pen," he said in his surprise, really much more to himself than to his father.

He stared at it in his hand, his astonishment complete.

How on Earth did that get there?

He had no recollection at all of appropriating it. None. If things were not already so very dire and calamitous—and in a far more serious way—he knew he would be in terrible trouble. Not only had he removed Gloriana's very best red crossing-out pen from her desk without permission, from her study without permission, from the house without permission, but he had travelled back in time with it four hundred or so years to a notorious Bankside tavern full of brigands and thieves. And a rogue monkey.

"Perfect," said his father, taking it from him. "And *Gloriana*, you say? Interesting. I shall watch out for her. Now, pay attention. Yes? Listen to me, I am going to write down a list of cities. And then I will cross them out one by one while you watch me do it. Understand?"

No, Mr Redmayne didn't understand, not at all, and his face fully betrayed his lack of understanding. Still, his father continued nonetheless, *Proceed Until Apprehended* being one of his many mottos.

"Now, my good fellow, you don't have to say or do anything. You will not be telling me anything, not consciously anyway. But I will be observing your responses. Thus, by dint of my superior intuition I shall find out what it is I need to know and your conscience will remain clear. As far as you are concerned, you will have told me precisely nothing. Is that acceptable?"

Mr Redmayne wasn't sure that he liked where this was heading. But his father had already commenced to construct his list of possible venues for his supposed death some four hundred years later (approximately).

In vain, he tried to peer over at whatever it was that the older (younger) Redmayne was doing. He couldn't see.

"Stop. Absolutely no peeking, now," said his father. "It will only influence your unconscious responses and spoil the result. I can't allow that."

"Look here, John, Mr Raven, please, listen," said Mr Redmayne. "Listen, I'm not at all comfortable with anything that's going on here, I don't think. And what exactly is your business in this tavern, anyway, may I ask?"

"What exactly is *your* business in this tavern?"

The pair stared at each other without a word.

"London," said the elder Redmayne, to his son's initial confusion.

Then, Mr Redmayne realised what had been said and determined to keep his face a perfect blank—no doubt a little too late on this occasion, for his father was crossing out the word London on the back of the envelope.

Mr Redmayne watched him do it.

"Shanghai," said his father.

Mr Redmayne frowned, and then tried hard not to frown. This was ridiculous. But Shanghai was already being crossed out.

"Lisbon." Mr Redmayne stared stoically ahead. Crossed out.

"New York." Crossed out.

"Paris."

"My son is missing," said Mr Redmayne. "Missing in time. He's eleven years old. Your grandson. That's the reason I'm here. That's my business in this tavern."

The elder Redmayne put down the pen. Paris did not get crossed out.

"When does this happen? The date. Tell me, I can help."

Mr Redmayne hesitated. Could he trust his own father? Probably not. But still, what choice did he have? All hands on deck in a storm.

"September 5th, 2019. London, Paris, or New York. One of those."

"And you're certain that the probable range of displacement is four hundred years, give or take?"

"No, not exactly. We're not certain at all, in fact. Not by any means, no. There was an accident of some kind, with the mechanism, or perhaps not. You see, some evidence exists of, well, manual tampering." At this point it was Mr Redmayne turn to scrutinise his companion's face rather closely. No joy. "Now, well, we're looking for signs of any impact he might have had—on the timeline, that is. It's not much, I know. Here, I have a likeness."

He reached inside his jacket again and this time pulled out one of the photographs of Emile that had been cleverly doctored by Felice to resemble a painted portrait. It gave his heart a genuine pang to see it again. Emile's face. He handed the picture to his father. The elder Redmayne studied it for a time.

"Emile," said Mr Redmayne, uncertain if he hadn't said too much already. "His sister prepared the portrait. Very clever."

"So, I have a granddaughter as well as a grandson?"

"Mr Redmayne smiled. "Yes, you do."

"Well, I'll help if I can." He folded the picture of Emile in half, and then in half again. "Watch out, here's my man, the worthless reprobate... He approaches. Beware. Will, what have *you*, sir?"

"John, what have *you*, sir? That is the question, if I may."

A tall, balding, dandyish if quite middle-aged man stood before them. It took Mr Redmayne a moment or so but when he suddenly realised the identity of the so-called "worthless reprobate" his double-take almost caused him to fall backward off his chair.

What? No!

The tall man regarded him most disdainfully, as if he were a bad smell. Or worse.

"Will, you must forgive my somewhat eccentric companion, here," said the elder Redmayne. "He is my kin, I'm afraid. My Uncle. Visiting from the countryside. A man of Kent. Ah, I see you understand. He is also *Will*."

"Ah, sir, no, forgive me. Truly if you are kin of good King John here you must be more than kind." He bowed to Mr Redmayne. A curt nod, nothing more. "Pray, forgive me, Will, as I *will* forgive you, Will. If you, *will*. 'As I *will*, you, *Will*. If you, *will.*' If you get my meaning?"

"What, sorry?" said Mr Redmayne.

"Really, for goodness sakes, Will, must you always babble so like this?" said the elder Redmayne. "And, please, please, I beg you, no more 'Will' puns. *Ever*. I find them very irritating. Everybody does. Understand? Yes, good. Then, to business."

The famous playwright nodded, obviously a little abashed.

"The volume you requested of me, John," he said, humbly, laying a manuscript on the table. "Although in truth I fear I must largely disown it as my own, so vilely corrupted stands the text."

The Tragicall Historie of
HAMLET
Prince of Denmarke

Mr Redmayne gasped. "The bad quarto—I mean, the first quarto of *Hamlet*?"

Will sighed. "You have heard of it, sir? As far as Kent? But, alas, you are right. It is bad. Very. Cobbled together by hacks and players from snatches of errant memory and parts retold one to another over and over. Ah, that it's damned infamy should precede me, even into the Kentish countryside, it would seem, and no doubt into parts still more distant yet. Wait but a little while, John, if you will. (Blushes.) …Sorry. No pun intended. A second quarto follows, a true and perfect copy, I can assure you, a volume as full as this is short, as right as this is wrong, as—"

"No matter. I already have one of those at home. No, *this* is the volume I require. One more thing. Take this pen and write your name on the front. There's a good fellow. Best be quick about it too. My blessed uncle and I have urgent business to pursue many miles from here. Many miles indeed."

"This is a quill?"

"Yes, it's modern. Made in China. Very common there."

"China must indeed be a realm of wonders. Forsooth, how smooth doth it write. Verily, it glides…"

"Yes, half the pressure, twice the speed, or so I gather. You'll find it very good for crossing out too," said Mr Redmayne, looking on in something of a state of wonder himself as the greatest writer in history used his wife's best pen for signing his name on a first edition copy of the most famous play in world literature. In 1603.

Will tentatively crossed through the line at the bottom of the page.

~~At London printed for N.L. and John Trundell~~

"You're right," he cried enthusiastically. "It is! May I keep it? I could put a quill such as this to good use. I have much to cross through. Constantly. And the blots are unsightly. They mar my work. Such ill presentation irks and distracts me from my glorious purpose… The poesy, you know?"

Mr Redmayne blanched at the prospect.

"Awfully sorry, no, I'm afraid not," he said, carefully extracting Gloriana's favourite pen from the clearly reluctant hand of the great playwright. "It is beloved of my wife, you see. And besides, the darned thing would doubtless soon run out of ink and be of no use to you, or anyone. So, thank you. Please, no. No. That's it. Let go. Now. Thanks. Yes."

The two Wills exchanged a look of, not exactly enmity, but it was hardly friendship either.

"This urgent business of yours," said the true Will, "what is it? Maybe I could be of service and win your patronage? I have many useful contacts, now that I lead the King's Players, no less."

"Our business is time-travel," said the elder Redmayne, much to the shock of his son. "What would you know of that? Anything, King's Player? Tell me true."

"Time-travel? Ah, by all means, sir. In truth, I know time travels in diverse paces with diverse persons. I can tell you who time ambles withal, who time trots withal, who time gallops withal, and who he stands still withal."

"Enough, man! Damn it! Riddles irritate me too. Take these and go. They're what you came for. Now, be off."

Mr Redmayne's father passed the great playwright what looked suspiciously like a small brown bag of modern confectionary. With a somewhat sour, petulant expression on his face, the latter accepted the bag and exited—such high, ill-grace.

Mr Redmayne looked on, aghast. "Father, John, did my eyes deceive me or did you just slip William Shakespeare a bag of M&M's?"

"Deal's a deal," replied his father, patting the copy of the first quarto of *Hamlet* before him on the table. "Besides, the man's quite mad for them. Can't get enough. I might try him with the peanut variety next time. Keep him sweet. Pun intended."

"I'm appalled," said Mr Redmayne, visibly taken aback. "Truly appalled. Such brazen irresponsibility. And what if he has an allergy? Do you even know he doesn't? For sure? There'd be no *Lear* or *Othello*, or *Macbeth*. Or what if he starts to write about them, in his work? Goodness, the possibilities! 'Shall I compare thee to an M&M, Thou art more lovely and more chocolaty!' Or: 'My mistress' eyes are nothing like an M&M, Except perhaps the blue one?' Where would we be then, I ask you? It doesn't bear thinking about, man! Chaos."

"Fiddlesticks! I collect artefacts. That's what I do. If you were my son you would know that."

"I happen to know the contents of your clearly entirely purloined library intimately, and therefore I also happen to know, Father, that this volume here does not exist in it. This has all been for naught. You may as well go and retrieve your M&M's. Immediately!"

"This volume does not exist in my library, *our* library, if you insist, because I happen not to have given it to you yet. There. Take it. It's yours. A souvenir of this special day. Something for you to remember me by—when I'm gone, and all too soon by the sound of things. Put it with the others because I'm collecting them all."

"Oh," said Mr Redmayne, taken aback. "I don't know what to say."

"*Thank you,* would do. Or perhaps you would prefer to have some M&M's? I've got another bag somewhere, I'm sure. No? I didn't think so. Now, to business. How are you to get back?"

"The house," replied Mr Redmayne distractedly. Wasn't it wrong of him to have acquired the famous 'bad' quarto in this way? And if so, how about everything else? "Gloriana's returning for me in what, half an hour. In which case, I must go. She'll be disappointed when I return empty-handed, without Emile. Or even news of Emile."

"Not empty-handed. No, you found—watch out, there!"

Mr Redmayne, startled, became aware of a red-brown streak scurrying lightning fast across the dark, ill-lit floor, toward them. It's movements were so rapid that it was at the table before he could properly register it as the monkey, the damned monkey from the other room.

"No, Iago!" cried the elder Redmayne. "Get away!"

But he was too late. The monkey had snatched whatever it had come for and was already scampering off. At speed.

"Great Galileo's Ghost!" said an astonished Mr Redmayne. "That monkey's stolen Gloriana's pen!"

20

The fate of Mrs Redmayne's best red crossing-out pen was, however, the least of her concerns and far from her mind. Like her husband, she also happened to be in London, albeit some four hundred and sixteen years or so after the events in the tavern in Bankside had taken place. Her thoughts were with him, of course; all of her hopes were pinned on his safe return and the possibility, however unlikely, that he might bring with him their son, or failing that, some clue as to his whereabouts.

Nothing else, Open Houses, parties, pens, mattered in the least. Not at all. None of it.

Guilt pursued her. What could she have been thinking all that time, she asked herself. Why would she waste so much of her energy on trivia—friends, guest lists, food, and the like? How could she have lost sight of what was truly important? Her family. Her precious boy. The pain was unbearable. The shame too.

Mrs Redmayne shuddered at the memory of just how distracted she had been over the last few months. She felt crushed…but not beaten. No. Hoped lived. If anybody could find a boy lost in time it was them. The Redmaynes. She was a Redmayne, after all. She would find him. She would bring little Emile home. Her funny little mouse.

And when she did, she would fix everything. Never again would she let anything distract her from what was truly important. Not ever. She would put it all back together. They would be the happy Redmaynes once more. That was her promise.

Even now she was working to that end.

Anomalies, anachronisms, distortions in the timeline, that's what they were looking for. George and Felice in New York, herself in London, the two places where Emile most likely ended up. It was a little bit of a thankless task, she felt, to be honest. So vague.

Anything at all, Eric had said, by way of guidance—what they were looking for could be, well, *anything*. Which wasn't much help (none, actually, in fact). But he was right. They just had to spot it, whatever it might be. Something strange or unexpected. Something that was out of kilter with how they knew the world to be. Because the house was immune to any changes in the timeline, any historical discrepancies should therefore leap out at them at once. If anything at all like that were evident, they would spot it. They would. And they were the only ones who could.

And so Mrs Redmayne had taken herself out to the Museum of London, over at the Barbican, which was but a short fifteen-minute walk from the house in Phoenix Yard. She imagined that any changes of the type they were looking for might be local in their impact, rather than national. Or short-lived, even.

Whatever it was Emile had changed (if anything) might have been popular for a while and then died out. It was a long shot, she knew. But she thought that concentrating on local history would bring a narrower focus to the task. Make it more manageable. That was the plan.

And so here she was, wandering through the displays and exhibits about London's grand and murky past as if she were a tourist on a day out. Although to a certain extent she *was* passing the time by being here, that was true too. Besides doing something useful, Gloriana was also occupying her mind until the three hours had elapsed before she would return to collect Eric from his trip. Needless to say, the temptation to return the house at once to the agreed collection time had been great. She could have gone back instantly for him, the moment she had dropped him off, and still arrived at the agreed time three hours later.

But as a principle they avoided mixing up their relative experiences of time. The thought of suddenly being even only three hours younger than her chéri was distressing to her. Next time it could be a week, or a month, or, heaven forbid, a year—or more! The wild idea that though some accident she could one day find herself much older than Eric was quite unthinkable. Then where would they be! No, time-travel required strong principles, which was probably why they had kept it from the children.

Might it have been better not to have concealed the truth from them? Maybe. Now there was no way to know. And doing so might have only led to some other catastrophe. It was all so complicated. Their lives...

Troubled so, distracted, Mrs Redmayne wandered into the section of the museum where they had tried gamely to recreate the typical Elizabethan street scene. Dark, narrow alleyways, period-style shop fronts, life-size (if lifeless) wax manikins in Elizabethan dress, it had a certain atmosphere, yes.

But it was nothing like the reality of the time. It had none of the filth or the squalor. Nor the smells! Sacre bleu! The smells!

To think Eric was suffering all of that right now (well, sort of right now). She looked around. Families were ambling around, the parents perhaps a little over-eager, the children perhaps a little bored.

No doubt it had been exactly the same here once for the Redmaynes too. Maybe they had not done their children any favours by allowing them to hold on to such a romantic, sanitised view of the past? The reality might have deterred them enough for none of this to have happened. Eric was right. Again. They were all equally at fault.

Mission. Mrs Redmayne tried to focus on the task in hand. But it was very difficult to do that when the task itself was so vague. *Anything.* Yes. She hoped George and Felice were enjoying better luck in New York. They might have more of an eye for this sort of thing than she did herself. She hoped so.

Elizabethan dress. Mrs Redmayne perused a long aisle of figures in the costumes of the day. Elizabeth, herself, in all her peacock regalia. Horrid woman, as it turned out. Swore like a

turnkey. Teeth black as coal. Credulous to the point of stupidity. Britain's blessing indeed!

And so it went on—one gorgeously fine, wide-bustled dress
after another. Such tiny waists! To think Gloriana had once
struggled into one of those herself. In fact, she still had the
loathsome garment somewhere at home, she was sure. But
never again. It had felt like the very life was being squeezed out
of her. Torture!

Courtiers next. Doublet, hose, gown, and ruff. Or doublet,
hose, cloak, and ruff. Eric had looked very fetching in the latter,
she recalled. Mrs Redmayne tried to read one of the explana-
tory notecards attached to the glass case but found that it had
been largely scratched through. Such vandalism. Sad to see. She
went on. Toward the end of the exhibit she came across the
sorts of clothes worn by the lower orders, the ordinary people. These were far less elaborate, of course, made from rough
cloth rather than silk or satin. No fur trim. Just plain wool or
linen. When she reached the final exhibit, Mrs Redmayne came
to a complete stop. Her face blanched. Her heart quailed.

A jacket. A modern suit jacket. Shabby, worn, unspeakably
old. A herringbone jacket. Eric's jacket! Or one just like it.

She leaned closer to read the card on the glass. Annoyingly
much of the text had been struck through once again, but she
could decipher enough to make her raise her hand to her mouth
in shock, dismay, and alarm:

> The jacket of an 'alien ~~artisan' from the early 1600s~~. Local
> feeling ran strongly against foreigners ('aliens'), particularly
> craftsman, ~~who were regarded as interlopers~~ taking English
> jobs and trade. Attacks were commonplace throughout the
> period, including the fatal assault by a mob on alien appren-
> tices ~~in 1517~~. This jacket is thought to belong to the Dutch
> stationer ~~similarly attacked by an enraged~~ street mob on
> London Bridge circa 1603. Notice its striking resemblance
> to the present-day herringbone jacket, a seemingly remark-
> able ~~anachronism~~, although such extreme heterogeneity in
> contemporary modes of attire was ~~far more commonplace~~

~~in the period~~ than is ~~presently~~ considered to be the case.

Mrs Redmayne felt weak at the knees. She thought she might faint. Her head span. My goodness! Eric! Chéri! What did this mean? Fatal attack? Surely not? No. She did not want to believe it. But the jacket, it was very much like the one he had left the house in that morning, not two hours earlier. And how many four-hundred-year-old herringbone jackets could there be? Goodness gracious! It was his. It *had* to be. There could be no other.

What to do? Mrs Redmayne pressed the palm of her hand against the glass of the display case, in part to steady herself but also to get as close as she could to the mysteriously errant item of her husband's attire. She did not want to speculate about what it might mean, the jacket being here like this. But she knew she had to return to the house at once. Whatever it was that had gone awry, she would fix. Whatever terrible thing had occurred, she would undo. She had that power. And she was ready to wield it without scruple.

She set off—immediately—brushing past one of those carefree, *ordinary* families that were idly clogging up the exhibition. Her heart was pounding. How did she get out of here? Now that she had to leave in a hurry the exit was nowhere to be seen. Was she on the ground floor level or was she in the basement? Vaguely she thought she might have gone down a flight of stairs on the way in. Or was it two flights? Or none?

In something of a panic Gloriana stopped and looked around. A sign? Was that a sign for the way out? No. Which way to go? She took a breath. At some level she knew she was being silly. No need to rush. Whatever had happened had taken place four hundred years ago—and she could undo it just as easily a year from now as she could this morning. Rushing about in a panic right this minute didn't help anything, or anyone.

She took another breath. Right. Stairs. There they were. Up. Gloriana strode across the lower atrium toward the staircase. She would not panic. No. She would make things right. Whatever it took. Yes. She would.

෨

Once outside, on Saint Martin's Le Grand, having pushed through the multitude of tourists lingering in the museum foyer, Gloriana was pleased to find that the street itself was very quiet. No crowds, little traffic. She swept along in the direction of Saint Paul's, the great dome of which soon came into view as she pressed quickly ahead. This wasn't a moment for sightseeing, however. Not at all. At the end of the street she turned left into Cheapside. It seemed odd to think that only this morning Eric had exited the house on to this same thoroughfare. Only this morning four hundred and sixteen years ago! That really was a very odd thought. One thing was for sure: whatever he had experienced would not have been anywhere near as orderly as these tall concrete and glass buildings. Orderly, clean, tidy, but also sterile. The old world had something going for it too—life! You had to remember that, along with all the filth. You always felt alive while you were there.

Good grief! What was she thinking? Her poor chéri, her poor Emile—were they feeling alive in the past right now? *In the past right now.* What did that even mean? It was all so very difficult to keep straight. *Focus, dear.* That's what Eric would say. *Will* say. Once again. She turned right past the church of St Mary-le-Bow and entered the rather narrow Bow Lane. The house had a tendency to present itself just a little off the beaten track. Of course, you had to know how to look for it—and it you. That's how it worked.

Gloriana looked for it in the place where she expected to find it. Where she had left it or rather, where it had left her. Nothing happened. Church, gap, wine bar. The house appeared in the gap. Phoenix Yard, Everywhere Street. Or rather, it didn't. It should but it didn't. Had she made a mistake? Maybe. But the house didn't make mistakes. Church, gap, wine bar. She looked around. All gap, no Everywhere Street. No house. It wasn't here. It had gone.

She was on her own.

21

Despite Gloriana's fervent hopes and wishes to the contrary, it would be fair to say that George and Felice were not enjoying any better luck than she had enjoyed herself in attempting to spot some sort of tell-tale anomaly in the timeline that might lead them to Emile. Still, with four hundred years of American history to trawl through, they suspected that it was always likely to be something of a thankless task. Futile, in fact, George believed, although he didn't go so far as to say this to his sister. They had to do something, even if only to distract themselves from the horrible fact that they were probably the reason why their brother was missing in the first place.

Or at least, deep, deep down, George felt that *he* was. Probably. Most likely. And he certainly needed to distract himself from that.

But what were they looking for anyway? Anything. And what they were finding was nothing. A big fat nothing. Nothing different, for sure.

Benjamin Franklin still signed the Declaration of Independence. George Washington still crossed the Delaware. The North won the Civil War. Neil Armstrong walked on the moon. Kennedy. Vietnam. The atom bomb. It was all still here.

Whatever the shrimp had done in the past it didn't seem to have had any effect on, well, *anything*. Assuming he had gone into the past, which George was now beginning seriously to doubt. The future? Or maybe he was still in the house somewhere, riding the mysterious elevator that George had never seen? The Paternoster. That was it. Why had he never seen that?

He looked over at his sister. Gosh, their lives were weird. None weirder. If he was sure of one thing, it was that.

No one had ever had a childhood as strange as theirs.

Felice temporarily lifted her face from the thick tome she was scanning and, with a silent downward flick of her eyes, exhorted her brother to resume the task in hand. *Read, damn, you, read.* That's what her eyes said. But the expression on her face was one of desperation. He knew that's what it was because that's how he felt too. Desperate.

George lowered his eyes back to the page before him. The first Disneyland still opened in California in 1955. July 17th. That was a fact. He knew that. Even if the year had been annoyingly crossed out. It was a fact yesterday and it was a fact today. Fact. This was pointless. Fact. Fact—fact—fact—fact—*fact.* George looked around again, distracted. New York Public Library. The Rose Main Reading Room. What a great space this was. Fabulous. He didn't deserve to be here. He didn't deserve anything.

Don't blame yourself, Felice had said. And he hadn't. Not until right then, anyway. Or perhaps he did all along but hadn't wanted to acknowledge it? He'd rationalised it away, the guilt. That's what he'd done. *We're all to blame,* his father had said. And George had bought into that. Because he'd wanted to—no, more than that, he'd needed to—but now... Now, he was as guilty as sin. Fact. Who else had shown Emile how to work the controls? And purely for his or her own selfish reasons? No one. That's who. No one except himself. George. Just George. They had to get Emile back. Pops was forgiving, but his mother? No, Mother would never forgive him. And George would never forgive himself. Shrimp! Where were you? What did you do? Something? Anything? Give us a clue. Please!

The silence was deafening. This was no good. He couldn't do it. But he had to do something. What? Maybe he and Felice could go back to the house and take it back in time for a little while in every year since 1600—and work forwards? Maybe if they did that, they'd find the shrimp standing right there in one year or another, exactly where the house should be, with that stupid grin on his face? Maybe. Maybe not. Probably not. But they needed a better plan than this one. This wasn't working.

He closed the thick reference book with a slam and the echo reverberated through the room. Its cover looked up at him reproachfully—

ENCYCLOPAEDIA of AMERICAN HISTORY
Seventh Edition
~~REVISED AND UPDATED~~

—indeed, much as did the older-ish woman in the tortoise-shell glasses sitting opposite him.

Guiltily, George smiled an apology and turned away, only to find that Felice was staring at him far more reproachfully than the woman whose glare he was trying to avoid. *What?* That's precisely what her eyes were saying now. *What?* He signalled to her with a nod of his head that they should step outside. She shook her head. He stood up, his wooden chair scraping noisily on the hard stone floor. Exasperated, Felice closed her book and stood up too (her wooden chair now scraping noisily on the same darn floor—causing her twice the embarrassment).

Despite his apology, as the pair departed the reading desk George in particular felt only too aware that the tortoise-shell-eyeglass lady was watching them both very carefully now. Library criminals. That's what they were. No doubt this was his fault too.[12] At a brisk pace he walked off to the stacks, quickly re-shelved his book and headed for the exit, with Felice in tow. Right now, walking away, he could feel her displeasure on the back of his head. But once outside in the narrow corridor he experienced it full on.

"What is with you?" she said, eyes blazing. "You can't want to quit already? George, we've only been at it for, what, an hour?" She checked her watch. "Less, actually. Not even you quit that easily."

"I need to think," said George. "This isn't helping. It's hopeless. Pointless. We've got to come up with a better plan."

"Like what?"

"I don't know. But did you spot anything? See, no, I didn't think so. Well, news flash, neither did I. Understand? We won't,

[12] Yes.

either, because there isn't anything to spot. Let's go outside. Get some air. I can't stand it in here anymore. Really, I can't."

He started toward the stairwell, stopped, looked back. "Coming?"

Felice growled in exasperation. But she followed him all the same.

Three flights down. And out. Down and out. Feeling very much more that way with every flight down. Bad. Very.

But, once outside, the sun was blazing and everything was seemingly right with the world. Normal. For everyone else, at least. Life was going on as if it were entirely unaffected by their extraordinary family tragedy. Which, of course, thought George, it was.

The traffic along Fifth Avenue, both human and automobile, was heavy. Standard.

Nothing was any different. George walked down the marble steps of the central concourse. There must be something he could do. He sat down on one of the steps. Felice joined him. She didn't say anything. Neither of them did, not for a while. They watched the traffic go by. Together.

"Mother will never forgive me," George said eventually.

And when, after a moment or so, no contradiction came from his sister, he knew that what he'd said was true, really true, and he felt worse. Much worse.

"If only this were a math problem I could solve it," he said. "Give me something logical. That I can deal with. But *this*…"

Felice was staring straight ahead. "Claudia isn't logical. Well, she is… But you and her, that isn't logical. Who'd have thought there'd be some connection between you two, my two arch-nemeses. Maybe that's why."

George felt stunned. "What? What are you talking about? And what's that got to do with anything that's going on now, anyway? Even if you were right, by the way, which you aren't."

"Oh, I saw you both. I didn't want to, but I did. For the record I told her you went to school in New York and were only home for the weekend, neither of which was strictly a lie.

Possibly, I don't think. Anyway, don't you see, George? The point is that life isn't logical. You can't solve it like a math problem or a crossword puzzle. That's not how things work. People are the variables and they don't work logically. Well, maybe you and Claudia do. But you're both freaks—and that's my point. Possibly. Possibly not. Maybe I'm just being illogical."

Neither of them said anything for a minute or so.

"Well, she is pretty cute," George admitted eventually, "and smart as a whip, I can see that. But, you know, I don't really suppose I'll ever see her again, not after mother banishes me to the furthest point of all frozen time and leaves me there to rot forever. Alone."

"Don't be silly. Maman wouldn't do that. Not literally. I don't think. Be brave. Chin up. We're not done yet. A little Patience and Fortitude, that's what you need, Georgie. Remember? Papa used to read us a bedtime story about them, these two lions here? One of them went missing in the library, I can't remember which one. Can you?"

He nodded his head, smiling. "I think so. Wait, it's coming to me, 'When you have Patience, you'll find Fortitude.' That was it. Damn, I really loved that book!" George reacted as if the memory of the book had suddenly turned from sweet to bitter. "And you know who else loved it? Emile. Emile did. That's who."

"I know, I know. Come on. Let's go for a walk. It'll do you good. Both of us, in fact. It'll do both of us good."

She got to her feet. George, as if wearied by everything all at once, struggled to join her. Felice helped him up. Together they started along Fifth Avenue, much as their father had done several weeks earlier after exiting the library himself.

"Anywhere in particular?" asked George. "I couldn't stand a 'family walk' around the park. Not right now."

"Nope. No agenda. Just a break, that's all. Might help us think. Let's cross. We got the lights." The pair crossed Fifth Avenue, moving from west Manhattan into east.

George was still feeling very pensive, troubled, in fact. It bothered him that he hadn't come entirely clean to Felice about

everything that he'd discovered about the house, about the letter he'd found in their grandfather's book, its date, 2766, and
the fact that supposedly it seemed to be addressed to him, that
it had actually encouraged him to make use of the house. He
didn't know what that meant but he'd kept it all to himself anyway. His secret. What did that say about him? Maybe he should
at least tell her now?

But what would she think? Secrets. They were the real reason everything had turned out so very badly. Their entire lives
revolved around keeping one enormous secret, about the house
and what it could do, and maybe that had made them the way
they were. Secretive, even with each other. It wasn't good. And
it had consequences. They knew that now.

"Hey, sis, listen," he said after they'd travelled a few blocks
north, in what was, unusually for them, total silence, "you know
the way we didn't get round to mentioning to anyone about that
M&M's wrapper, the one you found in the coal-cart, you know,
back on our trip? Yeah?"

"Yeah, that was weird. Maybe we should have said something? I'd put it out of my mind, to be honest. What do you
think?"

George came to a stop. "Yeah, about that. See, well, there's
something else, a bit like that, I think, something I never told
you about, even—something I discovered when we were researching the house in the library. Our library, I mean. I kept
it to myself. That might've been bad, I don't know. Wrong.
Whatever."

The pair were standing outside the large bookstore on the
corner of Fifth and East Forty-Fifth Street. Felice looked at
him a little anxiously. *What now?* That's what her face said. What
more is there? What more could there possibly be? George
hesitated, suddenly distracted.

Something odd about the display in the store window behind her had captured his attention. Something very strange.
His mind began to draw the dots together. Could this be it, the
thing they were looking for? Could it?

"Hey, forget that for a sec. Listen, sorry, but just now in the library, the public library, when you were reading through stuff, was there, like, all sorts of random words struck through? You know, crossed out? Like, totally randomly?"

Felice thought for a second. Then she nodded. "Yeah, there was. I was getting really irritated by it too. So what?"

George placed his hands on her shoulders and turned her around. She gasped. Her hand came up to her mouth.

The window display. Books of every title. All of them. Every single one. Words were struck out. Crossed through. Randomly. And not always even the same word on books of the same title. It was…weird. Disturbing. A little uncanny. Like waking up into a nightmare. A new reality.

The pair goggled wide-eyed at the display, taking it all in.

The posters, the advertisements, these had words struck though too. George took a step back. The shop title, above the store display, it read:

Barnes & ~~Noble~~

He looked around wildly. Other stores, billboards, they were the same—all randomly redacted in the same weird way.

"Shrimp, what did you do? What on Earth did you change for all this to happen? Hey, Sis, look! See?"

But Felice didn't turn around. She'd stepped closer to the store window and was peering hard through the glass. All at once she practically screamed, a genuine cry of shock.

"George, George, come here! George!" Her hand beckoned him furiously. "It's Emile! I've found him! See? It's him. It is! Here, in the window. He was in New York, George, all along. It's really him! See, in the display? There!"

George joined her at the window, not at all sure what to expect. The whole display was strange enough as it was. What was he supposed to be looking at now? He couldn't see it, not at first.

"What? Are you sure?" he said, confused. "Where?"

"There, idiot! Right there. *See?* The display. The big photograph. On the main stand, see? There. It's Emile, staring right out at us. For goodness sakes, George, can't you see him? Look, right there!"

Still confused, George tried to focus his attention as directed. In front of him on a stand was an old black-and-white photograph, very blown-up—in fact, it was a huge enlargement of the cover of the book that it was publicising:

~~Captured~~ on Camera:
Great Moments in ~~New York~~ History

George scoured the photograph. A street scene, possibly turn of the century. Or sooner, it was hard to say. A huge mass of people in old-fashioned clothes, top hats, straw hats, caps, other hats (so many hats!). Most of the crowd were facing away from the camera, except for the dignitaries in the top hats at the front. So, backs of heads, largely. What were they all looking at, he wondered. Then, George saw him. Emile, or a boy who looked a good deal like him, up front and off to the left, and unlike practically everyone else in the crowd he was staring straight at the photographer. Emile?

It could be him, his face. It could be. The clothes were hard to see, though. Could be modern. Might not. No hat. What had his brother been wearing that morning? George had no idea. What did the shrimp ever wear?

Still, it did look like him, the face. Very much so. The same scrawny, rat-like features. They had to buy this book, find out when the shot was taken.

Felice grabbed his shoulder, squeezing it a little too forcefully.

"George, look," she exclaimed. "Behind him, Emile, on the wall. There."

George looked. Graffiti. Was graffiti a thing back then? A figure sketched on the wall. What was that? An outline of something. It looked a bit like a giant lizard with fur. And an extra arm. Good grief!

"Is that? Wait, are you sure?"

"Yes, it is! George, once I've seen something, I never forget it. Never! It is!"

George looked again, closer. What, no! Wait. Felice was right. It was one of Emile's manga creatures on the wall. Right there.

It *had* to be. Yes! A sign, that's what it was! A clue for them to spot. This was it! He'd led them right to him! The shrimp! Emile!

They'd found him!

George quivered. A feeling like an electric shock surged throughout his entire body.

The two Redmaynes stared each other in the eyes. The electricity ran from one to the other and back again.

"George, it's Emile, isn't it? It is! It is! It is!"

"Sis, we've got to buy that book. Find out when and where that photograph was taken."

They went into the store. The interior seemed much like it ever had—books, bookshelves, table displays—except for the fact that words had been struck out all over the place.

The weirdest thing was that to everyone else it seemed normal. No one was paying it the slightest bit of attention. Maybe it was just a temporary thing, like a promotion for a particular book or something? But then why would it be everywhere? In the library? And outside on the billboards and such? No, something had been changed. This wasn't the world they were used to, no. Not their world. Not anymore. It was different. Alien.

"Whatever it was he did," said George, looking around, "we've got to find him before he does it. This is just too weird."

"George, over here. This is it."

Felice was standing not far away at a table display, mounted high with copies of the photography book that they wanted. George joined her. She had a copy open already, and he opened one up too. Together, they flicked through the pages. Quickly. So many photographs. George tried the index, but he wasn't sure what he was looking for. Felice found it first.

"Look, it's right at the front. George, the inside flyleaf. At the bottom. It tells us everything."

George flicked at once to the front inside cover. He read:

Cover photograph: 1900, Mar 24, Mayor Robert A. Van ~~Wyck~~ of New York broke ground at City Hall for the ~~New York subway tunnel~~ that would link Manhattan and ~~Brooklyn~~. RRR.

RRR? The initials struck George like a punch. What did *that* mean? Was it just a coincidence? He wasn't sure that he believed in coincidences anymore, not in their complicated and time-tangled lives. Or was it only that?

"George, come on," said Felice. "No time for dithering. Let's buy the book and go home. We can bring him back, George. Us. You and me. We can fix this. We can bring Emile home. Today. Now. Let's go. No time to lose! We know exactly where to go."

"And *when*," said George. "Don't forget the when. You're right, this tells us everything we need to know. Let's do it. What other choice do we have?"

But somehow, it struck him as a little too neat, too easy. Too convenient. Something else was up. He could feel it.

RRR.

22

Emile wanted to blame it all on Steven. He wanted it all to be Steven's fault, not his own. That would be nice. Neat. Done.

But while it was true that he wouldn't be here if it wasn't for Steven, stuck in the past, that is, the horrible, rotten past, without his family or anyone, Emile also knew in his heart that he largely had himself to blame, much as most of us know to be true most of the time about ourselves. Because, if he hadn't wanted to show off for Steven's benefit, for his *own* benefit, if he hadn't messed with the time mechanism levers and such, well, then it was also true that he wouldn't be here, stuck, like a bug on flypaper, a rat in a trap. A mouse. Without a house.

Okay, he mostly had himself to blame, Emile knew that, but he could blame Steven, too, at least a little bit. If his friend hadn't gone running in and out of the house in different times Emile wouldn't have had to go out after him and bring him back. The idiot. The *idiots*. Both of them.

None of this explained how he ended up here, though.

Emile had been out on the front step, looking for Steven. So, who was at the controls? George? He doubted even George would do this to him, though. Unless it was by accident. That was possible. The house had shook so hard while Emile had been standing on the steps that he'd lost his footing and fallen outside onto the street. And ended up here. Oz. Time-Oz. New York City, 1900. Strange.

And the past was a very strange place, he'd discovered. Different, but just similar enough for the differences to be weird. Emile had only been here for a short while but he'd had enough of time-travel to last him a lifetime. It wasn't all it was cracked up to be on TV and in books. He'd give practically anything to be able to click his heels three times and go home. Home. *Home.*

The first few minutes had been the worst. No, the first hour. No, no—actually it was once he'd picked himself up from the fall from the steps and he had looked around and found that the house was gone—his house, gone!—that was the worst. That first moment. Feeling stranded and lost. Cut off.

But then he'd kept expecting the house to return, to come back for him, to suddenly reappear. Any minute. Why hadn't that happened?

He'd stood there for an hour, two, more. Every moment expecting the old familiar sight of his house just to turn up. But it didn't. It *is* there, he told himself, just not right now. That sort of made sense. It was a nice thought. And he did kind of remember when it would be there. Properly, that is—actually, *there.* Pops had often said the date. 1900. That was when the house had first appeared here, in New York. March. He was sure of that. Well, fairly sure.

He just had to wait.

But at that point, when he'd first arrived, Emile didn't know exactly *when* he was, not right then. And so he'd had to go and find out.

New York City. Familiar but strange. Very strange.

Because everything, when you looked at it closely, was really just that little bit different. Odd, yet similar. Similar, but odd. Emile had wandered around in a sort of daze at first, taking it all in. The clothes, for one thing, obviously; all the big coats (topcoats!), the hats (everyone wore some kind of crazy hat or other), these were all so, well, old-fashioned. Heavy-looking too. Even people's faces seemed different somehow. Thinner, perhaps, or something. More serious, at least when they were staring at him, which they did, a lot. That really freaked him out.

And then there were all these lowish-storey buildings everywhere—with, like, only two, three, four or at most five storeys to them. Some were taller, yes, but Emile could even see all these church spires off in the distance, over the rooftops, that's how low-rise most of them were. That was weird. Or was it? Maybe it was just that he felt the lack of all the really, really tall buildings that he was so used to seeing all over the place in Manhattan, crowding down over everyone. No long canyons of skyscrapers standing there blotting out the sun, the sky, the moon. Everything.

And another thing, too, something that really, really, *really* nagged away at Emile but took him a long time to put his finger on, until it came to him suddenly.

The silence.

No background hum of traffic. Always in Manhattan, any time of night or day, you could hear that low-level noise in the distance. The city. People going about their business. But not here. Not now. That was strange. A bit eerie. To be in Manhattan and not hear any traffic. Weird.

But then it wasn't *his* Manhattan. He didn't belong here. Not at all.

First off, what he had to do was not panic. Sure, he was cut off from his family, friends, school—his entire life—by a hundred years or more, and was lost all by himself in a world so alien that he might as well be on the far side of the universe, on some distant planet or other in a galaxy gazillions of light years away. Plus, he had no way to get back.

Sure, all that was true.

But they would come for him, his family. They wouldn't leave him here.

They *wouldn't*.

And he was a Redmayne. He hadn't known what that had meant until now. He'd heard his father say it plenty enough times and now it meant something to him at last. Redmaynes coped with whatever came their way. Other people would freak (imagine Steven getting stuck here!) (and Emile hoped he wasn't stuck somewhere else). Because Redmaynes had experiences that other people didn't and couldn't have, or even understand, they coped with whatever happened in a way no one else could. They were Masters of Time, after all (which he thought was a pretty cool title for a comic book, one that he would definitely write when he got home).

And they would come for him. The Redmaynes. His family.

In the meantime he just had to find out *when* he was. And then find something to eat (this particular junior Master of Time was getting pretty hungry, he had to admit). And some-place to sleep, just in case they didn't get here before dark. But first of all he had to find a newspaper, because that would tell him the date. That would give him some idea about what he had to do next. Just in case he had to try and find *them*, rather than the other way round. And that's exactly what he was going to try and do.

Not panic. Not freak. He would find a way. Just in case.

Because he was a Redmayne. And that's what they did.

So, thus galvanised, the first thing the little Master of Time needed to find was the date. As it was, it didn't take long. Emile walked along as far as Fifth Avenue, by the corner of the park—what he would know one day as Grand Army Plaza. He scarcely recognised it. No stores or statues. No Plaza Hotel nearby. Big mansion-like houses everywhere, that was all.

But he did spot a newspaper seller, on the other side of the street.

Emile crossed. It was a little weird not having any cars to avoid, but there were plenty of other things he needed to watch out for. Like, horse-drawn carriages, for one (wait until he told Steven all about this!). These were everywhere, trotting in every direction—and they were nowhere near as predictable as the traffic he was familiar with. No one seemed to have the first idea about lanes!   Emile was obliged to stop—and start, and stop—all the way across (while also taking care to avoid the numerous 'deposits' left behind on the road—yuck!).

And then, when he was almost across, all at once came this crashing bell right behind him, so close that he jumped. A trol-ley car! Emile leapt out of its way.

A trolley car! An actual trolley car!

Its manic headlights and toothy grill made it look like it was grinning at him as it headed off into the distance, and not in a friendly way, either. Still, wow, he knew he really just had to sneak a ride on one of those things before he went home.

A real-life NYC trolley car!

Mission. Focus. The newspaper seller. The date.

Collecting himself again, Emile turned around and approached the seller, who as it turned out was a boy not much older than himself, in a flat check cloth cap. His 'stand' was nothing more than an upturned wooden crate with a pile of newspapers set down on top of it, with a small tin cup for coins on top of those. Emile wasn't sure if any coins he might have in his pocket (did he even have any?) would look the same as coins from this time.

And even if they did, he only needed to see the date on the paper; surely he didn't need to buy the entire damn thing just to do that? Or did he?

The newspaper boy looked up and down at Emile loitering for a second and then ignored him. He had a folded-up newspaper in his hand and he waved it at the passers-by.

"Day—*Lee*," he chanted in a loud voice, like it was the tiny chorus of a longer song. "Day—*Lee*! Get—*Ya*! Day—*Lee*!"

Emile edged closer. A tall, thin man in a black top hat (an actual top hat!) and a long, black coat with tails threw a coin in the tin, and the boy handed him the folded copy of the paper. The man took it, pausing to open it out right in front of Emile. Gratefully, Emile read the banner headline on the front cover:

TUNNEL DAY
~~MAYOR~~ VAN WYCK TO ~~BREAK~~ GROUND

This meant nothing to him, and although some of the words in the headline were crossed through he thought little of it, except that it was yet another minor oddity. He scoured the front page for the date. If tall-top-hat guy could just keep it still for a second. Was that too much to ask? *There*:

New York, ~~Saturday~~, March 24, 1900

March, 1900! That *did* mean something to Emile. March,

1900! The house would be here—and soon! He could go home. He wouldn't be stranded here forever. One way or another he was going to make it back. Home. By a week from now at the latest. Vaguely he wondered if he was going to be in trouble. Whatever. He would take that. Gladly. Happily. Bring it on.

The newspaper lowered suddenly and from behind it the tall man's pale eyes met his own. An old man. Very old. Big crazy moustache, grey beard. A hard stare.

Odd but familiar. Somehow.

Emile broke off. He would go now. Just then, however, the man—with a kind smile—spoke to Emile. "Ah, I can see, young fellow, that you are something of a student of the news. Or rather, as it were, of the *Times*? Am I right?"

He arched a lone eyebrow—and looked down at Emile, most knowingly. "Or maybe it is simply the date that holds some special significance for you? Very likely, isn't that the case, Emile?"

Whaa—aat?

Emile felt the world lurch in a new direction all at once under his very feet. He froze. This made no sense. What was going on?

"Oh, dear," said the man. "My. You need not look quite so entirely surprised, I don't think. It's very simple. Your father, he asked me to help him find you—and so here I am. Yes? And that's quite enough gaping for now, I should think. Come. We've an important mission to fulfil, you and I, one that's critical to your safe return home. And time, for once, alas, is not with us."

At once the old man, with a surprising briskness, folded up his newspaper, opened a black leather bag at his feet (much like an old-fashioned doctor's bag) and put the folded paper inside.

"You may carry my bag. Come."

Emile closed his mouth (until then he hadn't been aware that he *was* gaping) but otherwise did not move. Who was this stranger and how did he know who Emile was and how to find him? Emile thought about just running off right then while he still could, but didn't. Where would he go, for one?

And maybe his father *had* sent him? If so, again, who was he?

All of these contrary thoughts and impulses flashed through Emile's mind in an instant.

The old man paused, his eyes stern yet twinkling. "Ah, wait, I see you require proof? Evidence that my story is true? Very sensible. I would, too, if I were you. Trust no one. Except your family. And then, perhaps, not even them. Not all of the time, anyway."

Reaching down into the black bag on the floor he shortly produced a single sheet of paper, which he then held up to look at in the light for a moment before passing it to Emile. "The likeness is very good, I think. Indeed, very accurate. Yes. Be careful, the paper is rather old. Your father gave it to me three hundred years ago, or was it only this morning? Or both? Time-travel makes everything so very hard to keep track of, I find. Don't you?"

Emile looked at the faded picture on the ancient, brittle piece of paper. It *was* him, a painted portrait, or rather a photograph that had been made to look like one. He knew the original; it stood on his mother's dresser. Emile had brought it home from school, less than two weeks ago. That was weird.

And time-travel! He'd mentioned that, hadn't he? How could he know so much about them? Emile's mind raced but nothing made sense.

He handed back the portrait.

"Thank you, boy. I am quite attached to it after all this time. Your sister produced it, I believe. Felice. She must be a very talented girl."

"Felice? How? This makes no sense. None of it. Who *are* you?"

"My name, lad, in full, is Rufus Reginald Redmayne. Yes? Indeed, quite. You may know of me, perhaps, as none other than your grandfather. Yes, that's right, I am he, the one and the same—no less than the architect of the extraordinary house you grew up in. *My* house, in fact. Now, I think I've mentioned before about the gaping. And that we're on something of a time-sensitive mission, one that is critical to you going home today, among other things. So, yes, very important. Listen, Emile, tell me, are you ready to fulfil your destiny and become a true Redmayne? Yes, I can see you are, just about. Good. Excellent. Well, come with me. Now. No time to lose. You may carry my bag. You have my permission. Come, then."

Emile wavered. Grandfather? No, his grandfather was dead, wasn't he? That's what he'd always been led to believe. He'd died years before Emile was even born, hadn't he? But if he wasn't his grandfather, then why would he know so much about him, them, everything? That meant... Emile picked up the bag. It wasn't heavy. Not at all. He looked up. Despite the decades of testimony about his demise, the supposed deceased was already striding away down Fifth Avenue, in his top hat and tails, into the crowd. Making a decision there and then Emile ran after him with the black bag in his hand, even if he was still rather confused about what was happening.

He supposed it must all be true. Somehow. How could it not be?

"Wait, stop, even if I do believe you, where are we going? Tell me that," Emile called, a little breathlessly, catching up. "And why aren't we heading back toward the house? I don't understand."

"Because the house isn't there, boy. Not yet. We must make it turn up. That's what we're about to do. And today. Not tomorrow, today! It must turn up today. That's essential."

"Why? And how will we do that, anyway?"

"By taking a photograph. Obviously."

"What?" Emile really didn't understand. "How will that help? A photograph? What of?"

"Of *you*, boy. At a very special moment. In a very particular place."

Emile's grandfather stopped to consult his pocket watch. "It'll be like sending a telegram through time. Trust me. Or not. Up to you. Darn, we'll have to take one of those damned things there, see? Nothing else for it. Quick, now. To Third Avenue. Hop to it. Otherwise all my efforts down the years will have been all for naught and I will be exceedingly unhappy."

"You mean a trolley car?"

"Cable car. No trolley cars until 1907."

The elderly gent looked down at him as if he were an unpardonable ignoramus.

"I didn't ask to come here," said Emile.

"You know, you remind me very much of your father at your age," said the old man. "Really, you do. Now, let's go."

And he was off again at once, with Emile struggling along in tow.

"I don't get it," said Emile, practically running to keep up. "How come you're here in any case and not my father? Where's he? And where's my mother?"

"Your father is searching for you, boy, trust me. But in the wrong place and at the wrong time—and it's very important that he does too. But he'll be here soon enough. Don't worry. And your mother. We just need to take this photograph. That's all. That'll fix everything. Now, pay attention. We must cross from Fourth to Third in under two minutes. We may need to run. Can you do that? Good. Now, no more questions until we've made the cable car. Understand? It's essential that we reach City Hall before one-thirty. Now, *run*. Quick."

Emile ran, alongside his grandfather. Curiously, it was hard to stay with him. The old man's long-legged stride might have made it look as though he wasn't moving very quickly, but he was. Somehow he was running fast and slow at the same time, very upright in his gait, like a giraffe.

Meanwhile, Emile lumbered alongside him with the black leather bag. It seemed heavier, more awkward to carry, now that they were running.

His grandfather seemed to read his mind.

"Careful with the bag there, boy," he called to Emile. "You mustn't drop it. The camera's inside. Break it and we're doomed. *Both* of us."

Emile nodded. He looked ahead, through the many pedestrians. They were coming up to Third. Now that it wasn't so far off his grandfather slowed down, turning his jog into a walk. He didn't seem in the least breathless, unlike Emile.

Together, they approached the junction. Grandfather Redmayne checked his pocket watch again. He looked along Third Avenue.

"There. That one. Catch that and we'll make it. See? It's slowing down. Come on."

It was a cable car. An actual cable car. On its side, Emile read:

Bowery & 3ʳᵈ ~~Avenue~~.
City Hall To ~~Central~~ Park & Harlem Bridge

The rather ornate car had come to a halt now already, about twenty yards away, and many people were getting off. There were steps at the rear. Emile and his grandfather went up to it quickly.

Then, his grandfather was stepping on board.

Then, Emile was stepping on board.

He was on board. An actual cable car.

It was very busy. Passengers everywhere, coming and going. Confusing. And it smelled, he didn't know how exactly, all sort of new-leathery. Two adjacent spaces became free on the right-hand side bench and Emile's grandfather pounced on them, sitting down at once. He gestured for Emile to join him. In something of a daze, Emile did as he was beckoned.

Clang—Clang! All at once, with a jolt, they were moving.

On an actual cable car. In Manhattan!

Emile peered all around, taking it all in. He had the bag on his lap.

"I'll take that now," said his grandfather, lifting it from Emile. "Thank you very much."

After a moment or so, once he'd settled down a bit, Emile thought it was really actually a lot like being in a train carriage, but one in which everyone else was wearing fancy dress for some random reason, like it was World Book Day except for grown-ups. Also, a man in a blue tunic stood at the back in a fenced-off area, gripping two long levers that he moved back and forth all the time in a noisy scissor-like action. It reminded Emile of the levers in the secret room at home (which had gotten him into this mess in the first place!).

Then, another man also in a blue uniform was collecting fares, as best he could, anyway, the poor guy. The ride wasn't exactly smooth. He lurched now and then between strap-hanging passengers. No one was paying anyone any attention. That much wasn't different.

"The gripman and the conductor," said Emile's grandfather. "Fascinating, isn't it, how people used to live? I always think so. It's never boring. You know, I don't think I've ever been bored a single moment in my entire life—and that's the truth. Can you say that?" Emile looked up at his grandfather's long face. He shook his head. "Honesty," said his grandfather. "I admire that when I see it—if altogether far too infrequently, no matter what the era. Now, boy, are you hungry? I expect you are?"

Emile nodded. He watched as his grandfather opened up the black bag on his lap and rummaged inside. After a moment or so he handed Emile a familiar small brown packet of sweet confectionary.

"M&M's?" said Emile, looking first at the bag in his hand in surprise and then back at his grandfather. "Really? You've got M&M's in there? I didn't expect that."

"Always carry M&M's, my boy. Always. Golden rule of time-travel. You can acquire anything from anyone in the past with a bag of M&M's and the promise of more. Priceless art works, manuscripts, treasures." His grandfather's eye glinted at this last word. "Mark my words, lad, anything at all. Half the precious items in the house were acquired in exchange for a bag or two of M&M's, believe you me."

"Blimey," said Emile, tearing open the packet. "Think of what you could've got for a Chocolate Orange."

He offered his grandfather an M&M. The old man stared down at him, strangely wide-eyed.

"Good lord, boy, you're right! Why didn't I think of that? We'd probably own Versailles and half the Americas by now if I had. Darn it! All for the want of a Terry's Chocolate Orange or two. Good grief. The opportunities missed. Worlds."

"M&M?" said Emile, after a second, by way of commiseration.

The old man took one, with the very dissatisfied air of someone accepting a consolation prize. A very minor consolation prize, at that. Third place, when he had anticipated first. He stared off into space for a moment. Then he checked his pocket watch.

"Still, what is, *is*. And what *is* can be changed another day. That's my motto. Today we're doing this. And this is very important. Ten minutes. We should just make it."

"What are we doing again, exactly?" asked Emile. The cable car had stopped and started again already and he was watching the passengers come and go. He was just sort of going with it all now. Never did it occur to him to ask how his grandfather knew where and when to find him.

"Exactly? Well, I can show you." The old man opened up his bag once again and rooted around inside. "Exactly this, my boy. We're taking *this* photograph."

He gave Emile a newspaper; and it wasn't the edition he had bought some ten minutes or so earlier. This paper was old, yellow and very brittle. Emile read the headline.

TUNNEL BEGUN!
~~CITY~~ REJOICES

At first Emile didn't understand. Although it was very old the newspaper bore today's date—or at least the date of where he was at that moment: Saturday, March 24, 1900, the same as the other newspaper. That had been the *New York Daily News*; this was *The World*.

Then it struck him. This was the evening edition. It said so in small print at the very top. The yellow newspaper in his hand, technically, was from the future, although it looked really old (and also therefore was from the past). It was all very confusing.

Emile read on. The front page was all about the mayor of New York commencing work on the first tunnel in the subway system. It seemed like an event of great excitement: twenty-five thousand people had attended the opening ceremony, it said (was that why the cable car was so crowded?), along with headlines such as 'To Haarlem ~~in~~ 15 Minutes' and The ~~World~~ Boomed Out The Tunnel ~~Opening~~'.

All the crossings out were a bit strange. Emile wondered if that had been a thing back then, *now* (whatever). A black-and-white photograph filled the top right-hand column space: 'Record ~~Photograph~~: Rapid Transit ~~Scene~~.' Lots of people in hats. Emile's grandfather leaned over and pointed to a blotchy figure at the front left. It didn't look like much.

"That's you," said his grandfather. "That's why we're here. To take this photograph."

"Me? What? How can that be?" Emile's mind reeled. He looked more closely at the blotchy figure. It could be him. "If this is me, what would happen if I just jumped off the cable car now and ran away. Would this picture still exist? I mean, this doesn't make any sense."

"Nonsense, boy. It makes all the sense in the world. This picture would still exist in this newspaper, the one you're holding right there—because it's part of *my* timeline, here, now, right this minute. But it wouldn't exist in the edition that will come out later today—and nor would it exist in the book that your parents find it in one hundred and nineteen years from now, because it would be part of the new timeline following on from today's events. Understand? In a sense, everything exists and doesn't exist at the same time. Potentially. It's the happening that matters. And we have to make *this* happen. That's our mission."

Emile scratched his head. "But, if this is here, the photograph, then it already exists and we already did take it? I don't get it."

"It exists and doesn't exist at the same time. Always. We're about to select the option 'Exist.' Does that help?"

"Not really. Maybe. I don't know." He shook his head. "No, not really."

"I could go on, but I won't. Not now. One day you'll understand." He took the newspaper from Emile and folded it back into his bag. "What's important is that we take it. Everything from that moment will fall back into place. You'll see. When we disembark, which will be very soon, stay close. There'll be a crowd and we mustn't become separated."

"Well, obviously we don't. Otherwise…"

"*Anything* is possible, boy. That's what I'm trying to tell you. Nothing is written that can't be unwritten, or crossed out. Struck through. Erased. Redacted. Rewritten. Forgotten…much as the otherwise largely foolish, riddling bard once said. Remember that? No, well, never mind. Stay close, lad. That's all. Quick, boy, look sharp, this is us. Come, now."

His grandfather stood up and began to push through the standing passengers. Emile followed. At this moment he just wished that he was home already. Maybe taking this photograph would be the equivalent of him clicking his heels three times? Somehow he doubted it. Emile pushed through the cable car, trying to keep up. He could feel it slowing down. *There's no place like home. There's no place…*

This *was* no place like home. Emile stepped down from the cable car into a huge crowd. Noise. Excitement. Rushing. He could feel the anticipation in the air. The tall, top-hatted figure of his grandfather was already receding into the throng. Emile kept his eye on the hat. So many hats, though. It was tricky. People were bustling every which way. For someone who insisted that it was so important that they stay together, Emile's grandfather certainly didn't go out of his way to make sure that they did. He was striding ahead without so much as a glance backwards over his shoulder to check if Emile was still there. And so Emile struggled all the harder to keep up, despite the constant jostling. They weren't going to fail because of him.

City Hall. People everywhere. Was it familiar? Emile wasn't sure. He had been there before, once, over a hundred years or so from now in the future, and he might not have been properly paying attention at the time. He certainly was now, though. His grandfather had pushed his way toward the front. "There you are," he said, turning around at last to see Emile. "You kept up. Well done."

They were in a small clearing in the crowd. The old man had put his bag down on the floor at his feet. Now he opened it up and took out what looked like a small brown box. No one was paying them any attention. It seemed from the increased hubbub in the crowd as though the event was about to start. Emile's grandfather clicked something on the box and a lens concertinaed forward. It was the camera. It looked new and old at the same time. Old-fashioned, but new.

"Now, take this," he said (it was a thick piece of white chalk), "and go and write your name on the wall over there. Then stand in front of it and face me. Exactly there. Yes. Hurry, it's about to start. And expect fireworks. This is still America. There's always fireworks at this sort of thing. Now, go, boy. Hurry!"

Emile took the chalk and went and stood as directed. For some reason he didn't feel as though he should write his name. At the last second he decided to draw something instead, one of his and Steven's manga-style creations, something that was his. It was just an impulse, but he did it.

Then, he turned around—and the crowd erupted. Through a cloud of grey smoke an object fizzed into the heavens, leaving behind a trail of sparks. Then it burst with a bang, showering the heavens with innumerable brightly coloured, fluttering pieces of paper. Flags, Emile realised, after a second. The Stars and Stripes. Another bomb followed, and another. And so on. Emile stood transfixed. He was glad that he'd seen this. Here, now. It was something.

When, eventually, he turned back toward his grandfather, the old man wasn't waiting alone any longer. Standing by his side were George and Felice.

They'd come for him. He could go home. It had worked. Home.

જ

It was exciting, their reunion. Joyful. Something to see. The three children back together. The boy was lost and he had been found, against all the odds. Even the old man seemed really moved to see them reunited in this way. But something nagged away at George, as they walked north up Broadway through the crowds. He had too many questions, certainly about today and how they came to find Emile. But not only about that. He wanted to know about the house, how it worked and how it came to exist in the first place. He wanted to know about the mysterious letter that he'd found in the book, why it appeared to be addressed to him, and, in particular, why was it dated as though written in the year 2766? What was the significance of *that*? He wanted to know many, many things.

Most of all, however, he wanted to know about Rufus. Who was he and where had he been all of their lives? Why were they only meeting him now for the first time? What was his part in all of this? George looked on at Felice and Emile, enjoying their newfound grandfather, joking with him as they walked along. Felice admired his top hat and tails—and moustache, which seemed oddly familiar, probably from this portrait in Papa's study.

All very him, she said—without, George thought, any idea who he was.

Emile skipped along beside them both. George wished that he could be more like them, live in the moment. Relax. But he couldn't. He had too many questions—and he had to ask them soon or explode. *Pop*!

But now his grandfather was talking...

"I must admit I was expecting your parents, rather than yourselves. Although I can't deny that I am quite pleased overall at the way things have turned out. Yes, helps fill in the bigger picture. But any idea where they are? Exactly? Or *when*? It would be useful for me to know that, I think."

"We've stranded them," said Felice, her face a picture of guilt. "It was George's idea. Wait, I don't mean that in an it's-all-his-fault way. No, sorry, George; I really didn't intend it to sound like that. Just that it was your idea—and a good one. That's all."

George was walking a little bit behind the other three. He didn't say anything, and so Felice picked up the thread again.

"George and I were in New York, you see, in the present. In *our* present, I should say." She looked uncertainly at her grandfather for a second, unsure if he knew when that was. "Twenty-Nineteen, that is," she added for the avoidance of doubt. "Anyway, and so was Maman. Except she was in London, of course, as was Papa. Except he was in sixteen hundred and something or other. *Phew.*"

"Why is he there?" asked Emile, genuinely surprised.

Felice ignored him. "And so when we wanted to come here, now, to find you, Emile, George said we should bring the London exit with us too. You know, in case Maman came home and stranded us. Like, *here.* Even if we'd left a note she could miss it. That has happened once recently already. And then we'd all be even worse off. We didn't think she could take that. Not so soon after you going missing, shrimp. Short-term pain for long-term gain, that's what you said, isn't it, George? And you were right."

Old Rufus looked around at George, as if evaluating him. "Ah, a Redmayne after my own heart, I see. Must skip a generation. But, good, good. You made the right decision. One that I can respect. I would have done exactly the same thing in your place."

George didn't appear particularly flattered by this comparison. He walked on in silence.

"Am I in big trouble, then?" asked Emile, suddenly a little deflated.

"No, I don't think so. She'll just be so pleased to see you, to see all of us, back together. She'll be overjoyed, in fact. And Papa. We all really thought you were, well, gone. Lost. It was pretty grim for a time, I have to say."

"Well, no harm done in the end," said their grandfather.

"All's well that ends well, like the poet fellow says. You know, the babbler bard. Shakespeare, that's the one. Awful man. Very needy. Hardly any manners at all. And such terrible breath. Well, they all had that. Every last one. Except Keats, of course. Lovely little chap. Bad cough. But he came later."

"You know Shakespeare?" asked Felice, wide-eyed.

"As indeed does your father."

"Papa knows Shakespeare! He's never said."

"Well, he only met him this morning, to be fair. For me, it was over fifty years ago. That's 'Time' for you. You can give it a good run, and I have—better than anyone, believe me—but you can never entirely be its master. No matter how hard you try. This, I've learned. Take it from me."

They had walked a long way up Broadway by this point, as far north as Twenty-Third Street, where it joins Fifth Avenue. No Flatiron Building, although it appeared as though the site was being readied for construction. Weird. A cable car trundled past, heading north. It came to a halt just a short distance ahead. They all stopped to watch its passengers disembark.

"I've been on one of those," said Emile.

George could stand it all no longer. He turned toward his grandfather.

"Why aren't you dead? Huh? Sorry, but tell us that, if you want to tell us *anything*. Babbling on about Shakespeare. Keats. What's the point of that? Tell us things we need to know."

"George!" said Felice.

"Well, that's exactly what we do need to know. Why did we spend all our lives until now believing he was dead? Why did Pops believe he was dead if he wasn't? And you know Pops: if he didn't believe it was true he wouldn't say it. No way. And another thing: how come it was *him* who took the photograph of Emile just now, the one that led us here? I'll tell you why. He set us up. He's set us all up. He's played us all along—old Grandfather-Time here, me especially—and I want to know why. Or I'm not moving another step. Not one."

Felice and Emile looked ashen-faced, aghast, from one to

the other. Grandfather and grandson, angry, similar in so many ways, facing off on Fifth Avenue. In 1900.

Spring and winter. Winter and spring.

George didn't know what to think. He could see his grandfather was sizing him up, eying him shrewdly.

"George, no," said Felice again. "Come on."

"No, my dear, he's right," said the old man, as if almost relieved. "You do deserve answers. I admire your forthrightness, my boy. I do, truly. I respect straight-talking folk, always have. Well, then, yes, it's true. I'm afraid so. All that you say—and more. Guilty as charged. I'm sorry, Emile, I did strand you here. I plotted it all, pulled all the strings. I made it happen."

Felice seemed most shocked. She looked at her two brothers in disbelief.

"Why?" continued Rufus. "Well, it's simple really. I met your father many years ago. He was the man you know now. He was looking for *you*, Emile. Yes, he was. And he believed me dead. I therefore either had to be dead or make him believe it. I chose the latter. Given those options, what would you choose?"

"Not this," said George indignantly. "Anything could have gone wrong. Emile could have been lost forever. We all thought he was. Mother thought he was! You didn't have the right! For none of it! You're a…monster!"

"Really? Am I that different? No, no, I don't think so, George. And if I were you, I wouldn't be so certain about what choices you'd make under the same circumstances. Oh no, not at all. No. Indeed, what was it you said to your sister just a little while ago: 'short term pain for long term gain?' Think on that, my boy, if you will, at your leisure. I have other reasons, too, for all of this, but I really don't have time to go into those with you now. Things have to be this way. They must. What's about to happen, you see, can still go two ways. And I need to ensure we make the right choices."

"What?" George felt suddenly alarmed. "What do you mean? What reasons? Choices? What's about to happen?"

"I'm afraid I must take temporary repossession of my

house. *Our* house, if you insist. It's for the best, for everyone. Trust me, or not. Up to you. Your choice, my boy. Always *your* choice. That's the engine that drives the universe, you know, in the end. Choice."

"What are you babbling about?" George had a bad feeling.

His grandfather was turning away. George reached for him but he was too late.

Clang-Clang! The cable car was departing. With perfect timing the wily old man had stepped up on to its platform at the rear. He was departing. Motionless, expressionless, on the platform, he kept his eyes fixed on them as the car receded steadily into the distance.

The three young Redmaynes stood there as if transfixed, or in shock, watching him go—their grandfather growing smaller by the second. Disappearing.

"George, what's he doing?" asked Emile. "What's going on?"

"Isn't it obvious, shrimp? He's stranding us here. We're stuck."

23

Mr Redmayne was in something of a situation—a most unfortunate situation, at that. Inadvertently he had insulted a man's pig and now a mob had gathered and it was clear they were out for blood. His!

It had all happened like this. After leaving his father (and Gloriana's best red pen) in the inn (that damned monkey!) Mr Redmayne has hurrying back across old London Bridge toward the house. He wanted to be there when his wife returned, so that she wouldn't have to linger alone amid all of this mayhem. It was a very unruly time. You were prone to forget things like that when you hadn't visited the period for a while. He had forgotten it and so might she. Views of the past tended to be rose-tinted. Nostalgic. The reality was very different. If she ventured out alone, to look for him, say, should he be late, anything might happen. He had to be on time.

And so, he was in a rush. Also bothering him was the fact that he was no nearer finding Emile than he had been when he had set off, which was sure to disappoint his wife. And he truly hated to disappoint his wife. Not to mention that he had that strange meeting with his father playing on his mind too. What a tangled complication of emotions that was! You meet your long-deceased father and he's younger than you are? Who could deal with that situation and not be in something of a fluster? Or even sent partially insane? No, make that totally insane. That's how Mr Redmayne felt—somewhere on the wrong side of the thin, thin line separating 'partially' from 'totally' doolally, which was never a good place to be at the best of times.

Then, there was the whole time-travelling dimension to things. All of that was on his mind too. Had he said too much? What damage to the timeline might his revelations to his father have brought about? What harm had he done? Great Galileo's

Ghost! The portrait in his study—and the rest of it. Was all of that a result of their brief conversation today? Was that why Rufus had kept bringing him here when he was a boy? To make him familiar with the terrain, as it were? The era? Good grief! Emile! Was his father behind that? Mr Redmayne wouldn't put it past him. He knew his father. Anything was possible. Anything.

And so it was, with all of this running through his mind, that Mr Redmayne suffered the misfortune on the bridge of once again encountering the showman whose key contribution to the wide world of street entertainment—indeed to the wider world in general—was to offer passers-by the unique opportunity to view his two-headed sow, for a price, naturally.

Now it may be that to cater exclusively to low human curiosity about freakish and unnatural things on a day-to-day basis may in time colour your view of people in a none-too-favourable way—it might cause you to see people as intrinsically worthless themselves, perhaps, other than with regard to how they might be exploited for your own particular gain and pecuniary advantage. And maybe this was why he took so against the harassed-looking and very oddly dressed gentlemen who clearly wanted nothing more than to be on his way. Hard to say.

Or perhaps it was just that the unpleasantly baby-faced fellow took Mr Redmayne for an easy mark? Or that the gross take for two-headed pig viewing had been exceptionally poor that day? Possibly a pig with two heads wasn't any longer the landmark London Bridge attraction that it had once been, back in the good, old days under the old queen, God rest her soul? Perhaps all of these things? Who could know for sure?[13]

Suffice to say that on this second encounter Mr Redmayne found the troublesome fellow's overtures to be far more difficult to sidestep than he had on the way out three hours earlier. In fact, the damned mountebank was altogether extraordinarily pushy and aggressive, to the point that Mr Redmayne felt himself practically accosted and more or less held against his will.

This all took place toward the north end of the bridge, where

[13] Not you. Sorry.

the thoroughfare was most congested, and narrow, overhung, and dark, with very little room to manoeuvre, with the result that progress through the pressing crowd was slow, at best, to Mr Redmayne's immense frustration.

He had a place where he needed to be—and soon.

Unfortunately, the crowd seemed dedicated to the purpose of hindering his progress and at one point slowed down even further—and for what reason? None that Mr Redmayne could see, not at first, although after a moment he spotted—straight ahead—a stubbornly immobile, man-mountain-sized fellow who appeared to be deliberately blocking everybody's passage, or who was at least trying to do that. Luckily, people were still managing to squeeze past him, however, despite his efforts, and make good their escape.

Mr Redmayne really had no time for this. No eye contact, that was always the key to success in these situations. That had worked in the Vatican that one time, an unfortunate situation that had been in many ways very similar to this.

Looking the other way, he tried shuffling off to one side in an effort to sneak past, but alas only succeeded in inadvertent-ly shoving some other equally harassed fellow in the back, a matter of instant regret as the offended party at once returned Mr Redmayne's shove with interest, steering him directly back into the path of the over-sized, wobbly-jowled, unpleasantly baby-faced man-mountain that Mr Redmayne was hoping to avoid. Well, there was no avoiding him now…

…for he had grabbed Mr Redmayne by the arm, and he gripped it tight.

"Sire, riddle me this if you will," he said, manic-eyed, "if legs make four and heads but two, and yet withal I make thee breakfast, what am I? Faith, speak plain, and a rare opportunity doth surely be thine, sire, for a small fee."

"I'm terribly sorry," said Mr Redmayne, attempting to shake himself free. "But I really don't have time for any of this. Can't stop. Emergency."

He leered into Mr Redmayne's face, extremely close-up.

"The riddle, sire, canst thou guess what it doth be, the solution? Dost thou require a clue perchance? Very well. Faith, sire, if my first be in pen and my last be in plate, but happier by far be I in first than in last, for in truth, it doth be better to be written in Oink than eaten in Clink. Dost thou get me, sire? Dost thou? Canst thou guesseth? Methinks thou canst, surely?"

Mr Redmayne struggled to free himself.

"Unhand me, sir, at once. I must insist. I have pressing business elsewhere and have neither time nor interest in your childish riddles. Let—me—go!"

"The riddle, sire. Marry, can't thou answer it? Does thou know?"

Tiny dark eyes, staring. Blankly.

Mr Redmayne wrenched himself free. "What *is* with you all with riddles?" he said. "Honestly. Do you really have nothing better to do with your time? Pig. The answer is *pig*. Now be off with you. For I must away this instant."

"Nay, stay, sire! The prize is thine!" Then, he called behind, loudly: "Abel, bring forth the pig. Sire, nay, tarry! Thou'st never set eyes on a pig like it, for 'tis the eighth wonder of the world! My lord, behold the pig with two heads! Abel? The pig—now!"

"Now, look here," began Mr Redmayne, growing annoyed, "I would have neither the time nor inclination to view your pig if it had five heads, wore a dress, and danced the can-can for the Prince of Wales! Now, stand aside!"

Mr Redmayne tried to sidestep briskly to his right but the fellow moved with him.

"Prithee, see the pig, sire. Only sixpence. Steppeth this way."

It was clear the fellow had no intention of standing aside.

Under the circumstances Mr Redmayne wondered if it might not be expedient simply to give the scoundrel his damned sixpence and be done with it, much as he hated giving in to common ruffians, or clergy. He wedged the copy of the 'bad' folio of *Hamlet* that his father had given him so that it was secure under one arm and felt around for a coin in the pocket of his waistcoat. There.

He looked at the coin. Was that a sixpence? He thought so. "Here, take your damned sixpence, thou, fellow, chap, now, yes, and letteth me pass. Yes. For I profess I have urgent business elsewhere and I must away at once."

"Thank you, sire. Thou art kind. But thou payest thy money, thou seest the pig. See? Thou can'st not pay and *not* seest the pig, sire, if thou followest me? No, sire, no." Then, once more, behind, loudly: "Abel, by God's wounds, man, bring forth the damn bloody pig."

"Now, look here, you, thou, fellow, I have no time to see your pig! Let me pass."

"Pig's coming, sire. 'Tis but a slight delay, I assurest thee. And might I say, sire, that thy style of dress is very unusual. Very unusual indeed. Be it Dutch? Perchance, art thou a Dutchman, my lord? Pray, tell. Faith, thou look like'st thou could'st be a Dutchman. 'Tis the colouring, sire. Very Dutch."

"And see, look, aye, he's carrying paper, Bart," added a hitherto unnoticed accomplice, a by far smaller man, off in the shadows. "Dost he be one of them Dutch stationers, thou reckonest?"

"Look, I am not a Dutch stationer, I assure you. Now—" Mr Redmayne was growing very exasperated.

"No matter, sire. Here cometh my pride and joy now, I swear. My baby. Behold, my lord, if thou'st wilt, and avouch with thine own eyes the eighth wonder of the world, the two-headed paragon…the sow with two heads!"

Yet another of the fellow's accomplices emerged—finally—from the dark recess behind, in tandem, it must be said, with a rather cheerful-looking pig on a rope.

It trotted forth altogether quite amiably, in fact.

Mr Redmayne could see at once that while the poor animal had some kind of large fatty growth on the left side of its neck, which, while substantial, hardly constituted in any sense anything that might be regarded as a second head. The beast didn't appear to be in any discomfort, however, which was a blessing.

The pig itself looked up at Mr Redmayne with interest,

almost as if in the expectation of him having concealed something tasty somewhere in his eccentric Dutch stationer's garb.
Himself, possibly.

Regrettably, Mr Redmayne had loudly psaw-ed at the sight
of it, however, a potentially fatal error. And he hadn't stopped
there.

"Second head? What? That poor animal no more has two
heads than do you and I! Or the queen of England, for that
matter! You, thou, my poor fellow, are nothing but a cheap
huckster! This is a scam. A bad one at that. You should all be
ashamed! Second head! Now, out of my way or be damned!"

"What! Quick! Hold him, my lads! No one insults our blessed Gloriana! Now!"

"Especially no Dutch stationer! Grab him!"

With alarm, Mr Redmayne felt himself suddenly being seized
from behind by the arms, a fiercely tight grip. He struggled,
beginning only now to realise the gravity of the situation.

The trio of pig hucksters held him—and fast.

A crowd was gathering, too, or more precisely, a mob.

"Go through his odd doublet, seest what thou might find."

"I tell you, I'm no Dutch stationer! That, sir, is a play, by
William Shakespeare, the great playwright. He gave it to me
himself, not thirty minutes ago. And I didn't insult your queen.
I said she didn't have two heads! No more than you or I.
Technically, *not* an insult."

"Queen? Thou, sire, insulted my Gloriana, here! And most
grievously too. No man insults my pig! Not to her face!"

"Specially not no Dutch stationer!"

The lead—and by far the largest-pig huckster once again
leered directly into Mr Redmayne's face. Extreme extreme
close-up. Very unpleasant. Breath, bad. Complexion, greasy.
Ugliness, pronounced. Not so much baby-like now as unpleasantly piggy, he could see that.

Mr Redmayne turned away. The happy pig, he noticed, now
at his feet, was sniffing appreciatively (with its one head) (that
is, *one* head) at the hems of his trousers—and it didn't appear in

the least insulted. He thought about mentioning this. Decided against.

"Now, look here, I am an agent of the Crown. My Lord Walsingham—or no, wait, what's the year?—Phelippes will hear of this. Thomas Phelippes! You, thou all, don't want that, none of you, thou, oh whatever... But I can assure thee all of that. Yes!"

"Why, I do believe thou art correct, sire. Too very true. Abel, get the rope. Be quick!"

An undercurrent of murmured excitement seemed to run through the gathering crowd at these words. Now this was a show worth coming out for!

Mr Redmayne struggled all the harder but to no avail. He thought he heard the phrase "Dutch stationer" more than once in conspiratorial whispers from the lips of the assembled throng, in somewhat shocked tones...

"Look, for the last time, everyone," he cried out, "I am *not* a Dutch stationer! And what if I were? In what godforsaken world would that be a capital crime? Is Dutch stationery so perfidious?"

"He confesseth!" shouted a loud crude voice in the crowd. "Hangeth him!"

"Hangeth him high! Rope! Rope! Rope!"

Mr Redmayne felt the pig's warm, wet snout (singular, not plural) tickling his ankles, as unlikely a presage of imminent doom as he could imagine. Still, matters looked decidedly bleak.

The return of Abel with the thick coil of rope cranked up the level of excitement in the crowd to a new high. The murmuring changed into general calls and cries—the number of spectators packing the narrow, cramped, confused, and noisy space was growing by the second.

Matters indeed looked most decidedly bleak. Amid the wild melee Mr Redmayne could see no escape.

Then came a genuine presage of doom. The bridge began to shake. Violently. No mere tremble. Swaying, shaking, above and below—with a sound like the wooden buildings all around were being ripped from their foundations. Thick wood splintering, tearing, everywhere.

Panic. Moans, shouts—and the mob screamed as though one. Running, falling, trampling over each other to get away. The crush filling the narrow passageway was desperate. Cruel. Mr Redmayne felt the grip on him loosen and he took the chance to slip out of his jacket. He was free. His assailants seemed scarcely to have noticed. Mr Redmayne grabbed back the folio (it was, after all, signed by the author) but, as he reached to reclaim his jacket, a hand restrained him, a hand he would recognise anywhere, a fair hand—that, no less, than of his wife.

"Chéri, leave the jacket, yes. It's how I found you. Come. We must go. This way."

Mr Redmayne was astonished—but grateful beyond belief—to see his wife at all, let alone in full-period Elizabethan dress. Beautiful, as ever, a vision, the true Gloriana. Truly regal. He stumbled along behind her, led by the hand through the panicking crowd.

"When...how...what?" he struggled to articulate his questions, having so many.

Then she saw a door straight ahead that he recognised.

He stopped, astonished. "Great Galileo's Ghost! The house! You manifested it *on* the bridge! How on Earth!—"

"Don't stop, dear. We need to leave. No dawdling. Best not. I'll explain all later. Must go."

She went on ahead in her bustling dress and he followed. Speechless.

They went in. Never had he been so pleased to be home, to close that door behind him. Home! But she was right. They must leave at once. Gloriana was already striding on toward the library. He hurried after her.

"Dear, wait," he called, "we'll have to move the house first, I mean before we go back. Otherwise we'll end up in the Thames."

"Yes, dear, I know," called Mrs Redmayne back to him. "*I* brought it here, remember?"

He caught her up. "Yes, but *how*? I don't understand."

"Never mind. Just come along."

Obediently, he followed. So much had happened. He need-ed time to process it all. The hallway, he noticed, in passing through, appeared to be full of a thick dust of some kind. How long had he been gone? So many questions. His wife had en-tered the library—and all at once he decided to leave her to it. He went in, put down the folio (signed) and plonked himself in a chair, quite exhausted.

All in all, it had been a very unusual day. *Very* unusual.

He let the lovely, reassuring golden light of the library, his favourite place—*his* library, and his father's—seep into him, and didn't want to move or think about anything.

Indeed, it was only when Gloriana reappeared, resplendent in her dress, that he remembered that he must disappoint her, that he had no news of their son. In all the excitement, in his escape from the Jacobean lynch mob, and everything else, it had momentarily slipped his mind.

"Darling," he began, clearly crestfallen. "Emile. I'm afraid—"

"Dear, no, mon chéri, I meant to tell you," she said, her eyes excited (hardly the response he was expecting), "but I haven't had the chance. Emile. We know where he is—and when!"

"What! Are you sure? Dear, where? When? Tell me."

"New York. 1900. The children, George, Felice, they found him. Only now I don't know where they are! Something very mysterious is going on. I'll explain everything. But first, let us change, both of us. I look like a—well, I don't know exactly what. And you, you smell like, I don't know what either, some-thing far worse. We've the time, chéri, so let's do that. Now. Both of us. We'll feel the benefit. This dress—"

She pulled a pained face.

"I think it looks rather lovely. It still fits, I see."

"Yes, I know," she said, admiring her form. "But it's killing me!"

Mr Redmayne was astonished when his wife showed him the

photograph of Emile in the *Great Moments in New York History* book. He was ashamed to confess that he'd seen it before, weeks earlier, in the shop window, but hadn't paid it any mind, Emile being safe at home at the time. And afterwards he'd quite forgotten all about it. He felt like such an absolute ninny. All the pain he might have spared them if only he had joined the dots. He flicked through the pages, muttering to himself under his breath about his great stupidity. Gloriana asked him not to dwell on it so ("Don't, dear"). Context was everything. At the time, the photograph had no context, and so he couldn't possibly have been expected to realise that it *was* Emile, could he? No one could. She laid a gentle hand on his arm, by way of sympathy and comfort. And he did feel better, then. A little bit, anyway. Not a lot.

Mr Redmayne was even more astonished and intrigued to hear his wife's story about how she had returned home from spotting his jacket in the Museum of London (he absolutely must go see that, by the way), only to find that the house was no longer where she'd left it. That had been very distressing, to think him dead in 1603, Emile still missing, the other children alone in New York, and the house gone. She had been quite at her wit's end, she didn't mind saying (it was Mr Redmayne's turn now to lay a gentle hand on her arm, by way of sympathy and comfort). ("There, there, dear.") In the end she'd been forced to travel on the train from London to Paris ("the blessed train!") and enter the house from there. And when she did, it had been 're-set', as it were, in the interim. Somehow. Put back into its three original times and positions. And the book was right here, too, open at the very page so that she'd find it. Just like this. But—no sign of the children anywhere. It was all very odd. She couldn't explain it.

At this account Mr Redmayne grew suspicious. His father. He recounted the equally astonishing events of his day in 1603, about meeting his father in the tavern when the stubborn old rascal had been much younger (though still stubborn and no less the rascal), about how he now suspected Rufus might be behind it all—the crashing of the house during the party, Emile going missing. He wouldn't put it past him. His father was the arch-manipulator, the master puppeteer—no doubt he could teach even old Pierre Pierre a thing or two on that score. The crossword puzzle, the portrait changing, probably his own childhood visits to Elizabethan London, these were very likely all part of his plan. Mr Redmayne paused for a breath, to catch his thoughts, and then resumed:

"You see, dear, he wanted Emile to go missing because he wanted me to go and look for him," said Mr Redmayne with conviction. "He wanted, needed, our chance meeting to happen. He engineered it all. The unspeakable rogue."

Mrs Redmayne looked doubtful, if shocked. "But, Eric, dearheart, I'm sorry to say this, except, Rufus, he passed away, didn't he? Twenty years ago. Yes, he did. We arranged his funeral, you and I. I cried at his graveside. Remember? I was very sad—and so were you. Naturally."

"I'm afraid your tears were premature, dear. Look." Mr Redmayne pointed to the inscription on the inside cover of the book's cover. "The initials."

Cover photograph: 1900, Mar 24, Mayor Robert A. Van ~~Wyck~~ *of New York broke ground at City Hall for the* ~~New York subway tunnel~~ *that would link Manhattan and* ~~Brooklyn~~. *RRR.*

Mrs Redmayne raised her hand to her mouth in shock. The date, too, was compelling and could hardly be coincidence. The day *before* Rufus first moved the house to Manhattan. It was all true. He must have been planning this, everything, literally, in a sense, for centuries, all of their lives. All the time that they had known him he'd had this secret agenda, this plan, one that would involve losing their child in the past. No, it couldn't be. The deceit, it was monstrous, unthinkable. Yet, the evidence…

Mrs Redmayne rose from her seat, suddenly looking very anxious.

"Darling, we must go and retrieve Emile at once. Right now. I don't know what's going on, but I don't like it and it has to stop. We can figure all of this out later. I really wish I knew where George and Felice had gone off to in the meantime, but for now our priority has to be Emile. Come, let's go."

"We'll have to be careful, dear, you know, precise—in our timing, I mean. The house, it can't be in the same place more than once simultaneously. I know you know this, but we must make certain we're gone before Rufus, younger Rufus, turns up with the house on the morning of the twenty-fifth. Otherwise, well, we won't think about otherwise. Too horrible. Two small-mass black holes colliding—oh my, no... Anyway, the point is, we will only have a very narrow window of opportunity to find him in. Once we're there, the clock will be ticking."

Mrs Redmayne nodded. Gravely. And then she was off, with Mr Redmayne once again trailing in her wake. He struggled along after her, not knowing how she had gotten quite so formidable—since breakfast, that was. It really, *really* had been the most unusual day.

Sometimes in life, when things seem most bleak, when everything is at its most confused, most confounding, most troubling, you catch a break. Things turn around, go your way, work out, all at once, and this happens almost despite you, not because of you or anything you did. And all is well. Luck. Everyone has a moment in their lives like that. That's what Mr Redmayne firmly believed. Yes. And this was his moment of luck, and his wife's.

When they materialised the house at three o'clock in the afternoon on Saturday, 24 March, 1900 in New York, leaving themselves, they hoped, enough hours of daylight to undertake a thorough search of the city (with the aid of the handheld tracking devices), they hardly expected to find not only the child in question already waiting for them on the doorstep, like a bad penny, but indeed, to their great delight, they discovered no less than all three of their children languishing together on the kerb outside, glum-faced and looking up at the house as though it might contain the devil himself, rather than their loving, joyful parents. But so it was. Luck.

And all was well.

They came inside. Incredulity abounded. Astonishment. Relief. Mrs Redmayne first hugged Emile to her as though she might crush the very life out of him—and then all three together. Joy was unconfined. Tears fell, from all quarters. Tears of joy. Even Mr Redmayne was heavily moist-eyed as he returned the house to the present day. His tears travelled the ages with him, but in private. The important thing was that they, the happy Redmaynes, happily, most very happily, were reunited.

Never again, he vowed, to be split asunder. Not as long as he drew breath. Never.

Back in his study he found everybody talking at once. Questions, exclamations, shouts, cries, laughter, these punctuated the stories that each of them had to tell, their adventures. Meeting your father when he is younger than you are yourself (imagine!), Shakespeare, near lynching, riding a 1900 cable car, seeing the start of the New York subway, the fireworks, landing the house on old London Bridge, all of this came out in a stream of excited narrative. It was all very thrilling—and funny—to hear, in retrospect. A grand tale.

One person loomed large in the telling, however. Rufus. Grandfather, father, villain. His actions were unaccountable. Unforgivable. Ruthless Rufus. Mr Redmayne felt ashamed, chiefly by association, but also because it was his chance meeting, earlier that very morning (albeit in 1603), and the information that he had unwillingly and willingly imparted, to Rufus, which had set this entire fiasco in motion. But surely he could never have anticipated that his father would behave so very wickedly? That was what his wife said. And the looks of his children's faces assured him that they agreed. It wasn't his fault.

"Yeah, don't blame yourself, Pops," said Emile. "No way. I mean, I did something wrong too. It wasn't *just* you."

Mr Redmayne hugged his younger son at this point, largely for the sincerity of his endorsement.

"Yes, that's true," said Mrs Redmayne. "We all had a part to play. Lessons have been learned, I'm certain of that. By all of us."

"Secrets. That was the problem," said George. "That's what did it for us. Secrets. No more secrets. That's what I take away from this."

"What I don't get," said Felice, "isn't so much that he faked his own death. Well, I don't get that. But, it's the fact that he could cut himself off from us like that. He doesn't *know* us. He's played no part in our lives at all. It seems to me he missed out. I really don't understand."

"My father was, *is*," Mr Redmayne corrected himself, "a genius. A brilliant mind. But he's not like us. He sees things differently. Strategically. He has his goals and he doesn't care about consequences. Or people. He cares about the endgame. That's his priority. Not everybody's the same, I suppose. That's probably a good thing."

Mr Redmayne glanced wistfully at the portrait of his father that stared down at them all from the wall of his study. Something about it bothered him. *And he's not of our time*, he wanted to say, but didn't. That could wait. Instead, he said: "The important thing now is that we're all back together, safe and sound, at last. Home, where we should be. And hopefully all a little wiser for our adventures. I know I am."

"Cream tea?" said Mrs Redmayne, and everyone laughed.

And then they stopped. As one. Knocking. Someone was knocking on the front door. Who could that possibly be? The Redmaynes looked at each other in stunned silence. No one said a word. Their eyes said it all. What now? What possibly now?

The knocking persisted. Loud. Demanding. After a moment or so of this, Mr Redmayne went to see who it was.

When he opened the front door, he initially felt relieved. He recognised the caller. Watkins. The inquisitive chap from the public library who was always so very interested in the house. Mr Redmayne remembered with a pang of conscience that he had sent him an invitation to the Open House event. It must have reached him after all. That seemed like a lifetime ago. And he had brought two other fellows with him, which in truth seemed a little liberal of him with Mr Redmayne's hospitality. Still, none of that mattered now.

"Ah, Watkins, hello. You made it. And you brought friends. Well, this is awfully embarrassing, but I'm afraid the party's over. It finished early, you see. We had something of an incident. Nothing too serious, in the end. Thankfully." Curiously, he noticed that all three of them were wearing the same type of black Macintosh coat and identical bowler hats. "Normally, I'd invite you in but we're still clearing up the mess. Frightful business, really. I do apologise but, well, there's always next year, yes?"

Mr Watkins appeared oddly unmoved by this account. His expression didn't change. Instead, he looked around at his two associates, who were also very serious-faced, and then back at Mr Redmayne.

Finally, he said something that threatened to change Mr Redmayne's life forever:

"Thank you for the invitation, Mr Redmayne. Very much indeed. Very kind. Without it, we might never have found you. This house, we've been searching for it for ages. Literally, *ages.*"

"Centuries," said one of the two bowler-hatted men behind, with a sudden snap of enthusiasm.

He was silenced at once, however, by a stern glance behind from Mr Watkins, who then resumed:

"No, we're not here about the party, Mr Redmayne. Indeed not. No, we're the TDA."

TDA? Where had he heard that recently? Mr Redmayne had a very bad feeling, one of the worst he would ever have.

"Temporal Displacement Authority," Mr Watkins went on. "Surely? No? Well, as I say, we're not here about the party. May I introduce my TDA colleagues, Mr Wilberforce and Mr Wimberley. We're here about this house, actually—and time-travel."

Mr Redmayne blanched. "Really? Time-travel, you say? Right, well, in which case, yes, I expect you'd probably best step inside, then. All things considered."

He looked at the faces of the three men and supposed he didn't have much of a choice. Policemen. He should have guessed. They looked like policemen.

TDA, whatever. *Time* Policemen.

Mr Redmayne opened the door wider and, without any further ado, one-by-one the three bowler-hatted Agents of Time plodded inside.

24

The rear exit and the side exit had already been secured. Sealed, in fact, in perpetuity. The front exit would be sealed shortly, once everybody had vacated the premises. Again, in perpetuity. This was how Mr Watkins (Chief Investigator-in-Charge, TDA) began his summary of the 'brief proceedings ahead' to the bewildered Redmaynes, all of whom were still assembled in Mr Redmayne's study. Mr Wilberforce (Chief Detective, Timeline Enforcement) and Mr Wimberley (Detective, Time Displaced Objects) busied themselves in the room while he spoke, examining this and that. The latter had a handheld device, much like Mr Redmayne's own (which he now realised he had left in his jacket on the bridge), which flashed, beeped and buzzed continuously, much like some kind of over-excited, electronic bee, as he ran it over everything (and anything that beeped he rewarded with a round orange sticker, as if he were pricing it up for a discount offer in a sale).

The Redmaynes sat, listening—listening but not comprehending. "When you say 'vacated,' what do you mean by that, er, exactly?" asked Mr Redmayne.

"Exactly what you would think, Mr Redmayne. Vacated, emptied, abandoned. This house and all its contents are to be impounded forthwith. Everything will be examined. Any objects found to be time-anomalous will be returned to the era from which they were improperly and illegally displaced. Everything else will be sold to recoup costs."

"Everything? Sold? All my lovely things?" Mrs Redmayne held her hand up to her mouth in dismay once again.

Mr Redmayne looked distressed. "Just to be clear, we are going to be evicted from our own house, the home where both I and my children have grown up, and you will either take back or sell everything we own? Have I got that quite right?"

Mr Watkins nodded severely. "Yes, Mr Redmayne, you indeed have that exactly right."

The children, at this point, were growing quite agitated. Felice and Emile had huddled into their mother. To Mr Redmayne's concern, George's face was growing increasingly flushed. Angry. The boy had an impetuous streak, after all, and Mr Redmayne didn't want things to get any worse than they were already. He wanted to head that off.

"Now, now, everyone. Bad as things are, we'll still have one another. We'll get by. It'll take a while but we'll soon get back on our feet. You'll see."

"I'm afraid not, Mr Redmayne. You must return with us to your own time."

"What! What do you mean? This *is* my time. I was born fifty years ago, in Shanghai. There must be some mistake. I'll have you know, this is my era!"

"No mistake, Mr Redmayne. Yes, you were born in Shanghai, that's true, but not fifty years ago. No. We have in our possession incontrovertible evidence that proves you were in fact born in the year 2775."

"What? That can't be right. No, it can't!"

Mr Wimberley ran his handheld device up and down Mr Redmayne. It beeped.

"Anomalous," he said, and put a round orange sticker on Mr Redmayne's arm.

"You mean, I'm to travel with you to the future? What about my family?"

"I'm afraid they must remain here in their own time. They were all born here. This is their time. I'm sorry. Those are the rules."

Everybody grew very distressed at this point. George stood up most aggressively.

"You'll never take him! I won't let you!" he shouted.

"George, George, that won't help. Calm down. Sit down, that's right. Good lad. We'll sort this out. Now, why exactly must I return to my 'own' time, Watkins, fellow, if you will?"

continued Mr Redmayne, very calmly, by way of example. "What harm am I doing here? Tell me that. I have a family in this era. I live quietly, peacefully. Where's the danger to anything in that?"

Mr Watkins clicked his fingers in the direction of his other associate, Mr Wilberforce. Reaching into his inside pocket, Mr Wilberforce produced a small, zip-locked plastic bag and handed it to Mr Watkins. He held it up. It contained a thin, red object. A pen. Mr Redmayne felt his stomach churn. He recognised it at once.

"Is that my pen?" asked Mrs Redmayne, after a second or so. "My best red crossing-out pen? Is it? I've been looking for that *everywhere*. Where did you get it?"

"I'm sorry, dear," said Mr Redmayne. "A monkey took your pen. I tried to get it back. Really, I did. But it was too quick, the damned thing. We—"

Mr Redmayne halted there as he noticed that the Watkins fellow was waiting with interest to hear what he was going to say next. In fact, all three TDA agents were—and only when it was clear that Mr Redmayne had stopped talking, and wasn't going to resume, did Watkins then continue himself:

"Time is a delicate construction, Mr Redmayne, as I am sure you are only too aware. A series of events, a straight line from A to B and on to Z, and beyond. A true history of what *is*, as simple as that. That's time. But anything can break that straight line. Any object, taken out of its own time, can pollute the true timeline, can change history. Take this pen. We have reason to believe that circa 1603 either you or your father gave this pen to one William Shakespeare, a famous playwright of that era, very influential in his time and for many hundreds of years afterwards."

"We didn't give the pen to Shakespeare," protested Mr Redmayne. "Like I say, a monkey took it. Shakespeare wanted it, desperately, yes, but we, I, said no, he wasn't to have it. Not at all. No one respects the timeline more than I do, I can assure you."

"Be that as it may, Mr Redmayne, this pen destroyed the timeline. The playwright Shakespeare loved the pen, and spoke frequently of the smoothness of its action, its facility for crossing things out."

"It is very good for that," said Mrs Redmayne.

"Well, he grew obsessed with it, and used it obsessively in his work. It took him over. Let me try you with one or two examples. 'Shall I compare thee to a summer's ~~blank~~.' Anyone? Yes? No?"

"*Day,*" said Mr Redmayne. "'Shall I compare thee to a summer's *day?*' That's what it is. Obviously."

"Yes, an easy one. And you say 'obviously,' but no one out there, outside this house, in the *world*, knows that. Probably. Not yet. Not a single soul. Because it was erased, either by Shakespeare himself or by one of his followers, centuries ago. Erased from history. People speculate, of course, about what the word might have been originally: breeze, fête, pudding—these have all been proposed with one degree of seriousness or another. But no one *knows*. And that's just one example. Because of Shakespeare's reputation as the preeminent man of letters of his time, and beyond, the practice became a trend, a fashion, a way of life. Just the way things were done. Natural. And then it was everywhere. It caught on, and became inescapable. And none of it was meant to be. It took a full TDA task force six months to track down the root cause and remove it from the timeline before the damage could be done. And *this* was the cause."

He held up the bag. "So, Mr Redmayne, tell me, if a simple thing like a mere pen can so badly interfere with the timeline, how very far worse might you? You don't belong here. You potentially affect the future with everything you do. No, you must come with us. You face charges. And you will, of course, be interrogated about your father. Your father has singlehandedly done more to pollute the timeline than anyone in history. He started it all, in fact. Everything. The notorious Rufus Reginald Redmayne. *The* Time Criminal. Anything you might tell us about him, where to find him, *when* to find him, I dare say might work in your favour. It certainly couldn't hurt your case."

Mr Redmayne looked Watkins in the eye. "I haven't seen my father in centuries, I'm afraid. Can't help you, there."

"Well said, my lad," boomed the notorious Time Criminal, Rufus Reginald Redmayne, entering the room.

A collective gasp was shared by everyone present. If anything, the three TDA agents appeared more taken aback than the Redmaynes themselves. A true celebrity was amongst them—Time's most wanted. Flustering was evident. Extreme flustering.

"You can all close your mouths now, please. I can't abide gaping." The old man winked at Emile. "Yes, you too there. Watkins, isn't it? Now, what's all this fuss? I'll have you know, I was taking a nap upstairs. I do *hate* having my naptime interrupted. So, this had better be important. Well?"

Rufus looked around the room. Nobody did anything for a moment or two. No one moved.

George, Felice, and Emile all noticed how much longer and stragglier their grandfather's beard and great moustache were now compared to when they had parted with him in what had been, to them, only a few hours earlier.

Mr Redmayne looked on agog. Mrs Redmayne too.

Even if visibly overawed, Watkins managed to pull himself together first. He cleared his throat. No doubt he had rehearsed his next statement on multiple occasions. In a mirror. Privately.

"Rufus Reginald Redmayne, by the power invested in me by the Temporal Displacement Authority, you are under arrest for multiple crimes against the timeline."

"Fiddlesticks," replied Rufus. "What crimes against the so-called timeline? I invented the timeline because *I* invented time-travel. I invented it because I was *meant* to invent it. I was *meant* to travel through time, and whatever I do *becomes* the timeline. Don't you see? This *is* what *is*. You damned TDA, you're the pollution. Piggybacking on my work. You're unworthy of it. Time's Travel Agents, that's all you are! Pigmies. Wanting to take my house. Arrest my son. I don't think so. Now, get out!'"

"Father," said Mr Redmayne, but Rufus held up a hand.

The three TDA agents were converging on the elder Mr Redmayne and a struggle seemed inevitable. George was up on his feet again, grandfather and grandson against the world. Mrs Redmayne rose also. Mr Redmayne attempted to intervene. Bedlam. Hands were laid on Rufus. All three agents. George punched Wimberley. He fell down, holding his nose, his bowler hat sent flying.

"That's for putting a sticker on my Pops!" George cried out.

"George, no!" shouted Mr Redmayne.

"Right, that's it!" threatened Rufus. "I warned you. Now be off! The three of you. Go!"

Rufus held a small device with a plunger on top in his hand. It looked disturbingly like a grenade. He held it up and pressed it down. Watkins froze, his eyes wide. "You didn't!" was all he had time to say.

Rufus smiled. He had.

At once Watkins vanished. Wilberforce and Wimberley too. Instantaneously. Gone. Where the three agents had been standing was now just space, quiet. Calm. And a hat.

Mr and Mrs Redmayne looked at each other. Rufus was patting himself down, adjusting his clothing. "Last time you invite him to a party, I expect," he said, casually.

The children, especially, looked astonished. "What just happened?" asked George.

"Timejump," said Rufus, with more than a hint of pride. "A device of my own patent. When they closed in on me just now I set it up. Timejumped the three of them into the middle of next week. China. Qinghai. Very remote province. Bought us a few days. But, now they've found us they'll be back. By then we need to be long gone."

"Long gone?" asked Mr Redmayne. "Where are we going to go? And those fellows, the TDA, or whatever they are, the ones you just somehow disappeared, into thin air, they've sealed two of the exits, haven't they?"

"That's right. And I've sealed the other one myself. No one can get in or out. Not to worry, I've been making preparations. I always knew this day would come. Gloriana, how very nice to see you. You look as radiant as you ever did. Even more so. The years suit you. Now, everyone come with me. There's something I need to show you all. This way."

Rufus led the somewhat shell-shocked Redmaynes out into the hallway and then down the side-staircase into Mrs Redmayne's kitchen. Emile stayed close to his mother; despite his new trophy (the bowler hat, which he had picked up almost at once and tried on for size[14]) he seemed the most affected by everything he had just witnessed, although it would be fair to say that at that moment none of them were exactly at their very best.

Exhausted, George and Felice lingered together at the rear. George was still surprised that he had just punched a man in anger, any man, let alone some kind of government agent from the future—even if the lunatic had fully deserved it. No denying that. Felice, on the other hand, well, she was more than surprised by that particular turn of events. She was astonished!

Wait until she told Claudia, was the first thought she had, and then she realised that she never could. And then she realised she might never see Claudia again, the way things were going, and that just seemed strange—and, in truth, a bit sad. She was just getting to know her.

The Redmayne's basement kitchen, on the other hand, when they got down there a few moments later, appeared on first glance to be not in the least bit strange, or altered, but looked much as it ever did. Except it wasn't. Not at all. Mr Redmayne noticed more of that thick grey dust here and there. Rufus had been up to something, he now realised, as ever, and they were about to find out what that was. His father led them all to the far end of the kitchen, to the cooker, where he stopped and turned to face them all.

"I suppose you all think I owe you some kind of apology?

---

[14] Too large, at least for the time being.

Well, I'm sorry, I don't do apologies." He paused here, as if waiting for laughter, which didn't come. "No, okay, sorry, truly, all joking aside. I suppose, well, I expect, that looking at things from your perspectives, limited as they are, some of my behaviour must strike you as very, shall we say, *cold*. Especially the children. I imagine all in all that the feeling of abandonment in a past century that you all experienced can't have been very nice. Well, I apologise. There, I've said it." He looked at each of the children in turn. "But what you must all understand is that if my behaviour was cold, it was because it had to be. You see, when I say I always knew this day would come, that's because I knew this day would come. This *very* day—and everything that has just happened. I am from the future, after all."

"As am I, apparently," said Mr Redmayne.

"Yes, again, sorry," said his father. "But here we are. Let's go forward and see what happens next. Even I don't know that. This is the situation. The three known entrances to the house are sealed, and more than that they are spinning through time. I've set each of them on a random looping pattern, though history. The TDA will never find us. Those blasted fools thought they could take my house, our house, my life's work… Never! But it means we can't get in or out, either."

"You mean we're trapped?" said Mrs Redmayne, clearly not thrilled by that prospect.

"Now, no, wait a minute," said Mr Redmayne, thinking aloud. "What do you mean by *known* entrances? There are only three entrances, and I should know. Shouldn't I?"

The old man looked sheepish. "Well, to tell you the truth, actually, I've been doing a bit of remodelling," he said. "Finally I had you all out of the house, and so I borrowed it for a time, for some months in fact. You know, I think it's turned out rather well."

"What has? What on Earth *now*? And, oh, yes, Father, while we're at it, next time you need our co-operation with a crazy plan like this, you might think about letting us know. Just a thought. These are our lives you're playing God with, you know?"

"Noted. Now pay attention, boy. Behold."

Rufus pressed another button on his handheld device. Slowly the heavy-set iron range cooker began to move forward on one axis, like a thick iron gate on a hinge. It grated on the stone floor.

The Redmaynes were astonished. As one. Open-mouthed.

Rufus smiled, the magician who had saved his very best trick until last. It was another door.

చ

Where—and *when*—the door led to was the immediate point of speculation. But all Rufus would say in response was "Out" and "Now," before adding, "Whenever *that* is!" Clearly he was enjoying himself. The other Redmaynes were a little more non-plussed. The thought that they would need to leave their home after all was somewhat disconcerting, even if it was on better terms than those proposed by the nasty TDA agents. Rufus suggested it might not be forever. He had a plan, but that was all he would say. In the meantime, the house would always be here (wherever *here* was), but would only be accessible via the new door, wherever that led to and from, which only prompted more intense speculation.

In the meantime he had arranged alternative accommodations for them all, himself excepted, as he thought it prudent to maintain a safe distance between them for a time, so that they might not all be nabbed at once. Vigilance was required. Otherwise he expected they would be entirely comfortable. They needn't bring much, just whatever few personal possessions, clothes, and suchlike, that they couldn't bear to part with, even if only temporarily. One case each should suffice. And in the end, after much to-ing and fro-ing, that is what they did. Mrs Redmayne too.

Which led them back to the question of the door and where it came out. And when. It was a low, wide door, wooden, with two iron bands and a thick black lock. It narrowed to an arch at the top. George felt it looked medieval, and that they were about to spend some time in the company of jousting knights and fair damsels, which, on the whole, Emile considered would be fine by him. Mrs Redmayne replied that she sincerely hoped not. Medieval times were even worse than the Elizabethan era, and that was bad enough. No, she's had quite enough of the past for one lifetime, thank you very much. But, anywhere would do, so long as it was quiet and they could all be together. And Mr Redmayne concurred with that sentiment. Sincerely. Prudently. Happily.

When the time came to leave they all assembled in the kitchen with their cases. Rufus handed each of them a flashlight. Beyond the door lay a tunnel, a natural tunnel, part of a system of chalk caves in a series of hills. The door had to be hard to find from the outside and so it lay deep in the hill. But it would be very dark, hence the flashlights. And they needed to be careful, especially when pulling their cases, as the ground would not always be even and smooth. There was only one key, which Rufus handed to his son (Mr Redmayne didn't believe his father for a second that this key was unique and his alone but he accepted it anyway—a somewhat large and heavy iron key). He said he would try not to lose it—and both father and son smiled at what each of them hoped was a joke.

And so, they left. Their magical house that spanned space and time and in which they had always (mostly always) been so happy together. None of them felt particularly happy at that precise moment, however. Leaving is always hard. Mrs Redmayne may have suppressed a sob, for the sake of the children. Mr Redmayne's eyes may, once again, have been a little on the moist side too. Wet, actually. But he expected that no one noticed. Hardly anyone. Probably.

Rufus was right, as ever. The tunnel was very dark. Once Mr Redmayne turned the key in the lock and opened the door, they could all see only the bleak darkness ahead. It was a bit daunting. So, Rufus, stooping at first, flashlight on, led the way, and everyone followed. Mr Redmayne, leaving last, locked up and put the key in his jacket pocket. He had almost never lost anything from there. That's what he told himself.

They would all have to memorise the route, that was essential. Rufus promised to stay around for a little while so that they might grow accustomed to the caves and their winding passageways. That might not be easy. It seemed to take an age, but then things always feel like they take longer when you don't know for sure where you're going. That's what Mr Redmayne said when the children complained. Next time would be better, and the time after that, even better again. One day they would be able to do it without the flashlights. That's how these things went. Around and around, left and right and left again, and so on, until suddenly, when you least expect it, you find that you're already there.

The sun was coming up when they emerged from the hillside. Bright, warm.

Dawn, a good time for a new start. The hill sloped gently downwards and was gloriously green all the way. The air was fresh, clean. Everything seemed almost golden, such was the loveliness of the morning light. This would be a good place to paint, thought Mr Redmayne, inhaling vigorously and taking it all in, all of it at once, glad to be free and with his family. Reunited. Safe.

A short distance away from the foot of the hill stood a farmhouse, with a barn. No other houses were in sight. And Rufus, not waiting for anybody, was striding headlong in its direction. That must be the place.

"Trees, see?" said Mrs Redmayne. "There. Apple trees. An orchard. Do you think it's ours? All of it?"

"Do you think it looks French?" said Felice. "I think it looks French."

George, shading his eyes with his hand, pointed up to the skies.

"Plane," he said.

High, high up, twin white vapour trails bisected the blue heavens. Not medieval times, then, in case there was any doubt. *Their* times.

Emile had dropped his case and his souvenir bowler hat and

was running, full speed, toward his grandfather. After a second, George and Felice exchanged a look and silently agreed to do the same. They took off.

Mr and Mrs Redmayne stopped to watch them all run. Emile was gaining on his grandfather, and George was gaining on Emile. Felice, a gallant third, just seemed happy to be running. They were enjoying themselves.

"It's idyllic," said Mrs Redmayne.

"Yes, it is, isn't it?"

They started to walk again, carrying their cases now across the field.

"Eric, chéri, I do hope we'll all be happy here, for however long we stay. It might be a little smaller than we're all used to, though, you know. From here, it looks very, well, little, in comparison, I mean. Charming, yes, but little."

"Yes, it does look rather little, dear, I have to admit," he said, smiling at her. "On the *outside*, anyway. You never know, on the *inside* it might be surprisingly roomy, for a little cottage, that is. You never know, we might find that."

"You're right, dear. You never *do* know. Let's go and see."

And walking together, gaily, practically in step, they speeded up.

The happy Redmaynes.

❧SONNET CLV❧

Who can'st escape the mortall claimes of Time
And see his debt from Deaths grim ledger struck?
Who mighst by wit alone and conceald rime
Evade his Fate and all ill fortun'd lucke?
Alas, none, my friend. Nay, nere the long-liv'd
Phaenix, nor the red-man'd Lyon mighst pay
That deadly reckening and yet survive
To breath Gods sweet air for an other day.
But one way be knowne to cloake thy bright page
From Fates long seeing eie: obfuscate all!
Crosse out thy trackes, erase thee from the stage,
Be ye not found when the Reader doth call.
Hide. Forsake love, and be as one forsook,
Strike out, or else by Time's red pen be struck.

WS 1603

❧

ACKNOWLEDGEMENTS

Heartfelt thanks go to my good friend Matt Redmond, the screenwriter, whose time will come (remember, pal—I have *seen* the future), for his daily support and coffee; to Frank Richardson and his intrepidly bookish son, James (then aged 12), who read the manuscript—and *liked* it; to Dr David Hornsby, *mon Professeur*, who corrected my schoolboy French; to my long-time pals & enthusiastic readers, Leigh Williams, Sofia Dimoglou, and Graham Bathe, who took in all the stories down the years and were always open to more.

But most of all, of course, I am grateful to my lovely wife, Donna, for all of her special support, encouragement, eagle-eyed editing and general literary advice, and my two fabulous daughters, Ellie and Maisie, without whose company our many exciting family adventures in London, Paris, and New York would have been much diminished.

Now, ready, everyone? Okay, let's *go*! That farmhouse is waiting...